WHEN I WAS SUMMER

J. B. HOWARD

WHEN I WAS

SUMMER

VIKING

VIKING
An imprint of Penguin Random House LLC
New York

First published in the United States of America by Viking,
an imprint of Penguin Random House LLC, 2019

Visit us online at penguinrandomhouse.com

LIBRARY OF CONGRESS CATALOGING-IN-PUBLICATION DATA IS AVAILABLE
ISBN 9780451480200

Printed in USA   Set in Diverda Serif Com

1   3   5   7   9   10   8   6   4   2

For Brandon
and all the melodies that make him

CHAPTER I

*D*aniel's left hand rests on my waist. His right hand presses the wall behind me, supporting us both. He's leaning in, eyes closed, lips parted. My chest tightens around the timpani-thumping of my heart. This is it. Daniel Teague is going to kiss me.

Someone exits the club through the back door, and the alley fills with noise, which ricochets off the walls, amplified in the empty corridor. I don't look to see who emerged, but I hear them jog away from us, probably toward the entrance, or the parking lot. Before the door closes, I hear voices coming from the greenroom, which is a generous term for the sticky, closet-sized space where bands wait for their turn onstage. I think I hear Flynn's laugh, then Cameron's. They seem worlds away.

The door slams shut, and the alley is quiet again, but Daniel's hand is gone. He steps sideways and falls against the wall next to me, looking up between the buildings at the light-polluted sky.

"Sorry," he says. "I don't know what I'm doing."

"Don't worry about it," I say, as something inside of me deflates.

"No, we're in a band together. I can't—I mean—Jesus, I'm sorry, Nora. You should have punched me or something."

"Nah, I'd have let you down easy," I say, reeling myself back into this elaborate charade in which I am just his bandmate, his platonic friend.

He laughs. In these shadows, the dark circles beneath his eyes look like bruises against the unhealthy pallor of his skin. It's clear he hasn't been sleeping. Most days, I try not to resent Darcy for being the one he wants, but I have no problem resenting her for hurting him like this.

"You know what you need?" I bend down so I can look at his face, which is angled toward his feet.

He answers without looking up. "What do I need, Bass Girl?"

I wish he wouldn't use that nickname. It feels too much like an endearment, makes it harder for me to play my part. But I ignore my accelerating heartbeat and say, "You need about thirty minutes in front of an adoring crowd."

He steps away from the wall, looks at the back door of the Rowdy. "Then I've come to the right place?"

"You know you always feel better after a show."

He looks at the sky again, and I wonder what he sees. The stars are obscured by the marine layer, which is creeping inland from the ocean. All I see above us is a flat, featureless blanket of clouds.

"But Darcy is—*was*—" I so do not want to hear whatever he's going to say next. "Darcy's special, you know? Maybe she's *it* for me."

I'm standing right here. How can he not see what we could be together?

The door opens again, and Flynn steps out, holding his drumsticks. His freckles are whitewashed by the dim light; his short curls look uncannily tidy. Daniel and I both shrink into the shadows, but he spots us anyway. "What are you two doing out here?" His sharp voice cuts through the spell that had briefly settled between us.

"Just getting some fresh air," Daniel says, a little too quickly.

Flynn pauses, seems to measure the distance between Daniel and me. "Kraken's on their last song. The solo section could take another fifteen minutes, but we should get to the wing just in case."

"Yeah," Daniel says, pushing himself away from the wall. "Thanks."

He reaches the door first and holds it open for Flynn, then me. As I step forward, he touches my elbow, and I stop.

"Could you not tell Cam and Flynn about this?" he whispers.

"Of course."

"Temporary insanity."

"Obviously."

He looks relieved as I move past him into the dense cacophony of backstage.

♪ ♪ ♪ ♪

MY SISTER WOULD NEVER FALL FOR SOMEONE WHO'S clearly in love with someone else. She actually told me that once. It started as a conversation about *The Great Gatsby*, which I, full disclosure, didn't read. Under normal circumstances, I can mention the title of a book, and she'll launch into a helpful diatribe about the book's merits and weaknesses; with a little prodding, she'll also monologue about characters, plot, themes, and anything else I think might appear on a reading quiz. But when I asked her about *The Great Gatsby*, she just snorted and said, "Oh, my God. I hated that book."

I remember my stomach sinking. I hadn't even read the summary on the back yet, and the cover wasn't at all illuminating. I could probably have skimmed the SparkNotes before class, but my English teacher that year had a Spidey sense for students who were regurgitating information from the internet. Panicked, I asked, "What? Why?"

Irene, who was sitting shotgun as our mom drove us to school, looked over her shoulder at me and asked, "You liked it?"

I hedged, "It's okay, I guess."

Our mom chimed in neutrally, "*The Great Gatsby* is a classic."

Irene and our mom have identical wavy blonde hair. Irene pulled hers into a messy bun at the top of her head as she said dismissively, "Because of Doctor T. J. Eckleburg's eyes? What is it with literary critics and God metaphors? Equate an inanimate object or a sea mammal to the divine, and suddenly you're a genius."

I made a mental note: *Doctor T. J. Eckleburg's eyes are a metaphor for God.*

Our mom looked at her. "Do you challenge the book's literary merit?"

"I'm too busy detesting Jay Gatsby to worry about the book's literary merit," Irene said. "He spends his whole life pining for someone who has no interest in him. If he had a spine, or a brain, then he'd take his hard-earned new money and fall for someone way cooler than Daisy Buchanan, someone *likable*."

"So, do you think fictional characters must be likable?" my mom said. She and Irene have discussions like this all the time. When my dad's around, he chimes in, too. Even though my family and I look nothing alike, *these* are the moments when it feels most painfully obvious that I was adopted and Irene was not, because I never know what the hell they're talking about. When called upon to contribute, I've learned to read the tone of their voices and make decent guesses about what they want to hear. Based on the sound of this particular question, I knew the answer my mom wanted was *No.*

"No," Irene said. "But they do have to be interesting. And why should I be interested in a rich dude who's pining after something shallow and basically illusory?"

"Ah," our mom said, looking pleased. "But isn't that Fitzgerald's point? Daisy is the American dream—shallow, illusory. Gatsby is Everyman—compromising all in pursuit of it."

I was taking notes on my phone by this point. I'd review them quickly before class.

"Okay, but then we're talking metaphor," Irene said. "If Fitzgerald wanted to discuss the American dream, then he should have written an essay. If he wanted to write fiction, then he should have made the characters more compelling."

"Many readers do find Gatsby compelling, though," our mom said. "His quest is our quest—delusional, doomed."

"Whatever," Irene said, effectively yielding the argument. "I just know I'd never chase after someone who didn't like me back. I have better things to do with my time."

Our mom smiled at her, reached across the center console, and squeezed her shoulder as she said, "That's my girl."

I, however, am clearly not my mom's girl, because the second I saw Daniel, I started falling for him, even though the very next second, there was Darcy, standing by his side.

J. B. Howard

BACKSTAGE OF THE ROWDY IS A MESS OF PEOPLE. TONIGHT, Thursday, is Short Set Night, when four bands each play for thirty minutes, then one headliner plays for an hour. Tonight's headliner, Horoscope, is a bigger name than usual. Their first album was great, but their second has gotten wider recognition. I'm sure they booked this gig before their newest singles started climbing the charts. The Rowdy must be a dive compared to other venues they can play now.

Because Horoscope's on the marquee, the hallways are especially crowded. Everyone's probably hoping for a chance to slip them their demo or invite them to a party after the show. But as far as I can tell, Horoscope still hasn't shown up, and Daniel and Flynn are behind me, so I have to keep moving, be the one to push us through to the greenroom, which is thankfully empty except for Cameron, who's sitting on the limp yellow couch practicing the opening riff of our first song.

As we enter, Flynn says, "I found them."

Daniel ignores the irritation in Flynn's voice and starts unpacking his guitar. "We don't go on for five more minutes."

"Yeah, that's *totally* enough time to go over our set."

"But we all know what we're playing, right?" Cameron says. "'Fetch,' 'Long Morning,' 'Figure Eight,' 'Soul Fire,' and 'Love You So.' Easy."

Cameron and Flynn are wearing similar outfits—jeans, black T-shirts—and Cameron's thick black hair is just as well coiffed as Flynn's curls. Somehow, though, Flynn looks like an accountant on casual Friday, while Cameron looks like he's been transplanted from a Hollywood night-club. It's something about the cut of their jeans and the fabric of their shirts. Daniel and I have a slightly different look—tattered and fierce. I always wonder if people in the audience notice that out of the four of us, he and I match.

After a pause, Daniel says, "Let's not do 'Love You So.'"

Flynn widens his eyes. "You want to change the set *now*?"

"Wait." Cameron looks to the side. "Where's Darcy?"

Daniel shrugs, but at the same time he overcorrects the tuning of his A string. He's trying too hard to pretend this isn't a big deal.

"Oh, please," Flynn groans. "If you and Darcy had a fight, you can pretend you wrote the song about Beyoncé. But we're playing it."

I tell myself I'm just being helpful by suggesting, "Or we could do our cover of 'Blackbird' instead."

"We haven't played that in a month," Flynn argues.

But Cameron's already running through the guitar part. "'Blackbird' is short," he says. "We could do that and then finish with our cover of 'No Rain.'"

"You want to do two covers in one thirty-minute set?" Flynn says. "I thought we didn't want to be a cover band."

I have my bass out and am digging through my gig bag for a pick as I say, "It's just the Rowdy." This is a valid argument. The Rowdy is the third-largest music venue in Huntington Beach, which isn't known for its music scene in the first place. The guys and I all live half an hour south and inland of here, in one of the many quiet, manicured suburbs of South Orange County. We only make the drive up because the Rowdy is one of the few clubs that will let us gig without an album or demo. "And it's hard to go wrong covering the Beatles."

"We could open with 'Blackbird' and throw in 'No Rain' after 'Figure Eight,'" Daniel says. "So we still finish with an original."

I find a pick and stuff it in the back pocket of my jeans for later, then slap a run up the neck of my bass before saying, "Sounds good to me."

When Cameron stands, he towers over the rest of us. Onstage, he's the looming shadow on Flynn's right, standing almost completely still while he shreds his guitar. "Let's do it," he says, clamping a hand around Daniel's shoulder.

Daniel looks at Flynn, and something invisible passes between them. We've all been friends since the beginning of freshman year, but Daniel and Flynn go back further— Little League, I think, though it's hard for me to imagine. Neither of them is the baseball-wielding type. There's a pleading note in Daniel's voice as he says, "Please, Flynn."

Flynn sighs, then hits the wall twice with his drumstick. "Fine," he says. He looks at me. "Fine. We'll do it."

Daniel nods. "Thanks." He has a smile just for me as he plays a final chord.

The four of us file through the narrow hallway to the crowded wing of the stage. We circle up as the band before us plays its final chorus. Daniel wraps his arms around Flynn and Cameron, who have their arms around me. I love this part, when we bring it in before a show. There's an invisible line drawn around the four of us, separating us from everything it excludes. Whatever tension existed in the greenroom, or at school, or in rehearsal, fades, and we become bigger than the sum of our parts. We're not just four kids playing instruments; we're a *band*.

"What's the word?" Daniel asks, shouting over the noise from the stage.

I feel Flynn watching me, but when I look at him, he's staring at our feet.

"Ignite," he says.

Daniel asks him to repeat it, and he does.

The song ends as Daniel nods. "I like it. Ignite."

"I do love a fire hazard," Cameron says, but he seems distracted. For a second, I'm worried. Magic only happens when we cohere; that's how we came up with the one-word idea in the first place. We pick a different one for every show, but for that night it's our talisman. We weave it into the music. When our eyes meet onstage, we know what the other person is thinking.

"Ignite," I say, tightening my grip around Flynn's and Cameron's waists.

"Ignite!"

"Ignite."

The space between us is warm now. It crackles with energy. Thousands of bands just like ours are trying to get noticed, trying to make it, but in my heart, I know we're different. We have a chemistry that can't be learned or rehearsed. Maybe I spend a little too much time thinking about Daniel's eyes, and his hands, and his—whatever. That's not the point. The point is that I trust these boys above anyone else. We're more than a band, even. We're friends. We're family.

"Okay," Daniel says. "Let's light this place up."

We squeeze in for one more hug. When we break the circle, the sound of the audience floods back in. I'll never get used to this. I never *want* to get used to this. I always want it to be exactly this terrifying, this thrilling.

We run onstage, and Daniel, Cameron, and I plug in our instruments while Flynn sits at the drum kit. Once Evan in the sound booth gives us the signal, we'll be ready to start.

When I look at the audience, the first thing I see is Darcy. Her platinum hair is haloed by light from the bar, and she's wearing a clingy red dress that accentuates her unnaturally tanned cleavage, which is probably visible from space. I'm sure Daniel sees her, too, but he's doing a pretty good job of pretending he doesn't. I try to look away, but she has that same quality he has—once you see them, it's hard to stop.

I'm not surprised she's here. She and Daniel fight all the time, but they always reconcile with a passionate make-out session and promises not to do whatever-it-was ever again.

Evan in the sound booth waves at us, and Flynn taps out a measure. "One, two, three—"

Right before Cameron and I come in on the first note, Daniel shouts, "We're Blue Miles!"

I catch his eye.

Ignite, I think, and he nods.

We'll set this place on fire.

CHAPTER 2

We're nearing the end of our set, and the song substitutions are going just fine. Daniel's electric tonight, probably because Darcy's at the back of the room with a guy who's stereotypically attractive—all shoulders and chin. He's wearing a tight brown shirt that matches his skin tone so perfectly, it almost looks like he's shirtless; the impression that this gives is that seeing him shirtless would be a thoroughly pleasant experience. He and Darcy are standing shoulder to shoulder in the center of a pool of light, a fact I'm certain she's aware of. She's an actress; she knows her lighting.

I turn away from the audience and step toward Flynn, who's sweating a river over his drum kit. He and I lock eyes. Cameron steps closer to us, and now I can feel how he, Flynn, and I are breathing the same air, pumping the same blood. This lasts only thirty seconds, maybe less, but it's one of those moments I live for, when we disappear, and the crowd disappears, leaving only the music.

We strike our final chord, and the lights go black. I have a sensation of rushing back into existence, like I'd been suspended somewhere nearby. By the time the lights brighten again, Flynn has stepped out from behind his kit. We're all standing center stage, applause reverberating around us. Daniel leans in to his microphone and says, "Thank you! We're Blue Miles! Good night!"

We each handle our exit differently. Flynn bobs his head and waves. Cameron strums a chord. Daniel bends down and high-fives several of the people pressed against the stage. I get one last look at Darcy, who's whispering something to the underwear model. Then I stretch my fingers, power off my amp, and rip the cable out of my instrument.

Flynn walks up beside me. "You were on fire tonight, Wakelin."

I drape my arm over his shoulders, still too high off our performance to care that he's dripping sweat all over me. "You weren't bad yourself."

We press into the dark, cramped wing while the members of the next band jog past wearing electric-hued wigs and colorful face paint.

"Think they're compensating for something?" Flynn shouts at me.

"Yeah," I say. "Lame music."

We move single file through the hallway back to the greenroom. Daniel's in front, then Cameron, me, and Flynn. Cameron leans toward Daniel and shouts, "You okay?"

Daniel cranes his head back. "Yeah, yeah."

"You gonna tell us what's going on with you two?"

He hits the wall with an open hand. "That guy is directing the play she's in right now. He wrote it, and the script is terrible. Some autobiographical shit about his childhood."

"So what?" Cameron asks, not unreasonably.

Daniel looks back at him and shouts, "So, did you *see* that guy? And they've been spending, like, every waking moment together."

"He ain't got nothin' on you," Cameron says.

I shout, "Seconded," counting on my tone to conceal my true feelings.

Daniel glances back at us appreciatively as he opens the door to the greenroom, but then he stops short. Cameron runs into his back, nearly knocking him over. Flynn and I step forward more carefully and peer around their shoulders.

Two men and a woman are lounging around the greenroom. They're not wearing matching outfits, exactly, but they definitely have a *look*—all buckles and black leather. The woman has dark skin and black ringlets, which are gathered into several tight minibuns at the top of her head. The olive-skinned guy standing next to her has bleached hair that he's slicked away from his forehead. The other guy is sitting on a folding chair on the far end of the room. His head is shaved, and he has sleeve tattoos that start on the backs of his hands and spread up to his shoulders, twisting over his collarbones; the black ink contrasts sharply with his skin, which is as pale as bone. Peeking over the collar of his V-neck, I see an arc of tiny, precisely drawn symbols—their band logo.

"Oh, my God," I say. "You're Horoscope." Of course, I knew they'd be in the building tonight, but somehow I didn't expect to see them here, in the greenroom, hanging out like any local band.

The blond guy bows. "Guilty as charged." His accent is thickly British.

Daniel, Cameron, Flynn, and I move into the greenroom and let the door close behind us. The woman steps forward and shakes our hands.

"I'm Becca, drums," she says, in a slightly smoother, though no less British, accent. She gestures to the blond one. "That's Skeet, guitar and vocals." She points behind her. "And that's Jos, bass."

Jos nods. "Good to meet you." He doesn't sound British, more like Eastern European, if I had to guess.

I step past Daniel and Flynn. "I loved your last album. I mean, both albums, but especially that new opening track." I lift my instrument and play the bass line, which is funky but fluid, almost melodic.

Jos's eyebrows rise. "Girl's got chops."

Suddenly, I feel like I could leap to the moon.

"Yeah, and that's why we wanted to talk to you," Skeet says. "We liked what you did out there."

"You did?" Flynn says, sounding skeptical.

I dig my elbow into his side.

Cameron says, "You saw us?"

Skeet flops onto the couch and stretches out his skinny,

leather-clad legs. "We never pass up an opportunity to listen to live music."

"You groove together," Becca says. "You're good with your instruments, but you've got something else, too—attitude, verve."

Skeet adds, "And we like that you played those covers. Shows an admirable lack of ego."

Next to me, I hear Flynn humph.

"So, we have a proposal for you," Becca says. "We've got a gig at the Magwitch in San Francisco next Saturday, but our opener bailed. Some drama or other—"

The floor spins beneath me. "Wait," I say. "Do you want us to open for you at the Magwitch?"

"Yes, please," Skeet says, pressing his palms together and resting his chin on the tips of his fingers.

All the great bassists have played the Magwitch. John Entwistle. Carol Kaye. Jaco Pastorius. Esperanza Spalding. Victor Wooten. *All of them.*

"Yes," I say. "We'll do it."

"Wait," Flynn says, stepping out in front and facing the rest of us. "How would we even get to San Francisco?"

"Yeah, so that's the trick, isn't it?" says Skeet, sitting up. "Our tour budget doesn't cover travel for openers, which is why we usually try to recruit local bands."

Becca drums a triplet on Skeet's forearm. "But if you can get yourselves to the Magwitch in time for sound check on Saturday, then we'd love to give you the chance to play for a bigger audience."

Jos adds, "You never know who'll hear you at the

Magwitch." He stands, and I realize that he's basically a giant, a couple inches taller than even Cameron. "And this business is all about being heard."

I face Daniel, Cameron, and Flynn. "Guys, we *have* to do this."

"How?" Flynn says. He lowers his voice. "What about school?"

I cringe. I don't want Horoscope to hear us talking about our finals schedule and change their minds. "Finals are the week after," I say. "We can get home in time if we drive all day Sunday."

"Okay, but what about next week?" Flynn says.

"We can leave early on Friday," Daniel says. I knew he'd be an ally. "It won't hurt to miss one day."

I say, "Our teachers will understand," but Flynn makes a that's-total-bullshit-and-you-know-it face, so I amend my statement: "Our teachers will *have* to understand. And then we'll come back, take our finals. No one's going to care." I focus on Flynn, knowing he's the least likely to agree to this. "*Please?* You know we won't learn anything this week. It's all just review and busywork."

Then Cameron says, "You really think *your* parents will be down with this, Nora? This seems like the kind of thing Jerry and Megan Wakelin will veto on sight."

He has a point. Daniel's parents have both been supportive of his rock star ambitions since day one; Cameron's parents are too busy being brain surgeons to notice whether he's studying or smoking crack; and Flynn's parents know that he's congenitally incapable of breaking rules, so they pretty much trust him to make smart decisions on his own.

My parents are a different story. They keep me to a ten o'clock curfew even when Blue Miles is playing a gig, and they only let me play in the band on the condition that "school comes first." I've probably heard that a million times.

Time to put down your bass and finish that geometry homework, Nora. School comes first.

Are you sure you can afford to play a show on Sunday? School comes first.

Music is great for cognitive development, but it's not something you can do for a living unless you want to be a bum, which is why school always comes first.

My dad's an attorney for an environmental nonprofit, and my mom's in the California State Senate. They assume that Irene and I will both eagerly follow in their footsteps— Stanford, law school, save the world one court case at a time. I haven't had the guts to tell them I have no intention of doing any of that. I've been afraid that if I do, they'll take music away from me forever. My current plan is to get Blue Miles a real record deal before we graduate, so I have a contractual excuse to put off my parents' pantsuit, power-lunch ambitions for me, hopefully indefinitely.

So, I dodge Cameron's likely true observation by reiterating, "It's *the Magwitch*. We *have* to do it."

There's a pause before Daniel says, "I say we go for it."

Cameron shrugs. "If we can get away with it, then I'm down."

Flynn looks at me for a long moment while I mouth,

Please, over and over again. Finally, he sighs and says, "We could take my van." I'm already turning around when I hear Flynn add, "But you're all chipping in for gas."

"We're in," I say to Becca.

"I knew you would be," she says. She probably means the whole band, but she's looking at me.

There's a soft knock on the greenroom door, and then it cracks open. Darcy's face appears in the gap. "Daniel?" She sees Becca, Skeet, and Jos and retreats. "Oh. Am I interrupting something?"

Daniel's at the door, opening it wider, letting her in.

"No," he says. "What's up?"

Becca, Skeet, and Jos are now talking among themselves while Cameron, Flynn, and I awkwardly pretend not to listen to Daniel and Darcy's stilted conversation.

"I just—" She shifts her position. "That was a great show. You know how to work a crowd."

"Yeah, well." He's looking at her through downturned eyelashes. "I learned from the best."

I sense more than see Flynn roll his eyes.

"You know that Lucas and I are just friends," she says. "He wanted to hear your music. He said you're really talented."

Daniel pushes a hand through his hair. "Tell him thanks, I guess."

Darcy sighs. "Could we go somewhere to talk?" She looks past him, to Cameron, Flynn, and me, then takes Daniel's hand and draws him incrementally closer. "Privately?"

After a beat, he says, "Yeah. Of course."

He picks up his guitar case and steps out into the hallway. But before he lets the door close, he looks back at us. "So, we're doing this?"

"Yeah," I say. "We are."

He nods, then steps out—his guitar in one hand, his other arm draped around Darcy's bare shoulders. Before the door swings shut, I see him lower his lips to her hair. The sight makes something cold and heavy settle in my stomach, and I know it's not just because he's usually my ride home. But I push the feeling down. There's no room for jealousy, or heartbreak, in a band.

♪ ♫ ♪ ♫

FLYNN DRIVES ME HOME, EVEN THOUGH HIS HOUSE IS IN A slightly different neighborhood. At this time of night, the roads are open, but Flynn has a thing about speed limits— the thing is, he never breaks them—so, as we cruise down the empty, foggy freeway at exactly sixty-five miles per hour, I let my mind drift back to what happened before the show.

I'd seen Daniel duck out of the greenroom, and when he didn't come back, I followed him out. I found him standing in the center of the alley, hands in pockets, face tilted toward the starless sky.

Even though I see him every day and we spend heaps of time together with the band, my heart still leapt at the sight of him standing alone, looking thoughtful and forlorn in the dim, narrow alley. It took me several seconds before I was able to reel my heart back into my chest and say, "Is everything okay?"

He sighed. "I'm glad she came, but it's—" Of course, I knew he was talking about Darcy. I'd seen her, too. "It's hard." He looked at me, and I saw that his eyes were red rimmed, shadowed. "We had a fight."

I stepped toward him. "You want to talk about it?"

"No." He moved to the side, then leaned against the building. "Maybe."

I waited.

He surprised me by saying, "Have you ever had a boyfriend, Bass Girl?" He looked equal parts earnest and embarrassed. "It's weird that I don't know that, isn't it?"

If anything, I thought it was weird that he'd asked. I spend all my free time with the band. Where and when would I have hidden a boyfriend?

"No," I said. "If you want dating advice, I'd better get Flynn or Cameron. I'll be useless."

Really, though, Daniel has more relationship experience than the rest of us combined. Flynn's been in several let's-hold-hands-and-eat-lunch-together relationships with girls from his church, and Cameron dated a guy from the drama club at the beginning of our sophomore year. But Daniel and Darcy have been more on than off for three years.

"No, that's not it," he said. "I just want to know something."

He turned his body to face me, but his head was still leaning against the wall, and we were *so close*. A streetlight illuminated half his face, but the other half was hidden, shadowed by the wall.

"Go for it," I said. All the little strings inside of me thrummed, stretching toward him.

"If you said you loved someone, would you mean it? And if you loved someone, would it last forever?"

"Yeah," I said quickly. "Of course."

"No, think about it, Bass Girl. Maybe I'm crazy for wanting something like this to last, for expecting it to."

"I have thought about it," I said, speaking more deliberately. "I've thought about it a lot."

"You have?"

"Definitely." I tried to keep my tone light. "You really want to know what I think?"

"I really do."

I studied him for a second, wondering how much to reveal. Finally, I said, "I think different people experience love in different ways. At school, I see kids who fall in love and break up and date other people like it's no big deal. But other people, like you, and like me, are all in or all out. For me, love isn't knee-deep. It's headfirst, swan-dive, someone-throw-that-girl-a-life-jacket." I forced myself to laugh, as though anything I'd said could be considered funny.

"You've been in love?" he said.

I just nodded, my heart climbing into my throat.

"But you've never had a boyfriend?"

"No."

"What happened?"

"It wasn't reciprocated."

"That's bullshit," he said. "Who is this guy?"

"It's not his fault. He doesn't—didn't—"

"You never told him?"

I shrugged.

"Poor guy. Doesn't know what he's missing." He smiled, and my chest caved in. "So, what about now?"

"What about what?"

"Do you still love him?" This was when he pushed himself away from the wall, leaving his right hand on the brick by my ear. He stepped in. His left hand found the side of my waist, and I felt the skin beneath my shirt there start to burn. His voice was breathy and—did I imagine this?—a little uneven as he asked, "If you start loving someone, can you ever stop?"

Flynn turns off at our exit and says, "So, what were you and Dan talking about before the show?"

I jump in my seat, abruptly reminded of where I am (Flynn's van) and who I'm with (not Daniel). "Nothing important. Just—you know. Darcy."

He shakes his head. "That kid has a one-track mind."

I definitely don't want to talk about Daniel's obsession with his girlfriend, so I let that statement settle into the silence. After a moment, Flynn asks, "You really think this is a good idea?" I'm startled, thinking that he's read my mind, but then he clarifies, "Road-tripping to San Francisco the weekend before finals?"

"For the Magwitch? Of course." I look at him. "You don't?"

He shrugs. "I don't know. When you take gas and mileage damage into consideration, we won't break even."

"It's not about the money, though."

"Yeah, okay," he says. "But what do we expect to get out of it? Do you know how rare it is to get noticed by a scout, even at a place like the Magwitch?" He's turning onto my street as he says, "And is that really what we want?"

"Of course it is. Otherwise we've got to record an album on our own, distribute it, promote it—" We've talked about recording an album this summer, so we can start playing other venues, but it would be so much easier with the help of a label. "This is the best shot we're ever going to get to be seen by someone who can help us."

"But even if we did sign with a label," he says, "that's no guarantee that we're going to 'make it.'" He lifts his hands away from the wheel long enough to put air quotes around the last two words. "It's not like signing with a label is going to solve all our problems."

"Uh, yeah, it would."

"Okay, sure. It *sounds* great." He's practically idling his van toward my house, giving himself time to make his point, but I'm mostly worried about beating my curfew. My phone says it's two minutes to ten o'clock. "But take Horoscope for example. By most standards, they've made it, right? They have a manager, a label. They're headlining at the Magwitch. But they're on the road all the time. They make a living, but they're not, like, Paul McCartney. Even with the success of this album, they're probably just starting to get ahead. Does that sound good to you?"

"That sounds *awesome* to me," I say. "They're playing music. Every day. That's all they have to think about."

Flynn pulls up in front of my house and parks. He's silent for a moment, and then he says, "I just don't see myself doing that, you know?"

"No, I don't." I'm thinking about my parents now, about the way they light up when they talk to Irene about Stanford, which is, unsurprisingly, the school she'll be attending in the fall. After this summer, the guys and I will be seniors, which means we have to start making things happen, and soon. Otherwise, we'll end up going different directions, and Blue Miles will eventually fizzle and die, and I'll get stuck in a job I hate, doing stuff I don't care about, for people who listen to jazz to seem sophisticated, but don't know Coltrane from Kenny G. "I mean, that's what we're working toward. Right?"

"I guess it just isn't for me."

I feel suddenly cold. "Wait. What are you saying?"

"No, I mean, the band is for me, but making a living at it someday has never been the point. The point is, it's fun. The point is, it's, you know"—he looks at me—"it's us."

"Yeah, but we've got to make a living someday, right? And it'll always be us."

He drums on the dashboard, then shrugs.

"Okay, you're being weird." He doesn't respond immediately, so I go on, "Is there something you'd rather do with your life?"

The car is lit only by the orange glow of a distant streetlamp. He takes a deep breath and says, "No, this is where I want to be. I just—" He looks at me again, but there's a shadow falling across his face, making it difficult for me to read his expression. "I don't know if there's a future in it."

Neither of us says anything for a while. I know I should go inside, but I feel strangely frozen. Maybe I'm just tired. Finally, he opens his door and says, "I'll get your bass."

"That's okay. I've got it." I beat him there and pull my instrument out of the back.

"You sure?"

"Please." I adjust my grip on the handle and secure my gig bag on my shoulder. "It's nothing."

It looks like he might insist on helping me, but then he says, "Okay, see you tomorrow."

I head up the short path to my house, fumbling around for my keys. Only when I get my door unlocked do I hear his van pull away.

CHAPTER 3

*I*t's a few minutes after ten o'clock when I shut the door behind me. I'm holding my breath, hoping that my parents are buried in work in their shared home office, so they won't hear me come in. It's hard to be quiet, though, when I'm carrying a bass and my gig bag, plus my school backpack and a U.S. history textbook that's roughly the size of my torso. I'm halfway up the stairs when my dad appears at the bottom and says, "Nora! We've been waiting for you."

My heart sinks—this will not be a good way to open my Magwitch negotiations—but then I see that he doesn't look angry. He seems distracted, almost nervous, as he adds, "Come to the office after you put down your things."

"Yeah, sure," I say, trying to sound casual.

He looks as if he's about to say something else, but then he turns and disappears around the corner.

A veil of dread descends over me. I know there's such a thing as parents who work too much—Cameron's parents come to mind—but I actually love it when mine are a little extra busy. They have a no-Blue-Miles-if-you-get-below-a-B rule, but last year when I got a C+ in chemistry, my mom was wrapped up in something in Sacramento and my dad's company was mired in a legal battle against an oil company, and no one noticed. Things get dicey when work is slow and they start to check my grades online and monitor how I allocate my time.

I climb the rest of the stairs slowly, trying to imagine what they could want to talk to me about. It's possible that I have a C in trigonometry, but I know I can bring it up before final grades are posted. I have some missing assignments in history, but they're only worth a couple points each; not doing them was actually a strategic decision.

As I pass Irene's bedroom, I see her sitting at her desk. Her blonde hair is braided loosely down her back, and she's bent over a piece of paper, muttering something to herself. When she hears me, she spins around in her chair and says, "Hey, Nora. Could I practice my commencement speech on you? I'm trying to start with a couple jokes, but I can't tell if they're funny or just awkward." She picks up the paper and looks at it. "Do you think people will laugh if I talk about how stale the cafeteria pizza is?"

"I think that's been overplayed." I adjust my grip on the handle of my bass case. "Besides, does anyone actually eat that pizza?"

She makes a mark on the paper. "Yeah, you're probably right."

Usually, the senior class president and the valedictorian

have to compete for the opportunity to give a speech at graduation. Irene is both, so she won the honor unchallenged.

I shift my weight, trying to keep my history book from slipping out of my arms. "Do you know what Mom and Dad want to talk to me about?"

Her eyebrows rise. "No clue." She sets her paper down. "Want me to go with you? Act as a buffer?"

I shake my head. "No, it's okay. It shouldn't be anything bad."

She seems to regret her assumption—though it's a fair one—and says quickly, "Yeah, of course."

I step toward my room as I say, "I'll come listen to your speech when they're done."

"Thanks." She smiles encouragingly. "Good luck."

As I drop everything on the floor next to my narrow bed, which is pressed up against the wall under my window, I make a mental list of everything I have to do tonight before I can go to sleep—physics homework, history homework, trigonometry homework, read about three hundred pages of *Great Expectations*, because somehow I've fallen two hundred and fifty pages behind. There's never enough time. Something is always bound to suffer, and usually that something is me.

I find my parents in their office. My mom is sitting at her desk, and my dad is leaning against the table near her, arms crossed over his chest. He's still wearing his suit, but my mom has taken off her makeup and changed into cotton pajamas. When they see me, my dad gestures to his desk chair and says, "Take a seat, kiddo." As I walk slowly over to it and sit down, he goes on, "Your mother and I have some good news." He looks at her, which is apparently her cue to take the lead.

"We know you've had a difficult time finding an internship for the summer." It sounds like she's trying (and failing) not to let judgment creep into her voice. "So, we did a little digging and found some options for you."

"Two opportunities, both solid résumé builders," my dad says, loosening his tie. "You can't go wrong. You'll learn a great deal either way."

I vaguely remember something they said to me a few months ago—that this was an important summer, the one before my senior year. They urged me to search for internships; I wasn't sure what they meant, but I said I'd look into it. Later, when they followed up, I lied and said I'd applied to a couple things, but hadn't heard back. I figured that would be the end of it. There's an awkwardly long pause before I say, "What?"

"The communications office at the state capitol has an internship open, and they've offered it to you," my mom says. "It would be a wonderful learning experience, a chance to get away from home—"

"Hold on, hold on," my dad says, smiling. It's clear that he's trying to keep the tone light. "Don't start selling it yet. Let her hear *my* proposal."

Unlike my mom, who's petite, compact, my dad is over six feet tall and built like a bear. He's been balding forever, and a few years ago he leaned into it and started buzzing his hair short. He and my mom look nothing alike, and yet they've always seemed like a matching set to me. Somehow, they just *go* together.

"My nonprofit has hired lobbyists to influence federal-level legislation for the fall term, and they have two internships available, newly created this year," he says, leaning forward. "You'd be in D.C. for the summer, working alongside the movers and shakers of the federal government."

I don't at first understand what he's getting at, but when I do, my heart rate accelerates to a drumroll inside my chest. They want to send me away for the summer.

"You have a few days to decide what you want to do," my mom says carefully. "You really can't make a wrong decision, though, sweetie."

But I don't need a few days. The word *no* wheezes out of me before I know that I've thought it.

My dad's carefully neutral expression falters. "To which?"

"Both," I say. "I can't go away. What about Blue Miles?" I think about how Daniel looked as he leaned toward me tonight, his face half-shadowed in the dim alley. But I also remember what it felt like to be onstage, to disappear under the current of the music as I became nothing but sound.

My dad's voice is sharp as he starts, "Nora, you have to—" But my mom puts her hand on his forearm, and he cuts off his sentence with a deep breath.

"Blue Miles will be here when you return, sweetheart," my mom says. "But these opportunities will only come once."

She sounds so reasonable. This is what makes her great at her job; by speaking clearly and never losing her cool, she can convince people of almost anything. But I'm not letting her play her Jedi-politician mind tricks on me.

"This is the best chance we'll get to record our demo," I argue, trying to match her tone. "We'll never have time during the school year."

"Nora, we can't let you continue to waste your time like this," my dad says. "You may not realize it now, but time is your most valuable resource."

Based on the way my mom closes her eyes and sucks in a breath, I can tell that this is something they've discussed privately, but weren't planning to say to me. When she opens her eyes, she looks even more tired than usual, and I wonder if she's been worrying about this conversation. Did she anticipate my reaction, but hope to stave it off by framing their ultimatum as something positive? That would be *so* my parents. Finally, she says, "I know we said you could play with Blue Miles as long as you kept your grades up, but you're about to start your last year of high school, and it's time to reassess your strategy, get serious about your future."

I think, *I am serious about my future,* but I don't say it out loud. I'm afraid that would make things worse.

"You will take one of these internships, Nora," my dad says, using his addressing-the-jury voice—stern, yet persuading. "This may feel like a punishment now, but someday you'll thank us."

"You have a few days to decide," my mom says again. She never repeats herself, which means she *must* be tired. "But, like we said, either one would be an excellent opportunity."

When I stand and step quickly out of their office, they don't try to stop me. I run up the stairs, past Irene's room ("Hey, Nora, are you ready to—?"), and slam my door. Well, I don't slam it, exactly. Histrionics don't get you far in my family; we're encouraged to *use our words*. So, I close my door firmly, open my bass case, pull out my instrument, and start running through scales as fast as my fingers will move. I slide down to the floor, leaning against the wooden frame of my bed, and fold my legs beneath me. My fingers ache, but it's a good feeling, like they're draining the frustration and anger out of my heart, metabolizing it through movement. I only realize that I'm crying when my fingers start to slip on the salt-water-slickened strings.

A few minutes later, someone knocks on my door. I ignore them.

"Nora?" It's Irene's voice. She sounds worried. Based on her tone, I'd guess she didn't know what Mom and Dad were planning. Maybe she still doesn't. Maybe she thinks my grades have dropped and I'm being grounded until I bring them up again; it's happened before. "Nora? Are you okay?"

I play harder. My bass isn't hooked up to an amp, but it's still loud enough to be heard through the door. Anyone who knows music would understand from the way that I'm playing that I'm both angry and terrified, that more is pouring out of me right now than I can possibly shape into words, that I want nothing more than to be left alone.

"Nora? Talk to me. What happened?"

Irene plays viola for the orchestra, but she doesn't really

get music. To her, it's just another skill to be perfected, not a way of being. She cracks the door open and peers around its edge.

"Nora, what happened?" she repeats. When I don't respond, she steps inside my room, closing the door behind her. "Maybe I can help."

If I asked her to leave, she probably would, but I'm not sure I can say the words, so I just tune her out and keep playing scales, until my fingers are a blur across the strings. After a moment, she crosses to my side and takes a seat next to me.

She shakes her head, staring at my hands. "Holy crap, you've gotten good at that," she says. "Remember when Flynn Ross said you were the best bassist at the school?"

I look at her, surprised she remembers that. It happened the night the guys invited me to play with them, first semester my freshman year. We were in one of those interminable tech rehearsals for *Grease*, the school's fall musical. Daniel and Cameron were in the chorus. Flynn was an assistant stage manager. I was playing bass for the stage band. Irene, who was a reporter for the school newspaper, stopped by to interview the leads, including Darcy, who had caused an upset when she landed the role of Sandy Olsson as a sophomore.

During a break in rehearsal, the guys came over to the band box and asked if I wanted to join them in their "mission to make nonsucky music"—that's how Daniel phrased it.

"Introductions first, Dan," Flynn said, moving to his side. "Be civilized." I think his freckles might have been more pronounced then; I remember thinking that he probably had a billion of them. Reddish speckles dotted every inch of his pale cheeks and arms.

Daniel widened his eyes at me as if to say, *Can you believe this guy?* Even though Daniel and I were the same year, I felt flattered, like I'd been singled out by someone important. "This is Flynn Ross, our drummer," he said, jabbing his thumb in Flynn's direction. "The giant on my right is our lead guitar, Cameron Zamani."

"Pleased to make your acquaintance," Cameron said, bowing. His skin was warm, olive colored; his eyes were brown and thickly lashed. It occurred to me then that we looked sort of alike—similar skin, same eye color, same hair, both relatively tall—so later, when I found out that his grandparents had emigrated from Iran, I added that to my private list of possible biological heritages. Over the years I've alternately believed that my biological parents might have contained any combination of Southern European, East Asian, South American, and—after seeing an old movie starring Catherine Zeta-Jones—Welsh genes. Everyone seems to assume I'm white, especially when they know my family, but it's always felt weird to me that I don't know for sure if that's right.

Daniel moved forward again. I'd recently discovered the music of Nirvana, and Daniel reminded me so much of Kurt Cobain when he was younger—same ice-blue eyes, same messy blond hair, same reckless intensity. "And I'm Daniel Teague," he said. "Rhythm guitar, vocals, songwriter."

But I already knew who they were. My bass part for that show was mind-numbingly easy, so I'd had nothing to do during rehearsal besides observe the techies and actors in their never-ending whirlwind of drama. Even as a freshman, even in the chorus, Daniel stood out. There was that indefinable something about him that drew the eye. Flynn, on the other hand, stood out primarily because he seemed so out of place; collared shirts and rule following aren't exactly the drama-crowd aesthetic. And Cameron was easily the most coordinated male dancer.

I was saved from attempting an immediate response when Darcy stepped up next to Daniel wearing her final costume for the show—shiny black leather that hugged her curves. She looked at him like he was the only other person in the room and asked, "So, is she in?"

"In what?" Irene asked, appearing behind me.

"We're starting a band," Daniel said to her. "We want Nora to be our bassist."

"She doesn't have time," Irene said automatically.

That prompted me to finally find my voice and say, "Yes, I do," even though I'd been thinking the same thing. I was already committed to jazz band and orchestra, and both the drama teacher and the choir teacher liked to use me whenever they needed a bassist. And my parents had never asked if I wanted to take honors classes; they'd just signed me up for them. I couldn't remember the last time I'd gotten a full night's sleep.

Irene leaned closer to me. "Mom and Dad are not going to let you play in a *rock band*."

Daniel laughed. "You say *rock band* like it means *Satan worshipper.*"

Cameron unhelpfully chimed in with, "We only honor the Dark Lord on the Sabbath."

Flynn stepped forward. "We're not Satan worshippers, or delinquents. We're musicians, and we take this seriously. We're asking Nora because she's clearly the best bass player in the school."

Even though I'd frankly realized as much myself, it was thrilling to hear someone say the words out loud: *best bass player in the school.* After that, there was no way I was turning them down, especially when Daniel's lips lifted into a half smile and he said, "So, what do you say? Are you up for it, Bass Girl?"

Now, sitting here in my room two and a half years later, Irene shifts her position and says, "You might be one of the best bassists in the *state* now."

Finally, my fingers stop moving. I look at her. "They're sending me away for the summer."

"What?" She seems horrified, which makes me feel a little better.

"They got me a couple internship offers. Probably pulled strings." I think about the way my mom sucked in her breath, the way she and my dad looked at each other when I said *No.* "They want to get me away from my band."

"Ah." She doesn't look so surprised anymore. "What are the internships?"

"Does it matter?" I start forming chord shapes across the strings—plucking whole triads at once. "I don't want to be an attorney, or a politician. I want to be a musician." I slap a line that's all incoherent syncopation and dissonance. "I *am* a musician."

"Of course you are." She takes a deep breath, reminding me so much of our mom that I want to scream, but I keep my attention on my instrument and try to tune out everything else. Finally, she adds, "But it wouldn't kill you to spend a few weeks getting another perspective, seeing a bit more of the world. Besides, I bet you could find some people to play music with in another city."

But they wouldn't be Blue Miles.

I don't say the words out loud because the truth is, no one in my family understands. They *can't* understand. Our genetic codes were written in different languages. Too much is lost in the translation.

Irene pulls her knees to her chest and crosses her arms around them. "It's weird to think I'll be leaving home in the fall, isn't it?" The change of subject startles me, and I look at her. She's resting her chin on the groove between her knee-caps, looking oddly dejected. "Two months and seventeen days, to be exact." She looks around my room, as if trying to memorize it. "I hope my roommate at Stanford isn't a psychopath."

It's hard for me to believe she has any problems worth worrying about, but I can see how this possibility might be concerning. I nudge her shoulder with mine. "You'll be fine."

She leans against my bed frame and stretches her pale, athletic legs out in front of her. "When Mom and Dad told me I was going to have a little sister, I pictured you as Dora the Explorer, wandering through the world to get to us." She laughs. "I pictured you with a little backpack and everything. That's what I wanted them to name you—Dora."

I halfheartedly pluck my E string. Anger, it turns out, is exhausting. "I bet you were disappointed, then."

She looks at me, confused. "Why?"

I can think of a thousand reasons why I would have been a disappointing sister for her—my general disinterest in most of the things she talks about comes to mind—but what I say is, "Because I already had a name." I wish she'd leave. All I want to do now is lie down and fall asleep, homework be damned. Besides, none of it matters if I don't get to play with Blue Miles. "At least it was close, right?"

It takes me a moment to realize that something has changed. Irene looks uncomfortable, conflicted.

I ask, "What?"

She doesn't look at me. "Nothing."

"No, what's up?"

She stands, staring at the door, at her feet—anywhere but at me. "I should get back to my speech."

"Irene, what is it?"

Finally, she looks at me, and there's something in her expression that makes me think of a violin tremolo—one note bowed rapidly, conveying a sense of unease.

She seems to struggle to say, "You know your middle name is the same as Mom's, right?"

"Yeah, of course." Nora Jane Wakelin. Irene's middle name is Megan, so we both got a piece of her.

"So you know that Mom and Dad changed your name when you came into the family."

It takes a second for this to click, because I'd never even considered it before. I was two when the adoption was finalized.

"But not my *first* name. Right? I mean, I already had a name."

For as long as I can remember, I've known two things: first, that I was adopted, and second, that my parents hate being reminded of this fact.

"Yeah, of course." But Irene's discomfort is only increasing.

I set my bass down. "Irene, what was my name?"

She hesitates, but I can tell that the pause isn't because she doesn't remember the answer.

I add, "I have a right to know."

Eventually, she says, "Summer."

The word feels heavy and strange in the room. Above the head of my bed, there's a painting of my name, spelled out in musical instruments. Suddenly, it seems like a lie.

"That's what the adoption agency told us. I was only three, but I remember one of the ladies bringing you out and saying, 'Summer, meet your family.' You were so tiny back then, with these little bird bones."

I close my eyes, but my memory doesn't stretch anywhere near that far back. My earliest solid memories are of the day a music teacher came to my second-grade class to teach us how to play "Hot Cross Buns" on a recorder. I ask, "Did I have a last name?"

"No. No middle name, either, as far as I know. Just Summer."

"How did Mom and Dad choose Nora?"

"Could have been because it was semiclose to Dora," Irene says, picking at her cuticles. "But I think they chose Nora mostly because of that Ibsen play." I squint at her, and she clarifies, "You know, *A Doll's House*."

A Doll's House. I remember doing poorly on those reading quizzes.

I've always known about my middle name. I should have realized that they changed the whole thing.

"I thought you knew about this," Irene says. "I don't think Mom and Dad have kept it from you on purpose. They just—" Her next breath shakes. "They wouldn't have thought it mattered."

Of course they wouldn't. And of course they wouldn't have let me decide something like that for myself.

Her hand is on the doorknob. "Maybe I can practice my speech on you tomorrow?"

I say, "Yeah, sure," without really thinking about what I'm agreeing to.

Once I'm alone again, I pull out my phone and stare at the band's group text thread. Cameron, Daniel, and Flynn have all texted to say that they have permission to drive to San Francisco for the gig. Only now do I realize that I didn't even bring it up to my parents. Maybe if I agree to do one of these internships—not that they're really giving me a choice—they'll agree to let me take one day off school to play the most important gig of my life. Negotiation, compromise—isn't that what lawyers are supposed to be good at?

I text the guys that I couldn't ask my parents tonight, but I'll ask tomorrow.

FLYNN: I won't blame them if they say no.

DANIEL: But they won't. Have you seen how persuasive Nora can be?

CAMERON: If she convinced Flynn this was a good idea, then Megan and Jerry will be easy.

FLYNN: I'm not undervaluing Nora's abilities here. I'm just saying that they'll have legitimate concerns.

DANIEL: Don't listen to him, Bass Girl.

DANIEL: You've got this.

I text the flexed-bicep emoji, then close my phone. I don't have any remaining energy for words.

CHAPTER 4

*E*verything I know about my birth parents is written in dry legalese on my adoption papers, but this is how I like to tell the story:

They were in their midtwenties when I was born, living in Central California, and married. (This much I know is true.) But my birth mother felt trapped in the marriage, desperate to get out of suburgatory (I'm editorializing here), so she took off with me when I was still an infant. She and I went to Hawaii (that detail is, remarkably, included in the papers), where we lived until I was about one year old.

Sometimes when I close my eyes and slow my breath, I hear waves crashing on a beach. I like to imagine it's a memory of back then, when my birth mother and I lived in a little grass hut (I'm guessing) just beyond the reach of the surf. I used to picture a woman with shiny black hair leaning over me, like I was in a crib, or lying on a beach towel on the sand. In my mind, I would reach up to touch her hair and discover that it felt just like mine—smooth and fine. I know this isn't a true memory, just something I've imagined so many times it almost feels real.

So, anyway, my birth mother and I were apparently chilling in Hawaii, but then something happened, and she disappeared. A neighbor contacted my birth father, who brought me back to California. Apparently, he couldn't hack the single-dad thing, because a few months later he left me at Catholic Charities with some honest-to-God nuns and never came back.

And that's it. That's all I know.

When my parents adopted me, I could toddle, but I wasn't potty trained. According to them, I started calling my mom "Mama" almost immediately. My parents never talk about my adoption, but I've seen the papers. It was closed, which means there's no identifying information about my birth parents. I do know their names were Martin and Teresa, they were twenty-five, and they were married. They could have listed their racial background or where they were from, but they chose not to. They did, however, provide their professions (hers: *baker/entrepreneur*; his: *mechanic*) and favorite hobbies (both: *music*).

There are lots of things we don't talk about in my family, but the top three are the weight my dad's gained since he was promoted to senior director at his nonprofit, my aunt Jeanette (my mom's younger sister who died when I was little), and my adoption. Maybe that's why I never asked my parents about my name. Years ago, though, I started secretly googling "Martin + Teresa + Nora" + any other relevant terms I could think of, hoping that I might be able to find them and get some answers about why they gave me up and where I come from. Now that I know I've had one of the central details wrong all this time, I'm so angry I could cry. It feels almost malicious, like I've been sitting in a prison with invisible bars.

My parents and Irene have never given any indication that they think of me as a lesser member of our family, so every time I've searched the internet for signs of my biological parents, I've felt corrupted, like I've stumbled upon something filthy in a shadowy corner of the dark web. I've tried, instead, to focus on gratitude, because I know things could have been so much worse for me. I've heard foster care horror stories about abuse and neglect. But gratitude gets exhausting after a while. Sometimes I don't want to have to be thankful that I have a family. I want to deserve one.

All my life, I've made up stories to explain why my biological parents abandoned me. After seeing the movie *Elf*, I became convinced that my story was the opposite of Will Ferrell's, that I was really an elf being raised as a human. I'd imagine my birth mother appearing in my bedroom, telling me that I was a princess in her magical kingdom, that she had taken me to Hawaii to escape an evil witch, who had finally caught her, but not before she hid me among mortals to keep me safe.

Later, when music became my sole focus, I read about Joni Mitchell reuniting with the daughter she'd given up, and I became convinced that I was the child of now-famous musicians, who'd had me when they were young and struggling.

I stare at my phone for several minutes before I type "Martin," "Teresa," "adoption," and then, slowly, "Summer." Once the words are in the search bar, I pause.

Even if this is by some miracle the key to finding my biological parents, do I really want that? If I never find them, then they can be whatever I imagine, forever.

But it feels important to figure out what happened to them, now more than ever. Irene is a replica of our parents. She'll go to Stanford, major in political science, go to law school, become an attorney, save the world. And she'll know how to do it, because she's seen our parents do it. But I'm nothing like my parents; I can't replicate their life. I'm like a goose that's been raised by owls; now it's time for me to migrate south, but no one ever showed me the route.

I press search and start scrolling through the results, refusing to feel guilty this time, or at least refusing to let the guilt hold me back.

I FIRST SEARCH A GENEALOGY ARCHIVE FOR PEOPLE NAMED Summer born in California during my birth year. When I have a list of about twenty names, I start searching for traces of each of them on the internet, crossing out names that seem to match a person with an active social media presence or that appears in an article in a school newspaper. After about twenty minutes, I have five full names:

Summer Huerta
Summer Johnson
Summer Lee
Summer Saiyed
Summer Croft

I stare at the names for a full minute, wondering if it's really possible that one of them once belonged to me; the idea is almost too surreal to be believed. But I plunge onward, searching for a Teresa that might match any of the Summers on the list.

At the end of another hour, I've found three Teresas that seem promising. A Teresa in Santa Barbara married someone named Martin Huerta the year before I was born. Teresa Johnson of Reedley, California, gave up a child for adoption. Teresa Croft divorced someone named Martin Croft in Watsonville, California. I find all of this information via a mixture of the online white pages, the genealogy website, local news articles, and social media. I spend the next few hours searching for the whereabouts of Teresa Huerta, Teresa Johnson, and Teresa Croft.

I find a woman named Teresa Huerta living in a suburb of Santa Barbara. I can only access one picture of her on her social media site. It's a shadowy profile shot, but I think I can see some of myself in her features. Her jaw is round like mine is. Our eyes are similarly wide and brown. Her hair is lighter than mine is, but maybe she highlights it. Her complexion isn't quite like mine, either—a little cooler, like the sky before rain—but it's certainly darker than my parents'.

It's shockingly easy to retrieve her address: 2932 Willow Creek Drive, Unit 3, Goleta, CA 93117. I find the address on Google Maps and zoom in to Street View. The apartment complex is small, single level, and nicely maintained. There's a big tree in the front yard and a truck parked on the street. I find #3 and study it. There's a window to the side of the front door, but it's covered by a white curtain.

My birth mother could be behind there. The idea makes my heart race.

Am I really doing this?

I put my phone down, pick up my bass, and play scales again until my hands stop shaking. Then I write the Willow Creek address next to the name Huerta and move on to Teresa Johnson.

The article I found about her giving up a child is in the *Reedley Gazette* and is dated four years ago, but there's nothing specific about *when* she gave up her child. I try to find a record of her marrying someone named Martin, but just because I can't find a record doesn't mean it doesn't exist. I find her social media profile and study all the public pictures of her, but I don't really see any resemblance between us. Her hair is darker than my mom's, but not even close to black like mine. Her skin is tan, but I doubt it's a natural tan. And "tan" wouldn't describe my skin, anyway; my skin is sort of like the color of the ocean at twilight, an almost golden gray. Then again, I could take after my birth father.

I find two addresses for Teresa Johnson. One is a house

on Hope Avenue. Another is an apartment out past the college. I write down both addresses and move on to Teresa Croft.

At first, I find nothing. I can tell from the genealogy website that at some point a human being named Teresa Croft lived in Santa Cruz County, but there's no trace of her anywhere on the internet. I try searching for "Teresa Croft" plus "adoption." Finally, I try her name plus "bakery" and find an address for a business called Croft's Confections in Watsonville, not far from San Francisco. There's no proof that the owner of Croft's Confections was named Teresa, and when I click on the business's website, it's defunct. The street address now seems to belong to a nail salon, but that's all I've got, so I write down the address and then sit back and look at what I've found.

This morning, the idea that my parents were elves trapped in a witch's spell seemed as real to me as any other theory about who they are or where they might be. But now I have three full names, three addresses.

I could do this. I could find them.

But I don't want to write a letter or call. I need to get to them somehow, observe them. That's the only way I'll know if they're the real deal.

I text the guys: If we're driving all the way to San Francisco, we should play a few other gigs. Make it a tour.

There's a pause, then Daniel responds: Ohhhhhh I like this idea.

CAMERON: So, you got permission?!

ME: I'm working on it.

FLYNN: We can't miss more school.

I plot the addresses on Google Maps. We wouldn't have to travel too far off course to reach each of these cities. I'd just need time to go off on my own.

ME: What if we left Wednesday after school?
Played Santa Barbara that night. Then we
could play gigs Thursday and Friday night on
our way to SF.

ME: We'd only have to miss Thursday and Friday.
One more day won't kill us.

FLYNN: That's four nights in hotels instead of two.
That's expensive.

DANIEL: Cam's parents won't mind.

CAMERON: Honestly, they wouldn't even notice.

No one comments on this. We know that Cameron's credit card activity isn't the only thing his parents miss. This year, they gave him a birthday card that said *Happy 18th*, but he was turning seventeen. He brought the card to school, made it seem like a big joke—"This is a step in the right direction! Last year they completely forgot. Someday soon, they'll show me the same affection they show their cars!"—but it obviously hurt. That weekend, we threw him a surprise party at Daniel's house, and he got super drunk. We found him in Daniel's bathtub, covered in vomit and clutching a bottle of Jack Daniel's. We spent the rest of that night cleaning him up and convincing him not to drunk dial his parents to ask them if they wished they'd never had a kid. When we tucked him into Daniel's bed that night, he mumbled, "They regret everything about me."

I said, "They don't, Cam," and Daniel added, "Besides, who gives a shit what they think?" but Cameron was already asleep.

So yeah, I feel pretty okay with letting Cameron's parents pay for a few extra nights of hotel rooms. We all do.

> FLYNN: But where are we going to play? We can't just show up in Santa Barbara and start playing on a street.
>
> DANIEL: Why not?
>
> ME: But if I could book gigs?
>
> FLYNN: It's still the week before finals.
>
> DANIEL: What do you want to be, Flynn? A student, or a rock star?

I might be the only one in the band who knows what

Flynn's real answer to that question is. I'm not sure why he doesn't admit that he's not interested in taking our band all the way, but when he finally writes, Fine. If Nora can book gigs, and if her parents agree, then we'll do it, my whole body relaxes. I didn't realize I was holding on to so much tension until I finally let it go. It feels like the band is being threatened from without *and* within, and my best chance to keep it all from falling apart is to make sure we get to the Magwitch by Saturday night.

My phone pings again. It's a private text from Daniel: you're up late

I check my phone and see that it's after midnight. My group text probably woke Flynn up. I write back, Can't sleep.

DANIEL: something on your mind?

This is a perfectly neutral thing to say, but it seems almost tender. I do my best to ignore the fluttering in my chest as I write, Just everything.

DANIEL: like?

ME: Blue Miles. Senior year.

DANIEL: life? the meaning of existence?

ME: Pretty much.

Even though it's bound to cause me nothing but pain, I add: How did things go with Darcy?

He doesn't respond for so long that I think he may have fallen asleep, but finally he writes, fine, i guess

If things were happily resolved, wouldn't there be smiley faces and hearts or something? Wouldn't he be using capital letters? He seemed normal in the group text thread, but maybe he was just faking it for the guys.

> DANIEL: i thought she was pulling away because of that director, but apparently she's tense because she's graduating this year and i'm not.

> DANIEL: so . . . that's a relief?

> ME: Isn't she going to the JC? She'll still be living at home.

> DANIEL: that's what i've been saaaayyyyyyying

There's a pause, and then he starts typing again.

> DANIEL: go to sleep, bass girl.

That nickname will be the death of me.

> ME: You're okay?

DANIEL: hey, at least we've got Blue Miles, right?

ME: Yeah. We've always got that.

♪ ♫ ♪ ♫

THE NEXT MORNING BEFORE SCHOOL, I FIND MY PARENTS sitting at the kitchen table, passing each other sections of the *Los Angeles Times* and sipping black coffee out of identical mugs. I spent all night planning what I was going to say to them, but now that I'm here, the words catch in my throat.

"You're up early," my mom says, her voice neutral, as always.

I close my eyes and imagine the Magwitch, what it would feel like to play on that stage. Deep in my bones, I know *that's* what I was made for; I know that if I don't seize this opportunity, if I allow myself to stumble forward in my parents' footsteps toward a life that doesn't even feel like mine, then I'll regret it forever.

So, I open my eyes and do my best Megan Wakelin impression as I say, "I have a proposal for you."

My parents look at each other. My mom refolds her section of the paper and says, "Okay, Nora. We're listening."

I hand them each a stapled packet of paper, then retreat several steps. "On the first page of your packet, you'll find the bio for the band that headlined at the Rowdy last night."

I point at the lower left quadrant of the paper in my mom's hand. "At the bottom, you'll see a breakdown of their album sales over the last five years."

My dad sips his coffee, then says, "What's this about, Nora?"

"Last night, that band, Horoscope, invited Blue Miles to open for them at the Magwitch next Saturday." I hesitate, then say, "Please turn to your second page."

In unison, my parents flip the page, revealing several photographs of the interior and exterior of the Magwitch, along with a list of the most famous bands that have played there, organized by year.

"The Magwitch is a historically significant musical venue in San Francisco. It opened in 1959—"

My dad's nodding along. The nice thing about having maddeningly rational attorneys as parents is that they'll always listen to a carefully crafted argument. He sips his coffee again, then puts down his mug and says, "Your mother and I are aware of the Magwitch and its reputation."

This, frankly, shocks me. My mom mostly listens to classical music, and my dad has a soft spot for bluegrass, but neither genre is heavily represented in the long, illustrious history of the Magwitch.

My mom must notice my surprise, because she explains, "The apartment we lived in at Stanford was twenty minutes from there."

Well, that makes sense, then.

My dad's focusing on the stats at the bottom of the page. "Did Led Zeppelin really play there twice?"

I nod.

"And Ray Charles?"

"Yes. In 1972."

I'm tempted to explain to them exactly what it would mean to me to play on that stage, but I know that's not an argument that will matter to them. So, I stick to the facts. "This summer, Blue Miles was planning on recording our first album. Cameron owns the necessary equipment, and we know a bit about producing. But if I'm gone this summer, then that possibility is gone."

My mom puts down her stapled packet. "So, you want us to let you play a show in San Francisco next weekend." She looks at my dad, using the line of her mouth to communicate something I can't translate, then adds, "The weekend before finals."

My chest tightens. If my heart were a drummer, I'd tell it to stop rushing the beat. Instead, I swallow and say, "Please turn to page three."

They turn the page and find a map of our proposed route, hitting all the towns where I found a biological mother possibility. This feels like such a betrayal of them, but I remind myself that they've been keeping my original first name—the only thing I had left from my biological parents—a secret my entire life, and that feeling recedes.

"We've booked gigs in three towns along the way, so the trip itself won't be wasted. I was waiting until I had all the details before I asked your permission." This, of course, is a lie. I started making a list of possible gig spots in each town, but I haven't called anyone yet. If my parents ask for venue phone numbers and manager names, my best plan is to say I'll give them the details soon, then rush to figure something out, so I go on quickly, "If we leave Wednesday after school, I'll only need to take Thursday and Friday—"

"*Only?*" My dad's eyebrows rise to his nonexistent hairline. "The last two days before finals?"

I repeat the argument I used on Flynn yesterday. "The timing couldn't be better. We won't learn anything new on those days. They'll be dedicated to review, which the guys and I can do on our own as we drive. We'll probably accomplish more on the road than we would in the classroom."

This is another lie. Flynn's the only other member of the band in honors classes, but he'll insist on driving if we take his van, so he won't be much use as a study partner. But my parents don't need to know that.

The drummer inside my chest accelerates as I say, "Please turn to page four." I wait while they flip to a breakdown of income statistics for professional musicians. At the top of the list, I've thrown in a few rock stars making buckets of money, but most of the list consists of musicians backing up bigger names, or playing for live TV shows, or in studio sessions, or on cruise ships, or teaching lessons. No one's retiring at forty on those salaries, but no one's starving, either. Finally, I say, "Being a professional musician does not mean you're a bum."

My dad starts to say something, but I lean over and point at a smaller chart on the bottom of the page. "That's a list of the unemployment rates among people with law degrees over the past five years." I point at a number next to it. "Same for MBAs. Below that, there are statistics for depression and drug and alcohol abuse among doctors and dentists."

My parents are quiet. They appear to be studying the numbers.

"I understand you don't think being a musician is a valuable career." It takes a lot out of me to finally admit to them, "But it's what I want to do with my life. It's who I am."

My dad sits back in his chair as he and my mom make eye contact again. After a pause, my mom says, "We understand that this is how you feel now, Nora. But we still think it's important for you to have different experiences, see more of the world, before you make this choice."

I guess it was too much to hope that they'd realize how much music means to me and drop the internship thing altogether. I take a deep breath and say, "That's why I'll agree to do whichever internship you want, as long as I can have these days to tour our way up to the Magwitch."

My dad's pressing his lips together and nodding. "I'm impressed, Nora. You did your research."

That's not assent yet. I look at my mom.

She places her packet on the table and looks at me. "Your father and I would frankly prefer to keep both you and your sister here with us forever, but that would be negligent parenting." She's tapping her short nails on the table to emphasize certain words—*forever, negligent.* "Our goal, our *duty,* is to make sure you both have the tools to lead healthy, productive, meaningful lives." She takes a deep breath. "I'd love to introduce you to my colleagues in Sacramento, but I think the more promising opportunities for you are in D.C. I'd like you to accept that internship for the summer. I think you will benefit from the experience."

Even though this makes my heart turn sad and sluggish, I don't say anything, hoping against hope that there's a second part to her statement.

She closes her eyes and shakes her head, as if she can't believe what she's about to say, but then the words come out anyway. "Okay." She picks up the packet again and glances at the front page. "We accept your terms. As long as—" She holds up a finger. Thinks. "As long as you call us every night that you're on the road."

My dad chimes in. "And as long as you keep your phone's location tracker on the entire time."

My mom stares at some middle distance between us, probably trying to come up with some other condition to impose on my trip. When she can't think of anything, she says, "Agreed?"

I should feel more excited about this. True, I get to play the Magwitch. I get to tour up the coast with my band. But I'll still have to leave for the whole summer. I wonder what the guys will think about the deal I've just made. I quickly decide that I'll break the news to them after we get back.

I'm thinking about all these things as I say, "Should we get this in writing?"

My dad half smiles as he says, "I think, under the circumstances, a verbal contract is sufficient."

"I know you don't want to hear this, Nora," my mom

says, squaring the pages of my packet in front of her. "But you really would make a fantastic attorney."

I say, "I'll take that under consideration," even though I won't. Just because I *could* do something, doesn't mean I should. I'd think that two people as smart as my parents would recognize that.

It's not until I get to my room and text the guys, I've got permission for the tour! that it really begins to sink in:

We're driving to San Francisco. We're playing the Magwitch. And maybe, though it's a long shot, I'll find my biological parents along the way.

CHAPTER 5

*W*hen I reach Flynn's van after school on Wednesday, Flynn is loading stuff into the back, and Cameron has already staked out shotgun for the first leg, but there's no sign of Daniel. We don't have any classes together, but I usually see him on campus during the day. Today, though, he's been strangely elusive. If I wasn't certain he wants the tour to happen almost as much as I do, I'd worry that he's backing out.

When I ask Flynn if he knows where Daniel is, he shoves an amp to the side, using more force than strictly necessary. "You didn't hear? He and Darcy are having it out by the theater. Full-on shouting match in public. Super classy." He wedges my bass case carefully into the space vacated by the amp. Then he takes my overstuffed gig bag, which is all I brought for my clothes and toiletries, and places it gently at the top of the pile. "Should make Dan lots of fun to be around for the next five days."

I look back toward campus just as Daniel comes striding out through the gate. A second later, Darcy is there behind him. She's screaming something, and though I can't understand the words, I can see that her cheeks are red and tearstained. Daniel faces her, and the volume of their argument drops, but the intensity doesn't. She shoves him in the chest, and I think I see the muscles in his jaw clench. I can't stop staring at them even as I slide to the end of the van's bench seat.

Flynn gets into the front and slams his door. "Oh, my God," he groans. "They're like a soap opera." He looks at Cameron. "You know he's going to be impossible after this. And when we're back on Monday, they'll just kiss and make up, and we'll all have to pretend they didn't recently reenact Jerry Springer's Greatest Hits."

Cameron shakes his head. "I don't know, Flynn. This looks like it could be the real thing."

"Yeah, right. I won't believe those two are broken up until one of them is dead." Flynn looks out his window, which is facing the back of the parking lot. "They've been doing this since second grade."

Sometimes I forget that Flynn, Daniel, and Darcy used to live on the same block. When they were little, the three of them were supposedly kind of inseparable. It's hard to imagine now.

Daniel throws his arms wide, and I hear him shout, "Fine! Fine. That's it, then. Have a nice life." He turns around abruptly and strides toward us.

Darcy shouts something, but I can't understand the

words. She grabs a burrito from someone standing nearby and chucks it at his back. Flynn lets out one loud "Ha!" as the burrito explodes, creating a halo of gooey debris that rains down around Daniel's feet.

Daniel tightens his fists, but continues walking without looking back. When he reaches the van, he climbs onto the upholstered bench seat next to me, slides the door closed, tilts his head against the headrest, and says, "For God's sake, get me out of here."

Flynn looks at him. "Is there *burrito* on your back?" There's still amusement in his voice, but it's laced with actual irritation. "You're going to get my car dirty."

Without moving, Daniel says, "I will detail this van myself, as long as you get me out of this parking lot in the next thirty seconds."

Flynn must believe him, because by my watch we're pulling out of the parking lot twenty-eight seconds later. Several minutes after that, we're on the freeway, heading north.

Once we reach cruising speed, Daniel twists to his side and says to me, "Is there really burrito on my back?"

"Just a little," I say. "Hold on." I pull a tissue out of a box on the floor and wipe salsa and beans off his shirt. I use my fingers to pluck off a couple stray shreds of lettuce and cheese. I also wipe down the seat behind him, on which a couple beans have been squished. "All better."

He sits back again and stares at the tattered, sagging ceiling of the car. After one deep breath, his head rolls to the side, and his eyes land on me. "Love sucks, Bass Girl."

I can feel Flynn watching us in his rearview mirror, so instead of doing what I'd *like* to do—face Daniel, place my fingers gently on his forearm, say, *Only when we fall in love with the wrong people*—I shrug and say, "I guess it does."

♪ ⌐ ♪ ⌐ ♪

AFTER TWO HOURS OF CRAWLING THROUGH L.A. TRAFFIC, the buildings on either side of the freeway become less crowded, and the road angles upward, into the hills. Even though I've mapped everything out a thousand times, I tilt my phone away from Daniel and once again search for directions from our hotel to Teresa Huerta's. Time will be tight. It'll be possible for me to jet over there after we check into our motel and before we head to our gig, but barely.

Tonight, we're playing at a seafood restaurant a couple blocks from the beach in Santa Barbara, near Stearns Wharf. I told the guys that I also have gigs booked in Reedley and Watsonville, but in Reedley it's just a fast-food joint where we can play for tips, and in Watsonville, so far nothing. I've left messages at a few places, but haven't heard back. I'm hoping to get something ironed out before we get there, but if not, I'll say there was some miscommunication and apologize profusely.

I don't feel great about this plan, but it's all I've got.

As the van struggles up a steep stretch of highway,

Daniel leans forward and says for the tenth time, "How can both your radio *and* your tape deck be broken?" He reaches past Flynn to mess with the buttons, but Flynn swats his hand away.

Daniel sits back dejectedly. "When you drive by yourself, do you just sit in silence?"

"It's not that bad." Flynn glances at him. "Sometimes it's even nice. Peaceful. You should try it."

"I see how it could be meditative," Cameron says.

Daniel lets his head fall against the headrest. "Twenty hours of silence?"

"Focus on your breath," Cameron says. "Still your mind."

"Where's your phone?" Flynn asks.

Daniel pulls it out of his pocket and shows us its shattered screen. "Darcy threw it at a tree. The display still sort of works, but audio is completely busted."

I've been listening to the Stone Roses through my earbuds, but I take them out and offer them to Daniel. "Want to listen?"

He shakes his head. "What will you do?"

"Believe it or not, Dan," Flynn says, "there was a time before people listened to music every hour of the day."

"Yeah," Daniel says. "They were called the Dark Ages."

I add, "Medieval peasants would have killed for an iPod," and Flynn glares at me. But Daniel's the one I'm worried about. In the past couple hours, he's bitten his nails until they're almost bleeding. Even ignoring my feelings for him, he's still our lead singer, which means he needs to not have a nervous breakdown before Saturday. "We could share," I say, putting one bud in my right ear and offering him the left one.

He looks at me for a second, then takes the earbud from me. "Thanks."

It feels strangely intimate to lean against him as we find a position that allows us to keep the earbuds in place. I wonder if he notices how neatly we fit together, how warmth spreads pleasantly from his body to mine.

I hand him my phone, but he passes it back.

"You choose," he says. "Play something I haven't heard."

As soon as he makes the request, I know what to play. I scroll through my library until I find Victor Wooten's bass solo cover of "Overjoyed." It's from Wooten's first solo album, recorded between gigs with Béla Fleck and the Flecktones. As the opening notes come through, Daniel closes his eyes. This is the first time he's stayed still since we pulled out of the parking lot. His left ear drops a little closer to his shoulder, which is to say, to me.

"That's perfect," he says, maybe to himself.

"Have you heard it before?"

"No. Isn't it the best thing, though—finding something new?"

I notice Flynn watching us in the rearview mirror again. "Uh, yeah," I say, feeling self-conscious. I'm not doing anything wrong, though, so I try to ignore it.

When the song ends, Daniel takes the phone out of my hands and hits pause. "I actually have a theory that the song you choose when asked that question reveals who you really are."

This doesn't surprise me. I thought my American history teacher was kind of a jerk until I heard him listening to Cat Stevens during lunch, and there was a kid in my fourth grade class who used to tease me about being adopted, but then freshman year I overheard him saying that Nickelback was the best band ever, and I realized he was just an idiot, which made everything he'd ever said lose its power. I never really understand people until I know their taste in music.

"So, what does my song say about me?"

I feel like we have Flynn's attention, even if he's not watching us, so I lean away and stare at my hands, which are folded awkwardly in my lap.

"That you're a bassist."

"Wow. It's like you're psychic."

"Also, you're optimistic." He tilts his head to the side. "And romantic."

I look at him, searching for subtext, but don't find any. He's staring straight ahead now, watching the road. The freeway has narrowed, and we're coming over a ridge, descending onto a long, flat plain. Flynn moves the van into the slow lane, then looks back at us and says, "What are you two talking about?"

Daniel leans forward. "I asked Nora to play a song I hadn't heard."

"What did she play?"

"The Victor Wooten cover of 'Overjoyed.'"

Flynn laughs, looking back at me. "You're such a bass player."

It's true. I do play other instruments—I'm okay on guitar, decent on piano—but with bass it was love at first pluck. Flynn once asked me why I stick with bass when I could play whatever I want. I'd never thought about it before, but as I tried to answer him, I realized it was about control. "The bassist is the anchor," I told him. "Harmonically, rhythmically—the bass line is the foundation of everything."

"But why not let someone else be the foundation?" Flynn said. "The guitarist usually gets all the attention."

He was driving me home from a gig, because Daniel had been lured into some late-night shenanigans with Darcy—I think they and a few kids from drama hopped the YMCA's fence and went skinny-dipping in the overchlorinated pool. I could tell that Flynn approved of my refusing to join Daniel and his group, but the truth was I totally would have gone if not for my curfew.

"But the point isn't to get attention," I said. "The point is to make music. And it all starts with the foundation." I didn't like the idea of Flynn thinking I was morally superior to the skinny-dippers, which is maybe why I admitted, "I don't play bass because I lack an ego. I play bass because I know it's crucial, and I'm the only one I trust to do it right."

Flynn nodded at that and said, "I think that's why I play drums, too. Let the guitarists and the singers prance around up front. I'm more concerned with making sure everything doesn't fall apart at the bottom." I didn't know how I felt about it when he said, "I guess we're the same." But I didn't contradict him.

I hand Daniel my phone and say, "Your turn. Play me something I haven't heard."

He seems to know what to play, too, because a few seconds later a mellow blues guitar starts a riff I recognize, though I can't immediately place it. After a couple bars, I realize it's a cover of "Born to Lose." I look at Daniel, but he's leaning away from me, gazing out his window at the wide, flat desert.

Maybe for him this song is about Darcy, but it seems like there's more to it than that. The lyrics aren't just about losing one love; they're about losing everything, about being doomed to eternal unhappiness. He already told me that this game we're playing is about revealing who we really are. So, what's he trying to say about himself? I glance at him again, but he's still staring out the window.

Maybe he's trying to say he knows that if he and I got together, things would eventually end, and he can't risk it. Maybe he's trying to say he *wants* to be with me, but he's afraid of wrecking everything we have as a band. The thought swirls through me like a Beatles melody—dreamy and bright.

But what if I'm reading the signals wrong? What if he's simply regretting whatever chain of events led him to getting a burrito in the back a few hours ago? What if he's just missing Darcy?

When the song ends, I look at him and say, gently, "You never know. You could get back together."

"Not this time, Bass Girl." He chews on one of his nails.

"This was the big one." Before I can respond, he hands the phone back and says, "Your turn."

As I take the phone from him, I think of lots of songs I could play that would tell him all the things I could never say—"Bad Religion" by Frank Ocean, "I Will Wait" by Mumford & Sons, "Human Performance" by Parquet Courts, "Fake Happy" by Paramore—but decide against all of them. Instead, I tap on Miles Davis's live recording of "It Never Entered My Mind." I've always loved this track; at the beginning, you can hear the audience laughing and chatting in the background, but then Miles comes in and the whole room goes quiet until the final note, when everyone breaks into applause.

After the song ends, I ask, "What does that say about me?"

He studies me for a minute, as if he needs to read the meaning of the song on my face.

I always thought Daniel was beautiful—it's an objective fact—but I didn't notice myself daydreaming about him until we'd been playing together for a couple months. I think it started on the night Cameron's parents hired us to play for a New Year's party at their house. The event was for their work colleagues, and I'd never seen adults act so ridiculous. A woman who I later found out is a pediatric cardiologist danced on a table; Cameron's dad, a literal brain surgeon, dove into their pool wearing fifteen-hundred-dollar shoes.

That night, Cameron and Flynn kept wanting to take breaks, get food, wander around the house to watch all the doctors make fools of themselves, but Daniel and I just wanted to play. It didn't matter that no one was listening to us; that wasn't the point. For once, Darcy wasn't there to distract him—she'd gone to a New Year's party hosted by someone in the drama club—so all Daniel wanted to do was play music, which is all I've ever wanted to do.

Eventually, Cameron and Flynn did go inside, but Daniel and I stayed out under the pergola near the end of the yard and kept playing new songs—inventing bass-guitar arrangements along the way. The Zamanis' house is perched at the top of a hill, providing a view that extends across several cities—Mission Viejo, Aliso Viejo, Laguna Beach— all the way to the ocean. It's one of the most beautiful spots I've ever seen. Still, as it got later, more people abandoned the yard for the house, until it was just Daniel and me outside, facing each other, listening, responding in the music.

After several classic rock covers, I suggested we play "Nothing Else Matters" by Metallica. He knew the lyrics but not the guitar part, so I borrowed Cameron's guitar, and Daniel just sang. We were in the middle of that song when we heard everyone in the house erupt into applause. Through the long glass doors, we saw people embracing each other, blowing noisemakers, pulling poppers and releasing a storm of confetti. The year had ended, but we kept playing until we reached the end of the song.

There was a moment of silence before I put down Cameron's guitar and said, reluctantly, "I guess we should go inside."

Daniel lifted his guitar back into his lap and started

playing "Blackbird," but then stopped halfway through the verse. "Yeah, I guess we should."

I picked up my bass and played a line that would complement his guitar part, and then Daniel came in again. He started to sing, and then I found a harmony line above his. When we finished that song, he smiled at me and said, "I'm so glad we found you, Bass Girl."

To disguise how pleased I was by this, I played rolling triads across my strings. "I'm glad to be found."

He started playing something I didn't recognize, something he was writing. As he ran through the guitar part, he said, "I don't want to jinx this or anything, but I really think we could take Blue Miles all the way." He looked back toward the house. "Cameron's killer on lead. Flynn may be wound a little tight, but he's a great drummer." He looked at me. "And you and I—we *live* this. Don't we?" It wasn't really a question. Besides, I'd been thinking the same thing.

Since then, I've spent more time hanging out one-on-one with Cameron and Flynn than I have with Daniel. Still, I've always wondered if Daniel feels the way that I do—that we understand each other, maybe even better than we should. Maybe that's why my heart starts to race as he narrows his eyes and peers at me now, while we sit in the back of Flynn's van. I'm afraid that if he looks too closely, he'll see straight to the bottom of my soul.

But after a moment, he just says, "It says that you have good taste." He takes my phone out of my hand.

"And?"

"That you're not a fan of songs with lyrics."

"You can do better than that."

He looks at me. "And that the waters are deep."

He types something into my phone, and then a song by the Killers comes through. After a couple bars, I recognize that it's "Smile Like You Mean It."

I shake my head. "No good. I've heard this one before."

But he just closes his eyes and says, "It's so much easier to communicate through music than through words, don't you think?"

I'm glad he can't see me when I respond with, "Yeah, totally." Because if he could see my expression, he'd know that what I really mean to say is, *Why do you have to be so perfect?*

CHAPTER 6

I sit on the edge of my bed and stare at the image of Teresa Huerta's condo on Google Maps. Our motel is fairly close to the water, not far from the restaurant we're playing at tonight. Teresa Huerta's address is fifteen minutes away, on the edge of a town called Goleta. If I order a car now, then I can be back before we need to leave for our gig. The guys might not even notice I'm gone. The alternative is to go in the morning, but it might be harder to get away then.

The guys are in the room next to mine. Through the thin wall, I can hear them arguing about who has to share a bed with whom tonight. Flynn turned eighteen last month, and Cameron has a very convincing fake ID, so they were able to check into our rooms for us. But then after an awkward pause in the hallway fifteen minutes ago, the boys all filed into room 212, leaving room 214 all to me. This strikes me as incredibly stupid.

After I order my ride and see that I have seven minutes

before it gets here, I bang on the wall and say, "One of you can sleep in here. There are two beds."

There's a pause, and then the murmuring resumes, a bit quieter this time. Finally, Flynn says through the wall, "Who would you want as your roommate?"

Cameron's voice comes through next. "Me! You know I've got the best hygiene."

Flynn cuts in. "No way. He might have more hair products than a Kardashian, but you know he's a slob."

Cameron again: "Please don't make me share a room with Dan. He's literally in a fetal position right now."

"Well, I don't want to share a room with him," Flynn says. "Besides, I drove. I should get preference."

"Unfair," Cameron says. "You wouldn't let one of us drive your van if we begged you."

"Fine," I say. "Daniel can have the extra bed in here, and then neither of you has to deal with him."

There's silence on the other side of the wall, punctuated, eventually, by a quick knock on my door. I open it and find Daniel standing on the outdoor walkway, carrying his duffle bag and somehow looking both glum and triumphant.

"Thanks," he says. "Those two are impossible." The door swings shut, and suddenly I'm very aware of the two double beds, separated by a narrow nightstand. "And I was not in a fetal position. I was just resting."

"No problem." Does he look this happy because we'll be sleeping in the same room tonight, or because he loves beating Flynn in anything? I don't have time to try to figure it out; the car will be here in two minutes. I step toward the door, holding up my phone. "I'm gonna make a call."

I have my hand on the doorknob when he says, "Do you have a bed preference?"

"What?"

He points to the beds. "Do you care which bed you sleep in?"

"Not really."

"Are you sure?" He sits on the uncomfortable-looking peach-colored chair by the window. "Darcy would make up a preference just to make sure she got her way."

I shouldn't be surprised he's bringing her up, but it still irritates me. I can't keep all the frustration out of my voice as I say, "Then maybe she isn't as perfect as you thought she was."

"Yeah." He draws his knees in toward his chest: the fetal position. I almost wish I'd asked Cameron to be my roommate. The last thing I need is to spend the next five days listening to Daniel moan about Darcy. He starts to say, "You know, she used to tell me—"

But I hold up my phone and cut in, "I've really got to make this call."

He hesitates, then says, "Yeah. Of course."

I open the door. "It might take a while, but I'll be back before we need to leave."

"You'd better be. Without you, Blue Miles is three guys on a stage holding instruments and looking stupid."

I'm just vain enough for this to soften my frustration. Besides, they *just* broke up, and I don't really know the circumstances yet.

I lean against the door frame. "Are you going to be okay on your own for a little bit?"

He's been staring blindly out the window, but now he looks up at me. "Yeah, I'll be fine. Thanks."

As I hurry down the stairs toward the silver Mazda that matches the image on my car-ordering app, I imagine coming back to the room with Daniel tonight, too wired for sleep. Maybe we'll sit up late talking about the future of Blue Miles, then all the reasons Darcy was never right for him. Maybe to distract him, I'll suggest we play music, and we'll sit together on one bed as we invent something together, a new song, something lovely and lilting. After the final note rings to silence, maybe he'll look at me through those eyelashes and say, *Where have you been all my life, Bass Girl?*

But by the time I reach the car, my daydreams about Daniel fade to a background hum—not the current priority, but not completely gone. As I slide into the backseat, the driver asks, "Are you Nora?"

"Yeah," I say. Though, in my mind I add, *Well, sort of.*

I guess that's what I'm trying to find out.

THE DRIVER ISN'T VERY TALKATIVE. THE NEXT THING HE says to me after "Are you Nora?" is "Is this it?"

The apartment looks shabbier in person than it did on

Google Street View, but the light is gorgeous right now, with the sun drifting toward the ocean just a few miles away. When I open the car door, the air smells misty and floral. It reminds me of the opening notes of a song, though I can't place the title or the artist.

"Yeah, this is it. Thanks." I get out of the car, and as it pulls away, it occurs to me that this is an extremely stupid thing I'm doing. Even if Teresa Huerta actually lives here and is home, the odds that she's my birth mother are ridiculously small.

A beat-up green truck moves slowly down the street behind me. A few houses away, a man and a woman are arguing. I briefly wonder if police would be able to find me, using the location tracker on my phone, if I disappeared.

For some reason, the voice that pops into my brain is Irene's. As clearly as anything, I hear her say, *I would never go chasing after parents who demonstrably didn't want me. I have better things to do with my time.*

I respond to Irene-in-my-head with, *But you don't know what it feels like to be missing the instruction manual to your own DNA. You're an owl being raised by owls. I need to find my geese.*

To which she says, *Nora, you're not making sense.*

To which I say, *See. That's my point. To you, I don't even make sense.*

She starts to respond, but I cut her off by marching determinedly toward Teresa Huerta's front door. I hesitate for only half a heartbeat before knocking.

Through the door, I hear a man's voice, then a woman's. Crescendoing footsteps. What instrument would that be? How would I write this music?

The door opens, and I'm confronted by a man in tattered shorts and a grease-stained T-shirt. I smell something cooking; the flavors are spicy and familiar.

"Can I help you?" the man says. His hair is dark and shaggy, framing a youthful, brown face; his eyes are blue green and narrowed suspiciously at me.

A woman steps into view behind the man. "Who is it, babe?"

My stomach leaps into my throat, because she at least *looks* like she could be my biological mother. She seems to be the right age, the right build—tall, skinny—though paler than I thought, from her picture online. But I remind myself that if she's *it*, then she's only *half*.

"Are you Teresa?" I manage to say.

The man looks back at her, and the woman steps forward. She hesitates, then says, "Yeah."

Why didn't I figure out what I was going to say? I have no words at all.

"Are you selling something?" the man says. He doesn't sound annoyed, more like he's trying to be helpful. "Because we're probably not interested."

I shake my head, then force out, "I just—I wondered—I'm looking for—" I close my eyes, take a deep breath. What's more frightening? The idea that this isn't her or that it is? "Is there any chance that you could—"

They're both looking seriously worried right now.

They seem so nice, like a really great couple.

"Are you okay?" the woman says. "Do you need us to call someone for you?"

"No," I say. It's now or never. "I just wondered if you ever had a daughter named Summer."

The man looks back at Teresa, who's shaking her head. But something has changed in her expression; she's looking at me with dewy, tear-heavy eyes.

"It's just—" God, this is going to sound insane. "I was wondering if it's possible that you could be my biological mother."

The man puts his arm around the woman's shoulders. "Sorry, kid," he says. "But that's impossible. We tried to have kids, and couldn't."

From the way the woman looks at me, I can see that this is the truth.

"Oh." I feel like such an enormous ass. "I'm really sorry."

Teresa's shaking her head. "No, don't be," she says. "I wish we could help you. I wish we were what you're looking for." She looks past me to the street. "Are you here alone?"

"Yeah."

The man widens his eyes. "You probably shouldn't be knocking on strangers' doors by yourself." For someone who looks so scruffy, he sounds an awful lot like my dad.

"I know."

Teresa squeezes the man's waist. "Come inside. Let us call you a ride."

"She *definitely* should not be going into strangers' houses, though," the man says. He looks at me. "You're lucky we're good people, Summer."

"Actually, my name's Nora," I say. "My parents changed it when they adopted me."

"Do they know you're here?"

I shake my head.

The man sighs. "Well, you're welcome to come inside, but don't do this again."

I feel like such an idiot. And I really do need to get back to the motel as soon as possible. "I'll wait out here," I say, feeling like my insides have been punctured, like if someone cut me open right now they wouldn't find actual organs, but a handful of popped balloons.

Teresa steps past the man and joins me on the porch. "I'll wait with you."

The man hesitates, then heads into the house, closing just the screen door. Once we're alone, Teresa says to me, "Marty would have been a good dad."

I look at her. "Is his name Martin?"

She nods. "We've been married almost eighteen years. High school sweethearts. Everyone expected us to have a gaggle of kids, since we hooked up so young and everything."

"That's actually how I found you. My birth parents' names are Martin and Teresa."

"It's strange, isn't it?" Teresa studies her hands. "Around the same time Marty and I were trying to get pregnant, there was another Martin and Teresa giving their child away." She looks at me. "We could have traded lives."

I order a car, and I'm almost disappointed when I see that it'll be here in only a couple of minutes. I'm feeling reckless and hurried as I ask her, "Would you have wanted to?"

She shakes her head. "You know, even back then, when we were trying, and things were so emotional, I knew that if we never had kids, we'd be fine. We're"—she seems to consider her next words carefully—"*content*, just the two of us." She looks at me. "The people who adopted you, they must have wanted you pretty badly."

"Yeah," I say. "I think they did."

The truth is, I *know* they did. My parents could have had more kids biologically if they'd wanted. On the rare occasion when they talk about it, they've said they simply knew their second child was already out there somewhere, trying to find her way home. When my dad tells the story, he usually tears up.

None of this is making me feel better.

A blue Prius pulls up in front of Teresa's home, and its license matches the one on my app, so I stand.

Teresa stands, too, and walks with me toward the curb. She asks, "Do you live nearby?"

"No, I'm in a band, actually, and we're just passing through."

The left side of her mouth curls up in a half smile, and I realize that we don't look as much alike as I initially thought. Her lips are fuller, and her nose has a little dimple on the end. "Marty's in a band, too. He plays bass."

"*I* play bass."

We look at each other for a moment, and finally, she asks, "Are you playing somewhere tonight?"

"Yeah, a place called the Cove—"

"By Stearns Wharf?"

"Yeah," I say. "We start at seven and play until close."

The guy driving the Prius opens his door and asks, "Do you need help loading anything?" which I take as a subtle/not-subtle reminder that I'm wasting his time. I open the rear passenger-side door and say to Teresa, "I'm sorry for bothering you."

She holds the door for me as I get into the car. "It was no bother." Before she closes it, she adds, "Good luck, Nora." She stands there on the curb until the Prius reaches the end of her block and turns out of sight.

♪ ♩ ♪ ♩ ♪

WHEN I GET BACK TO THE ROOM, DANIEL IS SITTING IN THE same peach-colored chair, but he's no longer staring blindly out the window. He narrows his eyes at me as I step toward the bathroom.

"Do you need to get in here before we leave?" I say, even as I'm shutting the bathroom door behind me.

"No." I hear him get off the chair and follow me. When he says, "That was a pretty long phone call. Were you talking to your parents?" it sounds like he's standing right outside.

"Uh, yeah." I *will* call my parents before we go to bed tonight, so this doesn't feel like a total lie.

I'm rummaging through my gig bag for my toiletries when Daniel says, "Then why did you need to drive somewhere?"

My hands freeze. If the guys find out about my plans for the week, they'll know that there was no misunderstanding about the gigs in Reedley and Watsonville; they'll know that I dragged them miles out of our way and made them miss an extra day of school for my own massively selfish agenda. I need to deflect, so when I can move again, I open the bathroom door and glare at him.

"Were you *spying* on me?"

"No." He squares his shoulders defensively. "After you left, I decided to go for a walk, and I saw you get into that car."

"That is none of your business," I say, hoping that Daniel will just let it drop. Any minute, Flynn will come say it's time to leave, but I feel like a mess. I splash water on my face, then grab my eyeliner.

"It's my business if you're lying to me about it."

"No, it's really not."

When I finish with it, my eyeliner looks a little shaky, but whatever. I reach for my mascara next, even though it seems risky to put it on tonight, since I already feel on the verge of tears.

Daniel's gone silent behind me, but somehow this makes me *more* uncomfortable. I pull my hair out of its bun and try brushing it, but that only makes it look limp and greasy.

What I really need is a shower, but there's obviously no time for that.

Someone knocks on our door, and I hear Flynn's voice say, "Time to go. We'll meet you at the van."

I pull my hair back up into a tight ponytail and then turn toward Daniel, who's still staring at me with an expression I can't decipher. "What?"

His eyes search mine, and even though I'm half-panicked and more than a little irritated, I can't help thinking that I've never seen eyes quite so blue, or so kind, or so worried. Finally, he says, "Just tell me one thing."

"Maybe."

"If you needed help with anything"—his eyes narrow; I can tell he's trying to decode my reaction, so I keep my face as blank as possible—"you'd tell us, right?" I can't tell if he steps forward, or leans forward, or if the room just shrinks, bringing us closer together. "Or at least you'd tell *me*."

"Yeah," I say. "I would."

After a pause, he steps aside, letting me lead the way to the door.

CHAPTER 7

We got lucky with this gig. The Cove advertises live music on Wednesdays, but the regular band couldn't make it this week. I happened to call them before they started contacting their usual second-stringers. It's seafood with a surfer aesthetic. They specialize in battered halibut and fruity frozen drinks.

There's a small dais near the back, where we set up our equipment. The manager requested that we play as much Beach Boys as possible. We don't have any Beach Boys in our usual repertoire, but we added a few songs to our gig book to make them happy. When we were rehearsing these songs on Monday, Flynn said, "I don't know why we're going to all this trouble for a venue we'll never play again."

I said, "It never hurts to learn new music."

Daniel said, "And you never know who'll see us."

In rehearsal, Flynn played the bouncy, simple beats with

as little emotion as possible. But I know that once we're on-stage he'll rise to the occasion. He can't help it.

As we tune our instruments, Cameron asks what our word should be for the night.

Flynn plays a soft roll on his snare, then says, "How about *mediocre*?"

"Oh, lighten up," Daniel says. He gestures to the room behind him. "This place is cool."

Cameron says, "I wouldn't go that far, but it's definitely chill, like if Jimmy Buffett died and was reincarnated as a restaurant." He strums a chord. "How about *relax* for our word?"

At the same time that Daniel says, "I like it. Both an ac-tion and a command," Flynn says, "That's not how reincar-nation works, Cam."

Cameron responds, "How do you know?"

Before Flynn can launch into a lecture about compar-ative religion, Cameron starts playing the opening riff of "Margaritaville."

"Relax," I say. I try to let the word in, but it doesn't feel like there's room for it in my chest.

Daniel closes his eyes as he repeats it: "Relax."

"Relax," Flynn says. His tone suggests that he's not really taking in the meaning of the word, either.

The restaurant is only about a quarter full when we start playing our first set, but forty-five minutes later, the tables around us have filled and there's a crowd at the bar. People are talking over us, of course, but a handful of them pause to clap at the end of each song.

Our stage is small, so I spend most of the set sitting on a stool near Flynn. Daniel stands up front, and Cameron stands to Daniel's right. When it's time for the last song before our break, Daniel looks back at us and says, "Can we do an instrumental? I don't want to wear out my voice."

In response, Cameron strums a C-major chord, then an F-major.

"C blues?" I say, running through the scales.

He nods. Flynn switches to brushes and starts playing a light beat behind our groove. Daniel picks up the chord progression, and then Cameron takes the first solo. We've been jamming for several minutes when Martin and Teresa walk in. He's changed into jeans and a clean shirt, and she's wearing a summery halter dress and sandals. After a brief conversation with the host, they take a seat at the bar. They see me and wave—Martin also mimes playing a bass and then gives me two thumbs up—but for now all I can do is nod in their direction and smile. Luckily, the guys seem to notice none of this.

After Daniel announces our twenty-minute break, the manager of the restaurant turns up the radio to fill the silence. Daniel looks back at the rest of us and says, "Didn't the manager say something about free dinner?"

This will probably be my best opportunity to talk to Martin and Teresa, so I unplug my phone from where it's been charging behind the stage and say, "I've got to call my parents." I give Daniel a look that I hope he interprets as, *For real this time.* "Get me a burger, and I'll be there soon."

Cameron and Flynn accept this without question, but Daniel hesitates. I can see a question forming in his mind, but finally he says, "Don't let your burger get cold," then follows Cameron and Flynn across the room, to the kitchen.

Once my guys are out of view, I weave through the crowd to the bar. Teresa notices me first and says, "I hope it's okay we came."

"Of course. I'm glad you did."

"You're solid on your instrument," Martin says. It looks like he showered. His beard scruff is gone, and his hair, which was previously smooshed to one side, is neatly combed. "Way better than I ever was."

"Thanks," I say. "And thanks for coming. I never expected—"

"We know," Teresa says. "But we come to this place all the time anyway."

Martin sips his beer, then says, "My band has subbed here, too."

"Besides, we wanted to hear you play." Teresa squeezes his knee. "Marty always said that if we *had* had kids, then he would have wanted them to play music."

He smiles at her. "We would have needed a litter of kids to make the dream *really* come true. One to play drums, one to play rhythm guitar, one to play lead—"

"Of course, they probably would have picked up accordion, harp, and bagpipes, just to rebel."

"They'd *never*."

Teresa squeezes his knee a bit harder, which seems to tickle. He laughs and sits back quickly.

The person on Martin's other side leaves, and Martin gestures to the empty stool. "Sit with us. Let us buy you something to eat."

I shake my head. "Our dinner's covered. Part of our fee."

"Oh, yeah, of course." He looks past the bar. "Ask Eugene for a side of onion rings. You won't be disappointed."

Teresa's about to say something, but abruptly, I don't think I want to hear it. I don't want to let myself like these people. It's bad enough that I'm looking for my biological parents; I don't want to go around getting attached to strangers, too. There's only so much betrayal I can stomach. So, I give them the same excuse that I gave the guys, and then, even though it wasn't my original plan, I step toward the patio to call my parents.

Once outside, I go through the back gate to an empty space behind the kitchen, which is hidden from both the parking lot and the street. My mom answers the landline after two rings, and then my dad's voice is there beneath hers. They ask about the drive, the hotel, the restaurant. I tell them everything has been fine, easy, and safe, that I've been studying in the car and that after we checked into the motel, I took a brief nap. I tell them the guys are all sharing one room, and I have a room to myself.

I expected to feel better after talking to them, but instead I feel a thousand times worse, because I don't think I've told them anything true. My dad asks me something about traffic, but I cut in and say, "I'd love to talk longer, but I really need to get back inside for the second set."

There's a brief pause, and then my mom says, "Of course, Nora. Have fun—".

My dad cuts in, "And be safe!"

"We love you."

I feel an uncomfortable tightness in my throat as I press my phone against my ear and say, "I love you, too."

The call ends, but I don't leave my sheltered, shadowy spot. I know our break is probably halfway over, but I'm not sure I could eat a burger right now if I tried. Once I realize I'm about to cry, I hop up and down a few times, stretch my arms, square my shoulders. If I cry, the guys will notice, and then Daniel won't be the only one with questions.

I'm almost ready to head back inside when I hear Daniel call my name. I could use another minute to compose myself—my nose feels stuffy, and even though I managed to keep all my tears back, my eyes are probably red—so I press myself deeper into the shadows. But a second later he steps around the corner, looks right at me, and says, "Nora, our food's ready—"

I try to make my voice as even as possible as I say, "I'll be there in a second."

He hesitates, then says, "Okay." But he doesn't move. He doesn't step forward, but he doesn't leave. He just hovers. Eventually, he asks, "Is everything okay?"

The truth is, the weight of this secret is crushing me, but the thought of sharing it with someone makes some of the tightness in my chest release. I wrap my arms around my midsection and stare at my shoes. "Promise you won't tell anyone?"

"Yeah, of course."

"This afternoon, I—" I can't believe I'm about to say this out loud, to admit to someone what I'm really doing. "I went looking for my biological parents."

"Wow." He moves to my side, then leans against the wall. "Wait. Did you find them?"

"No," I say.

"What made you think—?"

I briefly tell him almost everything, aside from my impending exile to D.C. I don't tell him about the potential birth mothers in Reedley and Watsonville, but I do tell him about Martin and Teresa Huerta, and the fact that they're sitting at the bar right now.

When I finish, he's quiet. Over the sound of the chatter and clinking glasses and piped-in music from the patio, I think I can hear the ocean beating its rhythm against the shore. We're just a couple blocks away from the coast, so it's possible. It's also possible, though, that I'm imagining it, or that I'm really hearing the breeze through the landscaping. It's so hard to know what's real and what's illusion.

Finally, Daniel says, "Summer." He repeats the name a couple times, as if testing it, determining whether or not it fits. Then, "All of this seems like a stretch."

"Trust me, I don't need to be reminded that this is probably not going to work." I smudge tears off my cheeks as I say, "I know it's stupid."

"No, I get it," he says. He's picking at his nails again, a thing he does when he's nervous or uncomfortable. I have no idea why *he* would feel weird right now. "But I didn't know you were—" He stops, looks toward the sky, which is dark, once again blanketed by a low, thick marine layer. The air feels damp and heavy. "I didn't know you wondered about them."

"It's hard not to wonder," I say. "I'm so different from my family." I take a deep, shaky breath. I've never articulated this to anyone before. "I've always wondered if my biological parents are more . . ." More what? I finish, lamely, "Like me." I feel the tightness gathering in my throat again, and I can't continue. I look toward the light of the patio to my left and say, "We should probably go in."

Daniel nods, but as I step past him, he touches my elbow. That sends a brief spark through me, making me stop. "Are there others?" he asks. "Other people you're going to look up while we're on the road?"

I shrug, as if this is no big deal. "Yeah. That's the plan, anyway."

"Is that why you booked these gigs?"

I cross my arms over my chest. "Hey, a gig is a gig, right?"

I hear Flynn call my name, then Daniel's. He must be standing at the edge of the patio, staring out over the darkened yard.

Daniel groans, but he pushes himself away from the wall; we both know our break is over. As we head back into the restaurant, I don't bother to ask him not to rat me out to the other guys. It's not his style.

WE'RE NEARING THE END OF OUR LAST SET WHEN MARTIN and Teresa leave. They wave at me once, and I nod at them. As they walk out, Martin's arm is around Teresa's shoulders. She says something to him before they disappear around the corner, and I wish I knew if it was about me. But then they're gone, and I know I'll never see them again.

It occurs to me that this happens every day—paths cross and diverge, like non-imitative melodies in some massive polyphonic symphony. It's possible that one of my birth parents has come to a Blue Miles gig, and I just didn't know who they were. Maybe they didn't know who I was, either. Maybe they thought I looked familiar, or I had a sense of déjà vu, but then they went this way and I went that way. Maybe our paths bent back toward each other, only to bend away again.

I'm so distracted by these thoughts that I fail to notice when Flynn cues us to play a final time through the chord progression of "All Along the Watchtower." The band cuts out, but I continue playing my bass line for two awkward beats. The guys look at me like I just farted audibly, but the restaurant is mostly empty now, and no one else seems to notice.

We keep playing even when there's just one couple left at a table near the back and a handful of people hanging around the bar. For the last ten minutes of our set, we jam on a progression that Cameron invents. When Daniel does his final "We're Blue Miles. Good night," the only people left to applaud us are a bartender and the wait staff.

Ted, the manager, approaches us with the envelope containing our fee for the night—four hundred dollars for the four of us to split. "Nice job, kids," he says, as he hands the envelope to Flynn. People always give our fee to Flynn. They seem to intuit that he's the one who's least likely to misplace it. "On the phone, Nora said you're just passing through, right?"

"Yeah," Flynn says. "We're playing in San Francisco on Saturday."

"The Magwitch," Daniel adds.

Ted whistles, impressed. "Let me know if you're ever coming through here again. Wednesdays are hit or miss, even with the live music. But sometimes we have bands play on Saturdays. Do you play mostly covers, or do you have original music?"

"We usually play originals," Daniel says quickly.

Flynn jumps in with, "But we don't live in the area."

Cameron has already taken his guitar out to the van, so while Daniel and Flynn alternately try to get a follow-up gig at the Cove and dissuade Ted from offering us one, I head outside with my bass.

Flynn parked in the back of the lot, as per Ted's instructions. There are only a few other cars scattered across the badly lit space. After the heat and noise of the restaurant, the night air is refreshing. The marine layer has broken, and through a gap in the clouds I'm able to see a smattering of bright specks scattered across the inky sky. The air seems a little different here, so close to the ocean. I let my mind wander to what I'd be doing, what I'd be *like*, if I'd grown up here with the Huertas. Would I have a different cultural identity? A different set of values and beliefs? Would I be someone else, fundamentally? Am I a malleable thing, shaped by my circumstances? If so, then why have I never molded to fit with my family? Why do I still feel so outside of everything?

I don't see Cameron, so I'm under the impression that I'm out here alone, but then I hear voices coming from the other end of the parking lot, and after a moment I find them—Cameron and a guy I remember seeing inside. During our last set, I think he was sitting with some friends at a table in the back. Now he and Cameron are leaning against a shiny, sporty car.

I open the back of the van and slide my bass in next to the spare cables and amps that Flynn packed. Then I hesitate. Even from here, I can tell that Cameron and this stranger are flirting, and I don't want to interrupt something good. But I also see the stranger pass him a rectangular bottle, out of which he takes one long swig, then another, before passing it back. And I know from experience that Cameron and whiskey don't mix well.

I look back toward the restaurant and see Flynn and Daniel still talking to Ted by the bar, so I step cautiously toward Cameron, hoping that I'm doing the right thing. As I get closer, the guy he's with notices me and says, "Hey, you're the bass player, right? You are wicked on your instrument." His voice is deep and melodic.

Cameron leans toward me and says, "That's what we

should call you, Nora. Wicked Wakewin. Wickled Wakelin."
He snort-laughs. "That's hard to say."

I really hate Drunk Cameron.

"Cam, we should finish loading up."

Cameron laughs once, loudly—an abrupt, cheerless *Ha!*
"Nora, that sounded *dirty.*"

The stranger finds this funny, too, even though the unintentional innuendo was a stretch at best. The bottle ends up in Cameron's hand again, and he takes another gulp.

"Cameron—"

But before I can finish my thought, I hear the restaurant door swing open, and then Flynn's and Daniel's voices fill the parking lot. It sounds like they're arguing about the merits of gigs in restaurants. Daniel mentions something about free food, and Flynn complains that no one actually listens to the music.

"Cam," I say, stepping forward. "You know you don't want them to see you like this."

I can tell that even through the alcohol-induced brain fog, he knows what I'm talking about. Because Cameron getting shit-faced at his surprise party this year wasn't exactly a one-time thing. In fact, for Flynn at least, it was kind of the last straw.

"What does she mean?" the stranger says, teasingly. "Does she mean with *me*?"

"No," I say to him. "You seem like a nice enough guy, but Cameron's got to be up early tomorrow. We have another gig to play."

Cameron pauses, stares at the bottle in his hand. Then—and when he does this, I feel a thousand little muscles in my body unclench—he hands it back to the stranger. He places his left hand gently on the guy's cheek and says, "You have a beautiful smile." He leans in and kisses him once before pushing himself away from the car, moving to my side.

"That's it?" the guy says. He sounds like he's teasing, but I see real disappointment in his face. I almost feel sorry for him.

"Bass Goddess speaks truth," Cameron says. "We've got an early call time." He holds up his phone, suggesting, I guess, that they've swapped numbers. "But I won't forget you."

The guy doesn't look convinced as he says, "Good luck, Cameron." Before we have a chance to walk away from him, he gets in his car and turns on the engine. I really do feel sorry for him when the song that starts streaming through his speakers is by Young Fathers. I love that band.

As we head back toward the van, Cameron says to me, "Don't look at me like that, Nora." He reaches into his pocket and pulls out a pack of gum. He unwraps two sticks and pops them both into his mouth. "I'm not drunk. Just relaxed. That was our word for the night, wasn't it? I'm leaning into it."

I reach out for his hand and squeeze it, so he knows I'm not judging him when I say, "Maybe so. But if you relax again this weekend, then Flynn is going to make you take a bus to San Francisco."

He squeezes my hand back. "Fair point, Wicked Wakelin."

When we reach the van, he climbs into the back next to Daniel, probably to keep as much distance between himself and Flynn as possible. I climb into the front and pull a tube of berry-scented lotion out of my gig bag, hoping it will help mask the scent of the alcohol. It seems to work, because Flynn says nothing as he starts the van and maneuvers carefully toward the main road.

CHAPTER 8

It's a little after midnight when we get back to the motel. Daniel seemed to have boundless energy as long as we were at the Cove, but he was so quiet during our five-minute drive back here that I thought he'd fallen asleep. Now he's sitting on the edge of his bed—he chose the one by the bathroom—scrolling through something on his cracked phone, and I realize that he must be thinking about Darcy. I wish I knew *what* he was thinking about her. Is he missing her? Rehashing their last argument? Feeling relieved that it's finally over? I'm debating whether I should ask him how he's doing when he sighs and says, "I keep expecting her to text me."

I try to suppress my twinge of disappointment as I pull my toothbrush out of my toiletries bag and ask, "Have you considered texting her?"

"She threw a burrito at my back." He's still staring at his phone as he says, "I've got my pride."

I look over his shoulder at his phone. "Yeah, there's heaps of pride in stalking her Instagram."

He sets his phone aside, then leans back on his hands and looks at me. "What about your guy?"

"What?" I ask, my voice a pitch higher than normal. "What guy?"

"The one you told me about behind the Rowdy. The crush you've never confronted. When are you going to tell him how you really feel?"

I don't have a great answer for that, so I just say, "Fine. Stalk her on Instagram. I don't care."

I'm trying to figure out how to segue into brushing my teeth when he drops his forehead into his hands and says, "God, I really fucked up this time."

"Hey, it's not your fault." It occurs to me that I don't actually know this for a fact, but it seems like the right thing to say.

When he doesn't respond, I set my toothbrush down on the TV stand, then sit next to him, placing my hand on his back. I have never been so aware of my hand before; it feels like ice compared to the metabolic firestorm coming through his T-shirt.

"You two gave it a real shot. Three years—there are marriages that don't last as long." I wince, remembering that his parents are acrimoniously divorced, but he doesn't seem to make the same connection.

"I know." His voice shakes as he repeats, "I know." He sits up, squares his shoulders. "Sorry about that. I promise not to spend the rest of the week crying myself to sleep over this."

"I will happily banish you back to the boys' room if you do that, anyway."

That makes him laugh. My hand is still on his back, but now I slowly remove it. If this were Cameron or Flynn, then I wouldn't be pulling away. Instead, I'd bring him in for a hug, guide his head to my shoulder, and tell him to cry it out. But this is Daniel, and my rules with him are different.

"It's just—" He angles his face away from me. "She and I have known each other so long, you know? What if no one else ever gets me the way that she does?"

Irritation and sympathy war within me, but sympathy wins. "Hey," I say. "*I* get you."

"Yeah. You do, don't you." He doesn't phrase this as a question, more like something he's just realizing, much to his surprise.

Our eyes meet. Something like electricity passes between us, stealing my breath. We're sitting so close that the sides of our legs are touching. I can feel the heat of his body through both his jeans and mine.

He surprises me when he says, "You should go for it."

"Go for what?"

"Tell your guy how you feel."

I'm balancing on the edge of something dangerous, one breath away from leaning in to kiss him. I struggle to get out, "That's impossible."

"No, it's not," he says. "I promise, any guy would be an idiot not to want to be with you."

What sort of code are we communicating in here? It

seems like he *must* know the truth. He *must* know that there is no mystery guy. I consider saying something like, *Well, then he's the idiot for not making the first move,* maybe even adding, *especially when I'm sitting right here.* But I play it safe by saying, "No, he's in love with someone else."

"Oh." His posture sags, and I realize that he was simply offering me advice about my nameless crush. "I'm sorry."

The tension between us evaporates; our almost-kiss dissolves into the infinite ocean of could-have-beens. I don't have to fake my sadness when I say, "Yeah, me, too."

"God, we're a pair, right?" He clenches his fists. "Sometimes I wish I'd never met her, you know?"

"Don't wish that." The words come out easily, maybe because one of the things I love most about him is how thoroughly he's capable of loving. Even though it hurts to see all the sweet little things he does for Darcy—the notes on her car, the quick kisses between classes, the love songs—if he didn't do them, then he wouldn't be *Daniel.* "Think about everything she gave you."

"Like what?" he says. "Insomnia? Anxiety?"

"No, not that." I close my eyes and try to imagine what my life would be like if Daniel wasn't in it, if I didn't have to struggle against this unhealthy, impractical obsession. "I mean, she taught you what love feels like, right? What this kind of love feels like." I sigh. "If nothing else, she gave you a lot of good songwriting material."

He laughs bitterly. "How'd you get so smart?"

I catch myself studying the lines of his cheeks, which are highlighted by the weak glow of the lamp on our bedside table. Maybe he's in love with Darcy now, but he wasn't always. At some point he fell in, and that means he can fall out again. And his feelings for me are more than nothing; surely, they could grow.

"Same way you did," I say. "Disappointment. Heartbreak."

He tilts his head to the side, as if to see me from a new angle. "Why don't we hang out more, Bass Girl?"

The question catches me by surprise. Having a conversation with Daniel sometimes feels like playing along with a melody I've never heard before; the notes rise and fall and stop with no warning. He gets me to say things I *mean*, but I don't mean to *say*, like, "You've always had better things to do." I cringe when the words come out; to my ear, they sound petulant, childish. Luckily, he doesn't seem to notice.

"Not better," he says. "But it's so easy to get stuck, you know? With bad habits, with the wrong people." He looks up at me, and once again I feel a kiss sparking between us, suspended, tangible enough to touch. "You make me feel"—he takes a deep breath, lets it out slowly—"calm, comfortable." The words are so tender; I imagine they'd bruise at the faintest whisper. He ruins it a little by adding, "Darcy never once made me feel that way," but I don't even care. Because what he means is, I make him feel better than Darcy does, which has to mean he'd rather *be* with me than Darcy, even if his heart is still knotted up with hers. And that's something. Really, it feels like more than something; it feels like a promise.

My lips part, because I'm having a difficult time keeping my breath steady. We sway a fraction of an inch toward each other, and then there's a knock at our door, and the space between us widens again. Or maybe I imagine this. Regardless, when I stand, my legs feel weak. I answer the door and find Cameron hovering outside in a white shirt and fleece pajama pants, looking worried. His voice seems unusually small as he says, "Hey, can I talk to you?"

Behind me, I hear Daniel get off the bed. He asks, "Mind if I take a shower?" and I answer, "Go ahead," without looking at him. My heart is still pounding in my chest. I really hope that I'm not blushing, or that if I am, Cameron doesn't notice.

Daniel disappears inside the bathroom as I follow Cameron out to the walkway, letting the door close behind me. I wait several seconds for him to speak. When he doesn't, I say, "Look, Cameron—" but he says, "Nora, I'm—" at the same time.

Words are so stupid. It's infinitely easier to communicate with music, but our instruments are in the car.

He takes a deep breath, and I wait for him to spit out whatever he came here to say. Eventually he says, "Thanks for not telling the guys."

I fold my arms across my chest, not as a gesture of distrust, or discomfort, or whatever body-language experts would suggest, but because I'm cold.

"Yeah. Of course." After a beat, I ask, "How are you feeling?"

"What? Like, am I still feeling it?" He laughs. "It was, like, three sips. Wouldn't have affected a kitten."

I know I saw more than three sips, but instead of dwelling on that, I ask, "Did something happen?"

Now he's the one to fold his arms across his chest, and I think the body-language experts would probably be spot-on in their analysis of the gesture this time. "Like what?"

I wait. Because he knows what I'm talking about.

The first time I saw Cameron drunk was the summer before sophomore year. His parents had gone to a medical conference in Tokyo and left him home alone. They'd done things like that before, but this time they hadn't warned him about it. Instead, they called him from the airport, apologized for forgetting to tell him they'd be out of town for two weeks, and asked him to please give the gardener and the maid the checks they'd left in the foyer. That's what really stung, I think—the fact that they'd remembered to write checks for their gardener and maid, but hadn't remembered to let him know they'd be gone.

When we all showed up at his house to rehearse, we found him passed out in his backyard. He'd broken into their wine cellar—because they actually have a locked wine cellar—and drunk as many expensive bottles of wine as he could stomach. I wanted to call 911, but Daniel and Flynn carried him inside and made him drink a bunch of water, then held him while he vomited it all up, then fed him and made him drink some more water. None of us knew what to do, really. We were googling it as we went along. I don't think I've ever been as scared as I was when we found him there, facedown in the grass by his pool.

After a long pause, he steps away from me and leans against the wooden railing. He's staring to the side as he says, "I didn't ask my parents if I could come on this trip."

I lean forward. *"What?"*

"Don't worry," he says. His gaze moves to his bare feet. "It's fine. I didn't ask because I knew they wouldn't notice if I left." I'm watching his face closely, so I catch how his mouth briefly contorts before he goes on, "And they didn't. It just threw me tonight. I kept thinking they might call. I mean, I left my car at school and everything. But not a word. I had this whole"—he gestures tightly with his right hand, then tucks it back in under his left—"this whole *speech* planned for them, about how I would have asked them if I thought they'd care." He laughs quickly, through his nose. "And then they didn't call."

"Cam—"

"It's great, though. You know?" he goes on. "Because now I know where we stand. It's like, I'm finally free."

I don't know what to say, so I just follow an instinct and close the distance between us, wrapping my arms around his waist as I press my ear against his chest. I hear his heart beating against his rib cage. He doesn't move at first, but eventually he lets his arms relax around my shoulders. A moment later, I feel tension ease out of his body. When he steps away, he looks less terrified, more like himself. After he unlocks his door, he whispers, "Good night, Nora. See you tomorrow."

His hotel room is dark. Flynn is probably asleep in there, wearing noise-canceling headphones and an eye mask, intent on getting his eight hours. Now I have a whole new set of reasons to regret not asking Cameron to be my roommate.

If he and I were rooming together, we could have stayed up talking, laughing at the presenters on the QVC channel, messing around with music and our outfits for the Magwitch. The idea of him slipping into bed while Flynn snores on the other side of the room makes me slightly queasy.

Then I remember that Daniel needed me, too.

I turn back to our door, only to realize that I've locked myself out. While I wait for Daniel to get out of the shower, I lean against the flaking stucco wall and think about what almost happened between him and me. If Cameron hadn't interrupted, would Daniel have kissed me? What would I have done if he'd made the move?

I should not kiss Daniel. That way lies heartbreak and all the worst kinds of drama. As soon as I resolve on this, a tiny, pleading voice inside me sings, *But you know you want to.* Also, *What's the worst that can happen?*

When I hear the water turn off, I knock, and Daniel opens the door smelling like boy-soap. "What was that about?" he says, stepping aside to let me in. He's toweling off his hair so it flops in semidried clumps in front of his eyes. He's wearing a Sleater-Kinney T-shirt and black pajama pants that look appealingly soft.

"Nothing," I say. "School."

He nods, his interest immediately lost. I slip into the bathroom to get ready for bed. I wish I had something cuter to wear than loose cotton shorts and an enormous Reno Jazz Festival T-shirt, but that's what I packed, so I change and then step back into the room, where Daniel is sitting cross-legged on his bed, once again scrolling through his phone. When he sees me, he sets it aside and says, "I'm coming with you."

I force a laugh. "You have a habit of saying things out of context. It's really confusing."

He uncrosses his legs and leans forward. "I'm coming with you to look for your biological parents."

"Oh." I stare at him, not sure whether he's serious. "You don't have to do that."

"But I want to," he says. "Besides, you shouldn't have to do it alone."

That's when I decide that if the moment comes, I'll let him kiss me. Then I decide that's the most idiotic thing I've ever considered doing, and promise myself I won't let it happen. Then I remind myself that there's a third option: I could kiss him first.

"So, where are they?" he says. "You have addresses?"

I hesitate, reluctant to let him in on this. Then again, I could use some backup. "Yeah. A couple for the woman in Reedley, and a potential business address for the woman in Watsonville." I sit on the edge of my bed as I bring up the addresses on my phone, and he moves next to me in order to see the map. I force myself to sound calm, businesslike, as we talk about distances between our hotels and the addresses I've found. After we've come up with a sketchy plan for both cities, I put my phone down and say, "We should probably sleep."

He lets out half a breath as he looks at me. "Yeah. I guess so."

We both stand, and I expect him to retreat to his bed,

but instead he steps toward me. My breath catches in my throat. His fingers lift to my cheek.

Suddenly, here I am, living the moment I've been dreaming about. Only, it doesn't feel right. Everything between him and Darcy is so raw; it wouldn't be wise to rush into something, not when my whole heart is caught in the balance. And I know, though I don't like to admit it, that Daniel hates being alone under any circumstances. During previous breaks with Darcy, there've been other girls—nothing serious, just someone for him to hang out with—and this week, I'm the one who's here.

With difficulty, I say, "Daniel, don't—"

He lowers his hand, steps back.

The wiser half of my brain says, *Good job, Nora. That was close.* But then the levee of my self-control breaks, and I lean forward, closing the distance between his lips and mine. He hesitates, but then responds, wraps his arms around my waist, presses the length of his body against the length of mine.

"No, you were right," he says, pulling away. "You know I'm—" His breath is hot against my cheeks. "I'm such a mess right now."

"Me, too," I say. This is true, but not for the reasons he'd imagine.

We hover there for a long moment, suspended in indecision. Then, slowly, he leans down and kisses me again, and I kiss him back. And just like that, the decision has been made. I know he doesn't love me, but the fact that he wants to kiss me feels, in this moment, like enough.

My body seems to float, to disappear entirely. I feel electric, powerful, like I've manifested this moment through pure strength of will. Daniel's lips are soft. Our breathing synchronizes, and we find an easy rhythm as he nibbles on my bottom lip, then moves his mouth against mine. I let myself believe that he couldn't kiss me like this if he didn't love me at least a little.

We sit on the edge of my bed, lips connected the entire time. Daniel peels back the covers, then lays me down gently before stretching out on top. Suddenly, my whole body feels tingly and awake. But just as everything inside me is accelerating, he pauses, lifts his face away from mine. He rolls off to my right, leaving his right arm draped over me and his left arm tucked under my head. Against my cheek, he whispers, "Let's just sleep like this, Bass Girl. Okay?"

"Yeah," I say, feeling vaguely disappointed.

Seconds later, he's dreaming, but I lie awake until three in the morning, wondering what this means, wondering what will be different tomorrow.

CHAPTER 9

$\mathcal{T}$he first thing I notice when I wake up is that I'm alone, but before I have a chance to panic, I see Daniel sitting in that chair by the window, a pink doughnut box on the table by his side along with two unmarked paper cups, from which little ribbons of steam curl upward.

He sees that I'm awake and says, "I was up early, so I got us breakfast."

A happy flush spreads across my face and down my neck as I say, as casually as I can manage, "Please say there's something chocolate in that box."

He peers inside it. "One with sprinkles, one with nuts."

I climb out of bed, trying not to worry too much about my hair or my breath. "You're a saint."

He doesn't respond. Based on his distracted expression, I'd guess that he didn't even hear me.

As I sit in the chair opposite him, I place the doughnut with nuts on a napkin, then draw my cup of coffee closer.

I've never even tried coffee, but I know Darcy drinks it black, and that's what Daniel brought me. I don't want to be fussy, so I take a quick sip, then chase it with a large bite of doughnut, and wait. I tell myself I'm ready for whatever he's going to say, but when I hear the words "Look, Nora—" the truth is that they feel like a knife plunging between my ribs, puncturing everything essential. It's not that I expected him to fall in love with me while we slept, but I hoped he wouldn't regret what had happened between us so immediately.

He runs a hand through his hair and gets another running start. "I need to apologize for last night."

I sip my coffee, not because I want it, but because I need something to do with my hands. A few seconds later, I think I do a fairly good job of sounding neutral when I say, "For what?"

He shakes his head. "Because it was a bad idea to—" He shakes his head, closes his eyes. "Because there's so much at stake here, and I—" He tries again. "Because we're in a band. Because we're friends."

"I'm sorry, but I still don't really get what you're saying."

He rests his forehead on his hands, presumably trying to find the words that will get what he means through my thick skull, then says, "I know you're hung up on some other guy, and you know I'm hung up on Darcy, but these things"—his eyes drift to our unmade bed—"they can get complicated, even when two people start out on the same page."

I know that Daniel doesn't like being alone, but the thing is, I don't want to be alone, either. I tell myself I can keep my expectations in check. I can handle whatever happens after Sunday, but I don't want to spend the next few days lying in separate beds, not when I know how good it feels to fall asleep in his arms.

I keep my voice steady as I say, "So, it doesn't have to happen again. Or"—I pull an elastic band off my wrist and tie up my hair—"we could agree to not let it get complicated."

He picks up a paper napkin and starts shredding its edges. "You make it sound so simple."

I finish my doughnut, then take another swig of coffee, even though it tastes like curdled ash. Why anyone drinks it for *pleasure* is beyond me. I disguise a grimace as I say, "It's as simple as we want it to be."

Daniel considers this for a moment. "Either way, Cameron and Flynn shouldn't know."

I know he's right, but it still hurts. I think about his endless PDA with Darcy, the way his arm is always linked around her waist, but remind myself that I'm not her, and this isn't that. "Yeah, obviously."

"You really think it's possible?"

"Sure."

My parents were friends before they got together. They were in a study group at their law school, and one night the other two people in the group didn't show, and my parents ended up—cue a blush from my mom—doing a wee bit more than studying. Friends is a good place to start. Granted, I don't think that once they got together, they tried to pretend that they hadn't. Still, I try to sound unbothered as I say, "Friends with benefits."

This makes him smile. "Nora Wakelin, you surprise me. I wouldn't have thought you were the type."

As I reach for the other chocolate doughnut, I say, "There's a lot you don't know about me." This, at least, is true.

Daniel's relief is evident. He reaches into the box and pulls out a lemon-glazed doughnut, which he dips into his coffee as he leans back against the chair. My appetite, though, is gone. I excuse myself to the bathroom, where I take a longer, steamier shower than usual and try to convince myself that this is just the beginning.

♪ ♩ ♪ ♩ ♪

CAMERON'S STANDING A FEW FEET AWAY, SQUINTING AT the open fields around us, which seem reflective in the midday sun, like an enormous golden mirror. "Are you sure this is where our gig is?" he says. "It looks like a farming town."

"What's that supposed to mean?" Flynn asks. He doesn't trust the mechanisms that hold gas pumps into cars, so he's standing at the rear of the van, manually compressing the lever. "Farmers don't like music?"

Cameron swats at a fly that has landed on his shirt. "No. I'm just surprised there's somewhere for us to play."

"It's not going to be the Rowdy, if that's what you mean," I say. "We're going to have to play a semiacoustic set." It's not like I haven't warned them, but it's worth repeating: "The venue is definitely small." I still haven't told them that our only compensation for playing is whatever we collect in our tip jar; that's not going to go over well. But I have some time before I need to worry about Flynn's inner accountant. First, Teresa Johnson.

I have a good feeling about this Teresa. She seems to be the right age, and I know from an article I found that she did give up a child for adoption. How many Teresas could have given up children in California? She's got to be it.

I step away from the van, toward the hot, golden fields. I've been so focused on *finding* my birth mother that I haven't really stopped to consider how it would feel to meet her, to learn about her life. In all the times that I imagined her living somewhere, I never imagined her in a place like this. I wonder what she does here. As I turn around and face the street that bisects the town, I wonder what *anyone* does here. Though, maybe the people who live here would think our Orange County suburb is crowded and overpriced. They might drive through and wonder, *Why would anyone choose this place?*

It's less than a mile to our motel, but we drive past it twice before we realize it's the place we're looking for. The building looks like it used to be red, though now it's more of a brownish green, like the paint they used wasn't really meant for outdoor use. There are two rows of rooms ballooning out of the main office, but the walls are dotted only by thin windows positioned right under the roof, prison-style.

When we go into the office, we find out from the office manager that this building was indeed once the county jail. "Now everyone just gets sent to that big facility in Salinas or the women's center near Fresno," he says, digging through a drawer. "So the county didn't need this building anymore." He pulls out our keys, which are old-school brass things, tied to a room number by a piece of twine. "We don't get many reservations here. You've got rooms 12 and 13."

"Thanks," Flynn says, taking both keys.

Once we're out of the office, Flynn turns to Cameron and says, "How did you find this place? I'm pretty sure its primary function is as a brothel."

"You are such a snob," Daniel says, but he says it more like a joke than a jab. Ever since our conversation this morning, he's seemed unusually chipper. I've decided to take this as a good sign.

"It's not about snobbery," Flynn says. "It's about—" We reach room 13, and he takes out the key. "It's about bedbugs. And sexually transmitted infections."

"You can't get STIs from dirty hotel rooms," Daniel says.

"Are you positive about that?"

"Just open the door."

Flynn puts the key into the doorknob and twists. The door swings open with an actual creak, and the four of us stand there in the full noon sun, staring into the dark room, which smells distinctly of must and spilled beer, like a moldier version of the Rowdy greenroom.

"Oh, hell no," Flynn says. "No way. I'll sleep in the van."

"Maybe the other room isn't as bad," Daniel says. He

takes the keys out of Flynn's hand and opens room 12, which smells a little better than room 13, but is otherwise the same. He walks in and turns on the floor lamp. Cameron and I look at each other, then follow him in. There are two double beds, separated by a sticky-looking nightstand. The blankets are tucked in tightly around the edges of the lumpy mattresses. At the head of each bed are limp yellow pillows. The narrow window behind Daniel is thick with cobwebs and dirt.

"It's really not bad," he says.

Flynn points to a spot on the carpet. "Is that blood?" A woman in a short skirt and low-cut blouse walks behind him. He points after her and whispers, "Was that a hooker?"

"Why?" Daniel says. "Because she's wearing a short skirt? You are such an ass, Flynn."

The woman walks past us again, going the other way. This time she's carrying a kid on her hip and walking alongside an older woman, who's wearing jeans and a T-shirt. As they pass us, the older woman says, "How did you even find this place?"

The woman with the kid on her hip says, "I thought something off the beaten path would be interesting. Road less traveled and whatnot."

"Well, you can keep your off-brand interesting," the older woman says. "I'll be staying at the Motel 6."

Flynn looks back at us and says, "Okay, I'm an ass. But this place—it's—"

"It's rock 'n' roll," Daniel says. "It's Hotel California."

Flynn steps gingerly inside, glancing at the ceiling. "Hotel California isn't supposed to be a dump."

"Yeah, I'm not sure this is what the Eagles had in mind," Cameron says.

Flynn disappears around the corner, then comes back and says, "This room is definitely better than the other one."

I catch Daniel's eye and give a little shrug, which I hope he interprets as, *There'll be other nights*, then say, "So, let's all sleep in here."

I can almost see Flynn's objection balancing on the edge of his tongue, but he swallows it and says, "Fine."

We all look at Cameron, who hesitates, then says, "I'll return the other key."

Daniel steps back outside and says, "I'm going to see if they have a vending machine. Does anyone else want something to drink?"

I ask for whatever he's getting. Flynn says he's okay. Then Daniel and Cameron are gone. I pull back the comforter of the bed closest to the bathroom. The sheets look clean, at least.

Flynn scratches at a spot on the duvet, then seems to determine that it's just part of the design. Still, he says, "This place is objectively disgusting."

"At least it has character?" I say, though I can't help phrasing it as a question.

After a moment of comfortable silence, Flynn says, "Hey, Nora—" He crosses his arms over his chest, taps the edge of the bed with his heel, and stares at the ceiling. He's not usually the fidgety type, and it's making me nervous. Finally, he asks, "Do you think I'm a snob?"

I hesitate, surprised by the question. Eventually, I say, "*Snob* is a strong word."

"Is it accurate, though?" He sits on the edge of a bed. "I mean, as a description of me?"

"You want the truth?"

He nods, so I sit next to him. "You do—" How can I say this without being hurtful, or saying more than I mean? "You can sometimes come across as kind of judgey." He tenses, so I put my hand on the back of his wrist and say, "Don't get me wrong. You're a good friend. You're"—I look for the right word—"*steady*. You're dependable. And that's such an important quality."

"But?" He's looking at my hand, which makes it hard for me to know how he's going to react to the things I'm saying. Then again, he asked for it.

"But maybe *because* you're so steady, it's hard for you to understand people who don't make decisions the way you do. People might feel like they can't fully relax around you, or be themselves, because they know, or at least believe, that you'll judge them for it." I'm thinking about Cameron and his two sticks of gum.

Flynn takes a deep breath and brings his other hand around to rest on top of mine as he says, "Do *you* feel like you can't be yourself around me?"

"Honestly?"

He nods.

I think about how I felt when I first met him. While

Daniel was busy charming me into joining their mission to make nonsucky music, Flynn mostly stood apart and glared at his feet. For the longest time, I thought he didn't like me. Later, I realized that he's like that with everyone at first. Once you're in his circle he's different, but getting into that circle is a bit of a process.

I know exactly when he started to let me in. Daniel was meeting Darcy after rehearsal, so Flynn offered to drive me home from Cameron's house. At that point, I still thought he hadn't warmed to me, so I dreaded being alone with him for the fifteen-minute drive. But when we reached his van, he helped me load my bass into the back, then walked around to the passenger side to help me with my door.

"The handle's iffy sometimes," he told me. But that didn't explain why he held the door for me, then closed it once I was in my seat.

We drove in silence for several minutes before I asked if we could turn on some music.

Of course, he said, "The stereo doesn't work." I thought that was all he was going to say, but then he added, "This van is twice as old as we are. Hardly anything works anymore."

"But it's perfect for carting band equipment around," I said.

"That's why I got it." He patted the steering wheel affectionately. "My parents thought I was crazy, but Dan and I had been talking about starting a band, and it made sense for one of us to own something like this."

"You bought it yourself?" This idea baffled me. My parents didn't give me an allowance beyond some birthday money every year, which they used to teach me about wise investing and the importance of charitable donations, and they weren't showing signs of buying me a car anytime soon. Still, it had never occurred to me that I could get a job and buy one myself.

"Yeah," he said. "I worked at Quiznos all summer to afford it. It didn't even run, but my dad and I rebuilt the engine together. It'll cost another summer's worth of sandwich making just to repay him for the parts." He shook his head. "I'm hoping we start making money playing gigs soon, so I don't have to ever dice an onion again. Stings the eyes."

"That makes me feel so—" As usual, I couldn't find the right word.

"What?"

I said, "—inadequate," but that wasn't exactly what I meant.

His eyebrows pinched together, in the way they do when he's confused. Though, at the time, I thought he looked annoyed. "How so?"

"You've already given so much. If I'm going to be an equal member of the band, I should offer a blood sacrifice or something."

"You're doing plenty." He looked at me, and our eyes met, but it didn't feel as weird as it sounds. I felt something inside me settle. That's when I realized he didn't dislike me; he just took everything more seriously than Daniel and Cameron seemed to. "Don't worry about any of that. I was glad to do it, and I'm glad to have you in the band."

I knew he meant it, because even then I understood that

Flynn always means what he says. Which is why a few months later, when we were all at Daniel's house and Darcy convinced everyone (except Flynn) to go out and Saran wrap her neighbor's car, and Flynn later said, "I'm disappointed in you, Nora. I thought you were smarter than that," I felt so bad, even though I'd mostly stayed to the side and watched. And that's why a few months after that, when Flynn had to leave early from rehearsal, and Cameron, Daniel, Darcy, and I ate pot brownies together, no one told Flynn that it had happened. Because we all knew what he'd say, and we also knew he'd mean it.

So, do I feel like I can't be myself around him? I look over at him and say, "Sometimes."

His eyebrows pinch together. "Like when?"

"I don't know," I lie, mostly because there's no point in rehashing ancient history. "I can't give you an example. It's more of a—" If I had a piano in front of me, I'd play a D-minor chord with a suspended G mixed in; I'd let the sound of the chord just resonate until the air became still. "It's more of a *tension*. Like, you never seem to fully relax, so how can anyone else really relax around you?" He looks so sad. It's breaking my heart. "You know we all love you, though. Right? Daniel just likes giving you a hard time."

"I know," he says. "I appreciate your honesty." He takes a deep breath. "I'm going to work on it—on not being so uptight. I don't want to drive people away."

"Hey." I squeeze his hand. "We're not going anywhere."

He squeezes me back. "You're a good friend, Nora."

But am I? I have to force my smile as I say, "I try."

♪ ♩ ♪ ♩♪

AN HOUR LATER, CAMERON HAS GONE OUT FOR A WALK
and Flynn has fallen asleep facedown on the bed nearest the window. I've been sitting at the sticky desk trying to make my way through some physics notes, but now
I gladly put them away and get Daniel's attention with a
whispered, "Ready?"

He looks up from his phone and nods, then slides off
the bed and follows me out into the hot sunshine. It's a
little after 2:00 p.m., which should give us plenty of time
to walk to both of the addresses I have for Teresa Johnson
before we need to think about making our way to our gig.
As I study a map of the neighborhood on my phone, I say
to Daniel, "You can stay here, if you want. It's not a big
deal."

"It's a *huge* deal, and of course I'm coming with you."

To hide my relief, I study the map again. "The address for
the house is closer than the one for the apartment, so I figure we'll go there first. We should be gone about an hour."

"Lead the way."

I try not to notice the little thrill that passes through me
as we fall in step together, try not to notice that our strides
match perfectly, like we're moving forward to the same im-
perceptible, yet incessant, beat.

CHAPTER 10

The house is small and gray with white trim, surrounded by a chain-link fence. There's no grass in the yard, just weeds and dirt, but in the shade of the porch I see bright children's toys—a plastic tricycle, a wagon, a three-legged stool. I might have siblings living here, or at least half siblings.

"So, do we just knock?" Daniel asks.

All my breath has left me, and I don't even know how to begin to respond. I approach the house, forcing one foot in front of the other until I'm standing close enough to the yard to place my hand on the hot metal of the gate.

Daniel plants his hand on my shoulder and says, "Okay, I'm right behind you." Though, even his voice sounds weak right now.

I close my eyes and take a deep breath.

Of course right then my phone rings. The sound of the ringing alerts a massive, narrow-eyed dog that was hiding in the shade behind the plastic wagon to our presence. He leaps halfway across the yard in a single bound, and he'd be over the fence in a heartbeat if he wasn't hitched to the porch by a long metal chain. The dog strains against his leash, slobbering on the dirt, while I stare at the word *Mom*, which is flashing across the screen of my phone.

My thumb hovers over the green answer icon, but then the front door of the house opens, and a large, pale, shirtless man with a disorganized assortment of tattoos and a bushy goatee stumbles into the daylight brandishing a metal pipe.

I answer the call and say loudly, "Mom, can I call you back in, like, two minutes?" I'm hoping that the dog's barking doesn't sound quite as monstrous over the phone.

"Oh, my goodness, Nora. Where are you?"

"We stopped along the way," I say, counting on her not to look at the location tracker on my phone. I doubt she will; technology isn't one of her strengths. "And there's this dog. Don't worry. I'll call you back in two minutes."

"Okay, sweetie—"

And then I do something I've never done before and never intend to do again: I hang up on my mother.

The man with the pipe shouts at the dog, "Dawson, shut the *fuck* up."

"Dawson, as in *Creek*?" Daniel whispers at me. I dig my elbow into his ribs, keeping my eyes forward.

The dog keeps barking, so the man jumps down the steps and pulls on his chain. The dog yelps, then circles behind the man and lies down heavily in the dirt.

The man steps toward us, and from this distance I can make out some of the details on his tattoos. There's a cartoon-looking devil on his right bicep, a wide-branching tree tattooed across his sternum, and beneath his left collarbone there's a word written in elaborate script. As he steps closer, I realize that the word is *Teresa*.

The man plants one end of the pipe in the dirt and leans on it. "You want to tell me what you're doing here?" he says. "We don't need missionaries."

"No, I'm, uh"—I can't take my eyes off that name on his skin—"I'm looking for Teresa Johnson. Does she live here?"

His eyes narrow suspiciously, which is not the reaction I was hoping for. "Who's looking for her?"

"My name's Nora, and I—" I take a deep breath, but the words come out more easily this time. "I think she might be my birth mother."

"Not possible."

He says it quickly, leaving very little room for doubt. Still, I have to ask, "Are you sure? My birth parents named me Summer. I was adopted out of Santa Barbara County, but now I live south of Los Angeles."

"The girl Terry gave up lives in Denver. At least, that's what she thought last time she went looking for her. And she never named her nothing."

I pause, my heart drifting in the direction of my toes. "Are you *sure*?"

"Well, you never know anything for certain with a bitch like that."

I don't know whether that makes me feel better or worse.

"Is Teresa, or Terry"—I peer into the darkly shuttered interior of the house—"is she home?"

The man shakes his head. "No, kid. She's been locked up at that place north of Fresno since last month." He climbs back up to the porch. When Dawson attempts to follow, he shoves him back with his heel. "Bitch got high and stole some shit in the city. Got caught on camera and everything."

I let out all my air. I've considered lots of possibilities, but never this one. "Prison?"

"She'd only been out a couple months, too." He spits aggressively at the dust near his dog. "If she does it again, they'll throw away the key. Good fuckin' riddance."

Maybe the man says good-bye, but if he does, I don't hear it. The next time I'm aware of anything, Daniel's arm is around my shoulders, and he's guiding me back the way we came.

"Oh, my God." I feel like I might vomit.

Daniel's fingers tighten on my shoulder. "You okay?"

I stop walking and shrug off his arm, take a deep breath, then another one. My heart feels like it's trying to pummel its way out of my chest, but I need to sound normal for what I'm about to do. I take out my phone and call my mom.

She answers after the first ring. "Nora, are you okay?"

"Yeah." I step away from Daniel and close my eyes, focus on the sound of my mother's breath, on the sound of *my* breath. "We're on our way to Reedley now. But reception's not going to be great."

Daniel's eyes widen. I think he's impressed.

"Is everything okay? I thought I heard a commotion—"

"Flynn was gassing up the van, and this pit bull was barking at us through the window of a truck." I've always considered myself a terrible liar. I'm almost disappointed all these lies have been coming so easily to me.

"Well, be careful," my mom says. "And tell Flynn to be careful."

I hold my phone to my chest, then shout, "Hey, Flynn, my mom says to be careful."

Daniel leans over. "If he's any more careful, we'll have to walk to Reedley, Mrs. Wakelin."

I hold the phone back to my ear and say, "I'd better go, Mom. But I'll call you tonight."

After we hang up, I press my phone between my hands and sink to the curb. Heat from the cement bakes through my jeans, but I don't even care. Because my birth mother might be living in a prison north of Fresno.

"So, what's our move, Bass Girl?" Daniel says.

I open my phone and look up the place the man—I realize now that I never got his name; if it was Martin, then I don't even want to know—must have been talking about. It's a little over an hour away by car, and there's no public transportation around here, so car is the only way I'm getting there.

"I need to know if that's her."

Daniel sits next to me, close enough that his leg is touching mine. "Are you sure?"

He's communicating a thousand things with those three

words, but all I can manage in response is a nod, my eyes still glued to the screen of my phone.

He stands, then helps me up. "Then I guess we'd better find a way to get to this prison."

I have no words to communicate what I'm feeling right now, and it doesn't help when Daniel wraps his right hand around my left one and says, "We're in this together, Bass Girl." So I just try to focus on the feeling of his palm pressing against mine.

I don't know how visitation works at prisons, but I assume things start closing at around 5:00 p.m., which gives me just over two hours to get there and see Teresa Johnson. We're supposed to start playing at the restaurant at 6:00, which shrinks our timeline even further. Of course, *I* know that this gig isn't exactly high stakes, but I don't want the guys to know I know it.

Daniel follows me quietly as I retrace our steps out of the neighborhood. At the intersection of the next two main streets, there's a gas station, and at the gas station, there's a semitruck with Idaho plates. Half an idea leaps out at me. I turn to Daniel and say, "I know how to get there."

He looks baffled, maybe even concerned, as he says, "How?"

Even Daniel will hate what I'm about to do, so I say, "You should go back to the room. Stall. Tell the guys that I had some kind of issue and needed—" I see a skinny man in a red baseball cap stepping around the back of the truck. Even from here, I can see that his left arm looks more tanned and wrinkled than his right, probably from spending so much time on the road.

Daniel prompts, "Needed what?" But I'm already jogging toward the man in the cap. He's halfway into his seat when I reach him and ask, "Are you heading up the 99 through Fresno?"

Behind me, Daniel says, "No way, Nora," but I ignore him.

The man looks at me, then Daniel, then back at me. "Yeah," he says. "You lookin' for a lift?"

I nod.

"Both of you?" the man says, eycing Daniel again.

Daniel sighs. "Yeah, I guess."

I squeeze his hand once and say, "Thank you."

"How far do you need to be goin'?"

"Berenda or Chowchilla," I say. "About an hour north of here." The man is squinting at us, absentmindedly picking at a thin scab on his hand, and it occurs to me that he's wondering if he can trust us. I take a chance and tell him, "I'm looking for my birth mother, and I think she might be in the women's prison up there."

The man's eyebrows lift.

"I'm not certain it's her," I say. "But we're just passing through today, and this may be my only chance to find out."

The man nods, then gestures to the other side of his cab. "There's three seats. You both buckle up."

"Thank you so much," I say.

As Daniel and I run around the front of the truck, he says, "Just so you know, I'm coming with you because there is safety in numbers, not because I'll be able to bust out secret street-fighting moves if this guy pulls a gun on us."

I glance back at him and say, "Don't worry, I'll protect you."

I hoist myself up the steps and let myself into the cab, climbing to the center seat. As I pull the buckle across my lap, the man says, "You really shouldn't be gettin' rides with strangers." A little trail of goose bumps begins to rise out of my arms, but then Daniel's in his seat, and the man is putting the truck into gear. As he pulls away, he says, "But I got two kids of my own, and I know that when they decide they're gonna do something, they're gonna do it. I'd rather give you a ride myself than have you hitchin' with some other guy who might be up to no good." He looks over at me. "But don't you be doin' this again. You hear?"

He talks for the next hour without pausing or asking us a single question. He tells us about his kids (Samantha and Charles, twenty and twenty-two years old), about his wife (Lucy, a cop), about the house they live in (built in 1920; they don't make them like that anymore), about what he plans to do when he retires (fly-fish, exclusively). He tells us about the audiobook he's been listening to for the last several hundred miles ("John Grisham. Have you read any John Grisham? No? Well, you should read one of his sometime. That man knows how to tell a story"). And he talks at length about the joys and trials of driving trucks ("First year's the hardest, no doubt. There's a trainer driver in the cab with you most of the time, and you get the short runs, so money's no good. But if you stick with it, and you're comfortable with your own company, then the life can't be beat").

The prison is three miles off the main highway, but he takes us all the way. "It's five minutes for me, but an hour walk for you two," he says. "Can't let you go all that way by yourselves, now can I?"

I tell him I appreciate it, but he just goes on with the story he was telling about his wife killing a raccoon that had gotten into their garbage cans. Eventually, he slows down, pulling his truck over to the side of the road. On our right, there's an endless orchard—just fruit trees for as far as I can see. They're covered in blossoms now, so I can't tell what kind of fruit they're going to bear, but in a month or so, I bet the boughs will be heavy with them. On our left, there's a driveway, which is framed by a wide stone sign on one side and a colorful tile mural on the other. Down the road, I see a guardhouse situated between the incoming and outgoing car lanes. Behind that, a parking lot surrounded by limp evergreen trees.

"This's as far as I can take you, but"—he points to the driveway—"you head that way, and they'll be able to direct you to the person you're lookin' for."

Daniel opens the door and leaps to the ground.

"You take care," the driver says, as I follow Daniel out. "And good luck."

"Thanks." I glance over my shoulder at the guardhouse. The exit-side barrier arm lifts, and a silver minivan pulls through toward the road. "Uh—drive safely. And enjoy your fly-fishing."

Daniel and I retreat into the orchard while he pulls his

truck away. Once he's gone, the only sound is the soft patter of human voices coming from the guardhouse. The prison itself is set back from the road. The views to my right and to my left are identical—just the edge of an orchard and a thin line of asphalt disappearing to the horizon.

"'California Department of Corrections and Rehabilitation,'" Daniel reads off the sign. He glances at the road behind us. "This is not how I expected this day to go."

"Me, either," I say. "You can stay here, if you want."

"You can keep saying that, but you know what my answer's going to be."

That makes something inside me settle, making it possible for me to lead the way forward, between the sign and the mural, toward the guardhouse.

There are two women inside. On the far side of the guard station, there's a plump blonde woman with thin, curly hair, which is gathered into wispy mounds around her full, moonlike cheeks. She's assisting a car full of people passing through the other way and doesn't seem to notice us. On our side of the guard station there's a thin woman with midnight-black skin and slick gray hair, which is tied back into a tight bun. She's focused on her computer screen and doesn't seem to notice us, either. We stand there for several seconds, waiting, before I work up the nerve to say, "Hi," but the word comes out softly, on a breath. Finally, I take a deep breath and manage to say, "We're here to see Teresa Johnson."

Without looking at us, the woman says, "New visitors stopped being admitted two hours ago." She types something, her fingers punching rhythmically at the letters. "Did you miss an earlier appointment?"

It strikes me, suddenly, the way a cold sometimes just hits you in the back of the throat, that I should have looked into visitation procedures before dragging Daniel all the way out here. It's too late now.

"Not really."

The woman looks up from her computer, but not at us. Instead, she looks over our heads, clearly hoping to find an adult to speak to, or at least a vehicle for us to leave in. She's probably not used to having people approach the guard-house on foot. "The prisoner you're here to see isn't expecting you?"

"No."

"Are you on our list?"

I shake my head, pressing my lips together.

The woman stretches her neck so she can see as much of the road as possible. "Where did you come from?"

"We got a ride."

"Was this ride of yours that truck I just saw pull over and drive away?"

Until about thirty seconds ago, my plan seemed brilliant, destined for success. The rapidity of its reversal makes me want to evaporate.

"I just—" I take a deep breath. The sun feels hot on the back of my neck; sweat beads at the base of my skull. "I'm here to see Teresa Johnson. I think she might be my birth mother."

The car on the other side of the guardhouse pulls away,

and the blonde woman looks over at us before she turns to her computer.

Our guard's eyes go wide. "So, do you mean to tell me that this Teresa Johnson may not even know you exist?"

I shake my head again.

"This isn't a day spa. It's a *prison*. You can't just walk in, ring a doorbell, and ask for Terry."

"Can you at least tell us if she's here?" Daniel says, sounding much less panicked than I feel.

The woman takes a deep breath, then turns to the computer in front of her and punches a few keys.

"Teresa Johnson. She's here," the woman says. "Here's what I can do for you. I can have a letter delivered to her with your name and phone number, and she can call you tomorrow. But to *visit* an inmate, you'd need to write a letter to her requesting an application. She'd need to sign it, then send it to you. Once the visiting sergeant here received your application, she'd either approve or reject it. If you were approved, you'd get put on a visitation list. It could take *weeks*." Her tone softens. "I'm sorry I don't have better news, but we do have a phone number you could have called. This information is on our website."

Daniel says, "Thank you," because it's obvious that I'm not capable of speaking.

"Do you have some way to get back to wherever you came from?" the woman says.

The blonde woman on the other side of the guardhouse leans over. "I could drive them home when my shift ends."

Our guard looks at her like she's speaking the same crazy language we are.

"No, that's okay," I say, but Daniel elbows me.

"How else are we going to get back to Reedley?" he whispers.

"*Reedley?*" our guard says. "You hitched a ride here from Reedley?"

Daniel pulls me away from the guardhouse, back toward the road, and places his hands on my shoulders. "Nora, we need to text Flynn."

The sun is edging toward the horizon, but sweat is still streaming down the center of my back. I'm not sure I'll be able to take my next breath until my lungs stretch to gulp the hot, dusty air.

"Trust me, I don't want to call him any more than you do," he goes on. "But we need a ride, and we need to *not* get that ride from a stranger." He looks at the women in the guardhouse behind me. "I think we've exhausted our good luck in the rides-with-strangers department."

"Then everyone will know what I'm doing," I argue, weakly. But he already has his phone out and is typing a message, so I sit on the side of the road and stare at a trail of ants marching over the gravel—each ant in its place, following a prescribed path toward some inevitable destination. How relaxing that must be.

Daniel's phone buzzes, and he answers the call. "Yeah," he says, his voice quiet. "Yeah, the prison." He pauses. "We, uh, we got a ride with a truck driver." He holds the phone away from his ear, then brings it closer to say, "We'll be here."

I pick away the larger stones that are blocking the ants' trail, until they have a smooth highway through the dust. As I watch them march along the straight and narrow path, I wish that just once an enormous hand would reach down from above and clear the way forward for me.

CHAPTER II

*B*y the time Flynn and Cameron arrive, the guardhouse is closed. The blonde guard offered us a ride again before she left, but we told her our friends were on their way. I did, however, give her a letter with my name and phone number and asked her to deliver it to Teresa Johnson.

"So, what are you doing in Reedley?" the woman asked us. "That's an inconvenient place to stay, if you came to visit the prison."

"We're in a band," Daniel said. "We're playing a show there tonight."

I cringed, thinking about how disappointed he'd be when he realized that our "show" would be us standing outside a fast-food restaurant with a tip jar. But I couldn't worry about that yet. The blonde guard hovered a little longer than was comfortable, but eventually she left, waving at us as she pulled away in an old gray sedan. Daniel attempted to start conversations with me several times, but I just sat there, staring at the ants, trying to make their trek a little more straightforward. At one point, he placed the warm palm of his hand against the center of my back, but when I didn't react, he slowly removed it.

When Flynn pulls his van up and opens the door, the first words out of his mouth are, "Nora, are you insane?"

I shrug, then pick up a pebble and toss it at a tree behind me.

He jumps out of his van and stands over me. "You *hitch-hiked* to a *prison*? Do you have any idea what could have happened?"

"Dude, you're not her dad," Daniel says. "Just chill."

"And *you*," Flynn says. "You *helped* her *hitchhike* to a *prison*?"

"Seemed better than letting her go by herself," Daniel says.

I throw another rock, this time aiming for the orchard across the street. "I know, Flynn," I say. "You don't have to tell me how stupid this was. Because trust me, I'm fully aware."

"I didn't say it was stupid, I just—" Flynn squats down in front of me and puts his hands on my knees. "What are you doing, Nora? Why are we at a women's prison?"

I look to the side, trying to hold back the vast pool of tears that's growing behind my eyes. "Dan didn't tell you?"

"I wasn't sure you wanted me to," he says.

A large shadow looms over me, and then Cameron sits by my side. He puts one of his long, heavy arms around my shoulders and pulls me in. His shirt smells like laundry detergent and coconut. I bury my nose in it while he pats my back.

"I thought my birth mother might be here," I say, though I know my voice is muffled through the fabric.

"Say what?" Flynn asks.

Cameron rests his chin on the top of my head. "She thought her birth mother might be here," he repeats. His low voice resonates in his chest; it feels like something's purring between his ribs.

I hear Flynn plop down in the dust in front of me, then feel his hand on my exposed shoulder.

"I'm so sorry," I choke out.

Cameron smooths hair away from my face as he says, "It's okay. Don't worry about it."

Daniel crouches down in front of me and places a tentative hand on my knee. The four of us rest there for a moment, intertwined on the dusty and rapidly darkening edge of the Central California Women's Facility. I close my eyes and just soak in the sense of security that fills me. Even if I never find my biological parents, at least I have this.

"I hate to be the one to say it," Flynn says eventually. "But we're already late for our gig."

I peel my face away from Cameron's shirt and fold my hands over my knees. "Actually, I doubt anyone would notice if we didn't show up."

Now all the guys lean away from me.

"Nora, you want to bring us all up to speed?" Flynn says. "Because I think I'm still missing a few details."

I take a deep breath and finally tell them almost

everything, starting with finding out my original name was Summer and ending with the guard this afternoon telling Daniel and me that we'd have to wait weeks before we could get in to see Teresa Johnson. I don't tell them about my internship this summer. There's only so much grief I can handle at once.

"So, you're saying we're not going to be *paid* for playing at this restaurant tonight?" Flynn says. I shouldn't be surprised that's the detail that sticks with him.

I shake my head. "I don't know if you could even really call it a *restaurant*."

"And we don't have any gig booked in Watsonville, whatsoever?"

I shake my head again, then hold my breath and wait.

Finally, Flynn says, "Why didn't you tell us?" His voice is soft, almost drowned out by the sound of the breeze in the orchard across the street.

"About my birth parents?"

"About all of it. If we'd known that you wanted to go looking for them, then we didn't need the ruse about the tour and the gigs."

"You would have taken the time off school?" I say. "You would have spent the money on hotels and gas and all that, just because I wanted to find my birth parents?"

"Point taken." We all sit in silence for a moment before he reiterates, "So we don't *actually* have a gig tonight?"

I pick up another pebble and roll it around between my palms. "There's a guy named Juan at the burger place who said we could play on the patio for tips, but that's it."

After a long pause, during which I expect them to tell me off for wasting their time and money, not to mention for deceiving them both directly (lies) and indirectly (omissions), Cameron leans back on his hands and says, "Is there a reason why you're looking for Teresa instead of Martin?"

I look at him. My honest answer is that Martin's the one who ultimately gave me up, so I've always been less interested in him. Based on my understanding of the story, Teresa seems like the one who would be happiest to see me. But I hate talking about the circumstances of my adoption. It always makes people look at me like an abused puppy. So I say, "Not really."

"Then we should probably look for the Martins in these scenarios, not the Teresas."

There's a collective pause before Daniel says, "Explain yourself."

Cameron flicks an ant off the back of his hand and then stands, pacing along the side of the van. "You've been basing this off people born in your birth year named Summer, then looked for women with matching surnames, but what are the odds that your Teresa never married again, or changed her name—"

"Whereas Martin's surname would stay the same," Flynn says, nodding along.

"It's so weird that name changing is still a thing," Daniel says. We all look at him. "I mean, when you think about it."

"Did you find an address for Teresa Croft?" Cameron asks me.

"No," I say. "Though, I did find a defunct address for a

business called Croft's Confections in Watsonville, and my birth mother was supposedly a baker."

"So, someone with the surname Croft probably owned a bakery in Watsonville. Maybe the owner's name was Teresa, maybe not. But even if the owner was your birth mother, you should still search for a Martin Croft. He's probably the one you're more likely to find."

Daniel's eyebrows go up. "You may have a future as a detective, Cam."

He shrugs. "I mean, it just makes sense."

I look at the prison behind me. "But what if I've already *found* my birth mother, and she lives in here?"

"Then you'll find out when she calls you," Cameron says. "But in the meantime, we might as well keep looking."

My heart swells with gratitude. Daniel stands now, too, and I'm left sitting on the twilit dirt with Flynn, who pats my knee and says, "We'll find them, Nora."

I look at each of them. "What did I do to deserve you guys?"

Flynn stands, then extends his hand to help me up. "You're the best bass player in our school."

That makes me think of Irene sitting on the floor in my bedroom, telling me she thought I might be the best bassist in the state. I wonder what she'd say if she knew about my detour to this prison. I know she'd disapprove, but I'm not positive which reason she'd focus on. There would be so many.

"Plus, we like you," Cameron says, squeezing my shoulders.

But right now, I can't imagine why they would. All week I selfishly ignored everyone else's problems while plowing forward with my own insane agenda. If Teresa Johnson is my biological mother, then maybe it's hereditary. This thought feels like a fermata played on an out-of-tune instrument—not a temporary dissonance waiting to be resolved, but a suggestion of continuing discomfort.

We load back into the van, and then Flynn U-turns on the narrow road, heading in the direction of the highway. As the prison disappears behind us, I try to picture what the women behind those walls are doing right now. Eating dinner? Reading? Working? Are some of them writing letters to the people they're missing on the outside? Is my birth mother in there somewhere, wondering what happened to the girl she named Summer and then abandoned? Is she deciding, even this minute, to get her life back on track, to find me as soon as she has the chance? And what will I say to her if she calls me tomorrow and says, *Summer? It's me. It's your mother.* What will I do then?

As the fields between Fresno and Reedley rush past me, I think about a song I used to listen to over and over—"Little Green" by Joni Mitchell. It's the song she wrote about giving up a baby girl when she was too young and poor to take care of her. I used to lie on my floor and close my eyes as I listened to it, imagining that it was really my birth mother singing about me.

The van has gone quiet. Cameron's sitting shotgun, and Daniel's staring out his window. I don't have my earbuds with me, but I scroll through my music library anyway, find that song, and play it as softly as I can, holding my phone's speaker against my right ear while I rest my forehead on the window.

During the second verse, Flynn asks me what I'm listening to, so I lean forward and hold my phone up to his left ear. I see him glance back at me in the rearview mirror. He knows what the song means; everyone does.

Cameron asks to listen next, so I turn up the volume and start the song over. Joni Mitchell's voice fills the van.

Once the song is over, Daniel says, "I have a good feeling about Watsonville."

That makes one of us.

♪ ♩ ♪ ♩ ♪

AS FLYNN PULLS THE VAN INTO THE LOT BEHIND OUR MOTEL, he says, "So what do we want to do tonight?"

Cameron looks at him. "Aren't we playing at that burger place?"

"But we're not getting paid."

Daniel leans forward between their seats. "Since when are we such a hot commodity that we'll only play for money? A gig's a gig. It's all good practice."

Flynn glances at the time on his phone. "But we're over two hours late."

"Well, they can't complain, can they?" Daniel argues. "Like you said, we're volunteers."

"Besides, it'd be funny," Cameron says. "A full rock band playing on the patio of a fast-food restaurant. We should document this for our future *Behind the Music*."

I'm the one sitting right behind Flynn, so maybe I'm the only one who can see how his shoulders tense, how his neck and jaw become a little more rigid before he sighs and says, "Okay. Sure. Why not?"

Daniel and Cameron hop out of the car and head to the room, but Flynn waits for me to get out. We walk across the cracked asphalt together, falling further behind the other two. Finally, Flynn stops. I don't look at him, but I wait, because I know I deserve whatever he's about to say to me.

"Nora—"

The sky here is gorgeous. The thickest part of the Milky Way seems to pulse and quiver, like there are strings running through it and they were recently plucked. I wonder, if I sat here quietly and listened for a very long time, whether I'd be able to hear the music being played up there, if all the trembling vibrations would eventually coalesce into a melody.

"—why didn't you tell me?"

I wish we could just stand here in silence, listening to the stars, because I think I'm beginning to hear something unexpected but beautiful, a low, rumbling hum. No wonder heaven is often imagined as populated by harpists and a choir.

"I didn't want my parents to find out what I was doing. And I knew it was a lot to ask—coming this far out of the way, spending all this time and money."

"But you should have known I'd understand," Flynn says. "I mean, we're not just bandmates. We're *friends*."

"Yeah. Of course."

"And you know I care about you." When I don't respond immediately, he goes on, "I mean, *yes*, it's a lot to ask—coming here, when we all have finals to study for. But if you'd told me how much it mattered to you, I would have understood." His voice sounds tight. "I just—" He gestures broadly. "I feel bad, Nora. I think I've let you down."

I look at him. "What? No. Not at all."

"Yeah, I have." He steps forward. "I know I'm not as fun, or probably as likable, as Dan and Cameron"—he tries to laugh, but it comes out as more of a sigh—"but that doesn't mean I care about you less."

"I know that."

There's something strange about the tone of his voice right now. It's like these words are coming from somewhere deeper inside of him, and that's lowered his register.

"Nora?"

He says my name as if he's asking me to say something, anything, in response. He's not as tall as Cameron, but he's taller than Daniel. I have to angle my face up to meet his eyes. I reach forward and pat his arm. I don't know what he's going to say next, but I have a premonition that I don't want to hear it, so I say, "We should get ready," and then step toward the room. "We have a lame, free gig to play."

"Nora—" I think I see something new behind his eyes, something that makes my heart beat double time. Above us, the galaxy sighs a melody that's very nearly audible, but not quite. But then the expression is gone. "Yeah," he says. "You're right."

He digs his hands into his pockets, then steps forward and nudges me with his shoulder. The gesture is friendly, nothing more, but I can't help thinking about the way he froze when he found Daniel and me behind the Rowdy, the way he's mostly kept a safe distance between us. It's what I always did with Daniel, until last night.

CHAPTER 12

$\mathcal{J}$uan, the manager of JT's Burgers, tells us he's a musician, too, and he's been looking forward to us playing at his restaurant ever since I called. He's short and pudgy, probably in his thirties.

"You know Van Morrison?" he asks us as we set up. "'Brown Eyed Girl' is a good song." He strums an imaginary guitar and bobs his head.

"Yeah, we know it," Daniel says.

Juan points at Daniel, covers his mouth with his hand. "That's the first song I learned, man. It's a pretty good song. No?"

"Yeah," Flynn says flatly. It's clear he wishes Juan would let us set up in peace. "It's a classic."

But I like Juan. I turn to him and say, "Do you want to play that song with us? We cover it all the time."

Juan holds his hands up in front of his shoulders and

shakes his head. "Oh, no. I couldn't." But then he lifts his air guitar again and strums a few chords.

Cameron gestures to Daniel's guitar and says, "You should definitely play it with us."

"No, I'm not a real musician like you guys," he says. But he's already stepped over to Daniel's guitar. "This is a nice instrument." He drags a finger across the strings. "What kind?"

"Gibson Les Paul," Daniel says. The usual lightness is gone from his voice. The one thing he never jokes about is his guitar.

Juan nods. "I've got a pretty good one, too. Fender Squier. You know it?"

"Yeah, I know it," Daniel says. The Squier is Fender's starter guitar; the strings don't hold their tuning for more than a couple songs. But Daniel sounds fairly convincing as he adds, "It's a good one."

Cameron stifles a laugh as he says, "Hey, Juan, you should play Dan's guitar tonight, when you play 'Brown Eyed Girl.'"

"No, no, man," Juan says. But he immediately follows that up with, "Maybe I'll come play one song with you. Yeah? A little Van Morrison?"

"Great," Cameron says, pointing to him. "We're going to hold you to that."

Juan smiles broadly, then sings the *Sha-la-la* chorus of "Brown Eyed Girl" as he disappears inside the restaurant.

Cameron's thick eyebrows rise almost to his hairline as he says, "He actually has a good singing voice."

"Great." Daniel glares at him. "But he's playing *your* guitar."

"Fine," Cameron says. "Then I'm playing yours."

Juan squeezed the four plastic outdoor tables into one corner of the patio to make room for us, but there still isn't space for Flynn's whole drum kit. He sets up a few pieces, and I place my bass amp next to him. I can't stand without risking knocking over one of Flynn's cymbals, so I sit cross-legged on top of my amp and pull my bass into my lap. While Daniel and Cameron look through our gig book and discuss song order, Flynn starts drumming a simple beat. I feel the rhythm for a couple measures, then come in on a funky bass line—nothing too fancy, just a D-minor riff with plenty of space and groove.

As the progression evolves, I close my eyes and let my chin hang toward my chest. After the past few days, this is exactly what I need—to disappear into the music. I need a break from *me*.

I don't notice when Daniel and Cameron stop talking, but I do notice when they come in on the progression I'm inventing. Daniel's just keeping time on his guitar, but then Cameron takes a solo. As far as I know, no one is out here listening to us. We're just playing.

When Cameron finishes his solo, we bring it back to the groove. Flynn starts messing with the rhythm, and we're all listening and responding to each other. I'm reminded of the aspen trees I saw in southern Utah when my parents took Irene and me on a road trip to Yellowstone a few years ago. When they told me that the entire grove was a single organism, I didn't get what they meant. But that's what we're like now: four people circulating a single life force, only, instead of an interconnected root system, we have music.

I don't know how long we jam, but eventually the progression becomes steady and recognizable. When Daniel starts singing one of our cover songs, I open my eyes, letting the outside world flood back in.

We're in the middle of our second set when Flynn leans forward and says, "Hey, we forgot to come up with a word."

"Oh, shit," Daniel says.

"*Shit*," I say quickly. "I think that fits."

Cameron nods, as if seriously considering the word's merits. "I'm good with that. *Shit*."

Flynn plays a drum fill. "*Shit!*" he says, a little too loudly. The only couple sitting out on the patio glares at us.

"Sorry," Daniel says to them. "Our drummer has issues."

Cameron wisely starts strumming the opening progression for our next song. I meet his eyes as I come in on my bass line, and our word is there between us. Daniel can hardly sing through his laughter.

♪ ♫ ♪ ♫

JUAN ISN'T A TERRIBLE GUITAR PLAYER, AND WHAT HE lacks in skill he makes up for in enthusiasm. When we finish "Brown Eyed Girl," he says, "You know the band Creedence Clearwater Revival?"

Cameron nods. "Yes, we do."

"Yeah, they're pretty good, too." His fingers find the places for a C-major chord, then a G-major. I come in on the bass line for "Have You Ever Seen the Rain" by CCR, and Juan smiles at me so big I think his face might split in half.

Juan refused to sing on "Brown Eyed Girl," but as we play the intro to the song, Daniel points to Juan, then gestures to the mic. Juan shakes his head, but Daniel is already on the other side of the patio, leaning against the rusty metal fence.

"Go on," I say. "What's the worst that can happen?"

Juan looks at me. "I die," he says, and he looks like he means it.

"But that's true of driving to work in the morning, right?" Cameron says. "So, you might as well go for it."

Juan thinks for a second, then steps toward the microphone. He looks like he might be about to puke, but he opens his mouth and the words come out just fine. At the sound of a new voice, the people sitting on the patio—there are only six of them; one couple and another group of four—look up in surprise. When they see who's singing, they clap and cheer. Pudgy Juan does a little hip wiggle, tilts his face to the sky, and sings his heart out, sometimes hitting the notes, sometimes not, but it doesn't really matter. The worst doesn't happen.

As we're playing through the final chorus, two middle-aged white women step out onto the patio. They're about the same height, but one is broad shouldered and narrow hipped, wearing her gray hair short and gelled into erect and vaguely threatening spikes, while the other is soft and blonde, with smooth skin and small blue eyes. It could be my fatigue or the disorienting emotional stress of the past forty-eight hours, but I'm overwhelmed by déjà vu. I think I've seen them before.

Daniel's still leaning against the fence, but when he sees the women, he stands straighter and looks at me. He nods at them significantly, then mouths two words, but I just shrug to indicate that I haven't caught his meaning. He walks around the edge of the patio, moving carefully past the table of four, then squeezing past our instrument cases. He reaches me just as we play the final note of the song.

"That's the prison guard," he says. "The blonde one."

I see it now. She's changed out of her uniform, but her hair is pulled up into the same wispy bouffant.

Juan is basking in the applause from the now-eight members of his audience, alternately waving them down, as if he wasn't all that good, and bowing deeply, with a surprising flourish of his hands.

"You want to play another one with us?" Flynn says, but Juan is already lifting Cameron's guitar off his shoulder and handing it back. Even from here, I can see that his hands are shaking.

"No, no. Two good songs." He waves at his audience. "I'll stop while I'm ahead, right?" He presses his palms together in front of his chest, and I think he's about to thank us or something, but then there's a shine in his eyes, and he just steps toward the door. "I'll bring dinner. Burgers, fries, milkshakes—whatever you want." But without asking us what we actually want, he steps inside the restaurant. Through the window, I see him move quickly across the dining room, disappearing into the kitchen.

"I like Juan," Cameron says.

"Why not move somewhere else, though?" Daniel says, lifting his guitar strap back over his shoulder. "If he wants to do music, he should move to L.A."

"It's possible to *play* music without *pursuing* it," Flynn says, almost to himself. He's still looking through the window into the brightly lit dining room. "Not every musician wants to make a living off it."

"This is where his life is," Cameron says. "I get that."

Daniel looks over his shoulder. Beyond the decrepit fence, there's the cracked asphalt of a mostly empty parking lot, and, beyond that, the other half of this strip mall— a hair salon, an auto center, a liquor store.

"I don't," he says. "I don't get it at all."

"Now who's the snob?" Flynn says.

Daniel answers, but I'm only half listening to what they're saying, because the blonde guard hasn't taken her eyes off me since she stepped out onto the patio. The woman with the spiky gray hair has her arm around the back of the guard's chair. She's leaning toward the blonde's ear, having what appears to be a very one-sided conversation.

I've been trying not to look at the women straight-on, but my eyes drift that way. The blonde notices and waves at me.

Right then, Juan reappears carrying a tray full of food. The guys are already removing their instruments, so apparently we're on a break. Cameron and Flynn join Juan; Daniel takes a detour to the table of four that got here shortly after we started playing. The blonde woman keeps beckoning me over, so I approach and stand awkwardly in front of them, expecting her to speak first. When she doesn't, I say, "Long time, no see," which is maybe the stupidest collection of words that's ever come out of my mouth. Still she doesn't speak. "I didn't realize you were also driving down to Reedley," I say. "Do you live here?"

The gray-haired woman finally peels her gaze away from the blonde woman's face and says, "I'm Harriet."

All I can think to say is, "Oh."

The gray-haired woman looks back at the blonde and says, "Well, she does have your gift for gab, Mel." She stands and offers me her chair. "You sit. Mel's got something she'd like to say to you." She looks inside the restaurant and then adds, "I'm gonna hit the little girls' room. Take all the time you need."

Without looking away from my face, the blonde woman nods and says, "Thanks, sweetie."

Harriet crosses the patio in three long strides, then disappears inside the restaurant. Daniel's sitting with the guys now, unwrapping his burger. I hear them laughing at some story Juan is telling about a time he played guitar at his nephew's seventh birthday party. "I thought, he's a pretty smart kid, you know? I'll play him some Bob Dylan," Juan says. "But 'Blowin' in the Wind' is a long song, man. I didn't realize."

The blonde woman gestures to the chair vacated by

Harriet. "Please, sit," she says. I hear a faint southern twang in her voice that I hadn't noticed before.

As I sit on the empty chair, I catch Juan saying, ". . . face-first in his cake, man. Fell asleep right in the middle of the last verse. Was exhausted, I guess."

"I suppose you're wondering what I'm doing here," the woman says.

I expect her to continue, but when she doesn't I say, "Yeah, I guess I am."

"Well, I didn't have—" She looks at the dark sky. "I heard what you said to Beatrice at the guardhouse this afternoon, about thinking Terry Johnson might be your birth mother. And, well . . ." She looks at her hands. Before I came over here, she couldn't stop staring at me, but now that I'm here, she seems to want to look anywhere else. "I'm sorry, sweet-heart, but there's no way that woman is your biological mother."

"Oh."

There isn't any music being piped out to the patio from the restaurant. In fact, there might not be any music in the restaurant either. The table of four has finally left, as have the few other people that drifted out here to listen to our last set. The only people on the patio now are me, my band, Juan, and this woman. Around and through the sound of Juan's voice and my bandmates' laughter, I think I can hear my own blood whooshing through my ears.

"But I think . . ." The woman (did Harriet call her Mel?) is staring at her upturned palms, which are resting on top of either thigh. She's studying them, as if they might be where she wrote the script for whatever she came here to say. "I think *I* might be your mother."

The whooshing in my ears seems to stop. Everything seems to stop.

"What?"

She presses one of her palms against her chest and says, "My name is Melanie Teresa Klassen. Sixteen years ago, I gave up a baby girl for adoption. I was living in Morro Bay at the time."

I feel belief begin to seep into my bloodstream. The feeling reminds me of the night we ate pot brownies at Cameron's house; once the drug is in your bloodstream, it colors everything.

"But my adoption papers say my birth mother's name is Teresa," I say.

"Back then, I used my middle name a lot," Mel says. "I grew up in Georgia, but I'd run away from home, was working as a maid with a cleaning service. I was only seventeen, but I lied about my age, my name, everything."

"When was your baby born?" I say.

Mel says a date that is the year I was born, but the wrong day and month.

I shake my head. "That's not my birthday."

"But how do you *know*?" Mel says. "The papers?"

"What was your baby's name?" I ask.

"I didn't name her, at least not officially," Mel says. "For most of my pregnancy, I knew I'd be giving her up. I signed the papers in the hospital." Her eyes are dewy, but I'm not sure if that's because she's about to cry or because she hasn't blinked in a while.

Behind us, I hear Juan say, "Reedley is a small place, you know? Who would want to start a band with me? I'm not so good, anyways. I just like the good music. It's fun for me to play sometimes."

"I'm sorry," I say. "But there's no way that I'm the girl you gave up."

Mel wipes away a tear that I didn't see fall and says, "How can you be sure?"

"You have the wrong name. I'm the wrong age. I was given up for adoption at eighteen months, not at birth. And my birth mother named me Summer." I study the squareness of her jaw, the thin sharpness of her nose. "Besides, we look nothing alike."

She looks at me, her blue eyes sparkling in the dim light. "I should have known it was unlikely I'd find you so easily," she says. I resist the urge to correct *you* to *her*. "It's just, I've been looking for so long. The circumstances of the adoption were so—" She shudders. "How was I supposed to know what I'd want a year later?" She wipes away her tears again. "I'm so embarrassed to be crying in front of you, but it's just—I thought I'd have another chance, and it never came. I know there's no use regretting these things, but—" She stops herself, takes a deep breath. "Could you just tell me one thing?"

I nod.

"Have you been happy with your adoptive family?"

"Yes," I say, but that doesn't feel like the whole truth, so

I add, "I've been happy. But I always knew I was adopted."

"Was that a bad thing?"

I close my eyes and try to think about how I can put this into words. "I think it made me always feel like I needed to be—"

I pause so long that Mel tries to help me by saying, "—different?"

"No. *Careful*." I can see that Mel doesn't understand, so I try to explain: "I just—it's hard to get over the idea that the people who were biologically most inclined to love me still were willing to give me up. If *they* could abandon me so easily, then what's to stop *anyone* from doing the same thing?"

This is something I've thought about a lot, but have never said out loud. It feels weird to put this deepest fear of mine into words for a stranger.

Mel's eyes are dry now, but her eyebrows are lifted and pinched in the center. "I've spoken to a lot of people who've given up children," she says. "I belonged to a support group before I moved up here, and I'm still active on the message boards." She wraps her hands around mine and squeezes. "And I want you to know that no one makes the decision to give up a child lightly. We're not all equipped for deep thinking and future planning, so some people just follow the *feeling* of what they ought to do, but it's never easy. Someone wanted more for you than they had to offer. You weren't abandoned, sweetheart. You were set free."

Her words feel like cool water on a feverish forehead, but they don't solve the problem of the combustion inside me. I ask, "How do you know Teresa Johnson isn't my birth mother?"

"Because her daughter was adopted by a big family in Colorado—a pastor and his wife. There was an article about it in the paper a few years ago." She wipes away another tear. "When Terry Johnson was inside last time, the girl visited her."

Harriet steps back outside. Mel looks at her and shakes her head, and Harriet's weathered features soften into sadness. Mel stands and apologizes for taking up my time, or something like that. I'm not really listening. Instead, I'm watching Harriet watch Mel. The love between them is palpable, like there's an actual ribbon of it cycling physically on an infinite loop, from one body to the other. As they disappear into the restaurant together, I think, *At least she's not alone.*

"Nora, what was that about?" Daniel says, looking across the now-empty patio.

"Nothing." I join them at their table, sitting in the empty chair between Cameron and Flynn. "A misunderstanding."

"Why was she crying?" Flynn says.

"She thought she was my birth mother."

"What?" They all say it at once, so I have no choice but to explain the whole conversation. As I finish summarizing what I know, I look at the boys at this table, and I remind myself that I'm not alone, either. I know this. I've always known it. But it's easy enough to forget when the people who were supposed to love me first may not have loved me at all. Because no matter what Mel says, it's hard to believe that love wouldn't have been enough reason for them to keep me.

♪ ♫ ♪ ♫

WHEN WE GET BACK TO THE MOTEL, I CALL MY PARENTS. I tell them that the drive into Reedley was easy, and that our gig was smaller than we expected, but it was actually a lot of fun. I tell them about Juan and his cover songs. It feels good to say something true.

Daniel's the last one to get ready for bed. After some debate, we all agreed that Cameron and Flynn would share the bed on the far side of the room, and Daniel and I would share the one by the bathroom. Flynn didn't seem overly pleased with this arrangement, but he went with it.

While I wait for Daniel to get out of the bathroom, I think about something I learned in history last year about René Descartes and John Locke, philosophers of different ages. One believed in the primacy of nature and the other believed in the importance of nurture, but I can't remember which was which.

I imagine my parents lying in their bed, my mom's blonde hair spread across her pillow, my dad already kicking off the covers, rolling closer to her side of the bed. How can two people feel so intrinsic to my life and yet so foreign? If I do find my biological mother, will I feel differently about her, or will it be the same? With her, I'll have the blood ties I'm missing from my parents, but I won't have all this history.

Then I remember, René Descartes believed a person is born with innate knowledge, while John Locke, who came later, believed each person is born tabula rasa, a blank slate, upon which character is written by experience. I wonder what Descartes and Locke would say about my quest to discover my origins, to find the people who made me, in the most literal sense, *me*. If I've understood them correctly, then Descartes would approve, while Locke would tell me to get on with my life.

The door to the bathroom opens, and Daniel switches off the light. I hear more than see him cross the room and climb into the bed beside me. I lie still, hoping he'll believe I'm asleep, but when he whispers, "Nora?" I can't help responding, "Yeah?"

"I just wondered if you were awake."

When I swallow, it sounds enormous. I don't think I've ever been in a room as quiet as this one.

Neither of us moves for a long time, but his breathing doesn't change, so I know he isn't asleep yet. Finally, he whispers, "I'm sorry we didn't find her today."

"Yeah." I roll onto my back. "Me, too."

When his fingers brush against my skin, I'm so startled I almost jump. But then his warm palm presses into mine, and our fingers weave together. He repeats what he said earlier. "I have a good feeling about Watsonville."

I have a good feeling, too, but I think that's just because his hand is holding mine.

CHAPTER 13

$\mathcal{S}$urprisingly, we all sleep deeply, and late. In the morning, Flynn claims to have a stiff neck because of the limp pillows, but I think he might be imagining it, because once he's been awake for a few minutes, he stops wincing every time he moves his head.

None of us wants to step inside the questionable shower, so we just check out (the total cost of our stay is forty dollars, which causes Flynn's mood to improve drastically) and then pile into the van. It's my turn to sit shotgun. I'd just as soon stay in the back, but I don't want Flynn to think I'm avoiding him, so I climb into the front seat.

As we cross the river on the way out of Reedley, it occurs to me that if I'm going to find my birth parents this week, or even find a clue as to where they might be, then today is my last chance. Maybe someday I could hire a private investigator. There's an ex-cop named Frank Haines who advertises detective services on a lot of the adoptee discussion forums. Supposedly, he has a pretty high solve rate. He's also expensive. And who knows what will happen to Martin and Teresa by the time I've saved up enough? Who knows what's already happened? For all I know, they're both dead, or have moved to Australia, or have joined a cult and are permanently off the grid. Maybe I'm chasing ghosts.

The drive to Watsonville goes by in a blur. After we check into our hotel (Daniel follows me into room 309 without comment), we head to the address I already found for the defunct Croft's Confections. Last night, we tried searching for the whereabouts of a Martin Croft of Watsonville, but we didn't find anything promising— no social media profiles, no white pages entries. Croft's Confections is our only lead, and as far as I can tell it went out of business years ago. Its space in the strip mall is currently occupied by a nail salon called Princess Nails, whose windows are decorated with a disorderly mishmash of cartoon decals. When we get there, there's a tattered sign hanging from the door that says *Come on in! We're open!*

We pause outside. "You guys don't have to do this with me," I say. "I know this isn't what you signed up for."

"Are you kidding?" Cameron says. "You've given us a *quest*. Who doesn't love a quest?"

"Most bands would love to have a quest," Daniel adds. He leans against one of the brick posts supporting the awning of the building. "Once this is over, we should record a concept album about it."

Flynn tears his eyes away from a garishly cheerful kitten decal to look at me. "What do we ask here?"

"Whether or not they knew the previous tenants?" I say.

"Or if they know if the previous tenants were named Martin or Teresa?" Cameron says.

"Or if they know someone named Martin or Teresa who lives or used to live in Watsonville?" Daniel says. The three of us look at him. He shrugs. "It would be better than nothing."

Suddenly, the hopelessness of this task lands on my chest, crushing out all my air. I can almost hear violin strings snapping with a twang inside my rib cage. "This is a waste of time," I say. "I'm sorry we're spending all this money to stay in—" I gesture at the characterless strip mall. "In *nowhere*. But we're not going to find my birth parents in Watsonville. Just like I was never going to find them in Santa Barbara or Reedley. Maybe I should just"—I sit on the curb—"*stop*." As I cross my arms over my knees, I mutter, "I mean, what's in a gene pool, anyway?"

"Hey," Daniel says. He sits on my left, and Cameron sits on my right. "I'm supposed to be the emotional train wreck in this band."

Flynn moves in front of us and says, "That's true."

Cameron says, "Dan's right. You're supposed to be the stoic badass."

"I thought I was the stoic one," Flynn says.

"No, you're the anal-retentive one," Daniel says.

I squeeze my eyes shut, wipe away the twin tears that leak down my cheeks, then sit up. "I'm serious, you guys."

I gesture to the storefront. "My biological parents are not going to be inside Princess Nails."

"Well, obviously," Cameron says. "Because that would be a literal miracle from God."

"But we might find someone who can point us toward whatever dead end we're chasing, so we can cross this off your list," Daniel says. He's resting his chin on his knees, looking at me sideways. It's hard not to feel better when he's looking at me like this. "If we don't find your biological parents in the next twenty-four hours, it's not like we have to stop looking."

"Well, *you* can stop looking if you want," Cameron says, squeezing my shoulder. "But I need to know now. I'm invested."

Flynn looks behind him at the rapidly sinking sun. "Are we going to ask the Princess Nails people about Croft's Confections or not?"

"Dude," Daniel says, looking at him. "We're having a moment."

Flynn exhales through his nose, then walks around us and disappears inside the salon.

"He's also the efficient one," Cameron says. "Without him, we might never get anything done."

"I know that," Daniel says. "But don't tell him. His ego would never recover."

I stand and follow Flynn into Princess Nails. As I open the door, it warbles and chirps at me; as in, instead of a bell, there's a brief sound bite of singing birds. Flynn is already talking to the woman at the front desk, which is decorated with patches of fake moss in an obvious attempt to give it a woodland vibe. The walls of the salon are plastered with the same cheesy decals that decorate the front window. The effect in here is no more aesthetically pleasing than the effect out there.

The woman herself looks young, though she's wearing thick makeup that makes it difficult to tell for certain. Her hair's been bleached and then highlighted with bold streaks of cotton-candy pink. When I walk in, Flynn's saying, ". . . Confections. This was their address, though we're not sure when they closed."

The woman shrugs. Then, in a voice that's so high-pitched and sweet I almost feel myself developing diabetes, she says, "Sorry. I don't know. We've only been here a year."

I look at the empty stations, wondering if they'll make it through year two. "Do you know what business was in here before you?"

The door warbles again, and Cameron and Daniel join us.

"Welcome to Princess Nails!" the woman says.

"Wow." Daniel eyes the décor. "Is this *your* shop?"

"It sure is," the woman says. "Did you want a mani, a pedi, or a mani/pedi?"

"None of the above," Daniel says. "We're with—" He points at us.

The woman doesn't seem too put out. She directs her attention back to Flynn. "Before I moved in, this was Abracadabra Comics." She shakes her head. "But they were only here six months."

I'm surprised she's able to stay so upbeat when her shop is empty and the lineage of this location does not suggest business longevity.

"Can you remember any previous owners named Teresa?" Cameron says.

The woman shakes her head. "Sorry. I wish I could help."

"Have you ever heard of someone in Watsonville named Teresa Croft?" This is my last-ditch effort, and I can see that she's about to apologize again, but then Cameron says, "Or Martin Croft?" and her expression freezes.

"My mechanic's name is M. J. Croft," she says. "I think his initials might stand for Martin John, but I couldn't swear to it. I'm friends with Julie, his office manager."

The guys look at me. I told them my adoption papers say my biological father was a mechanic.

I ask, "Do you know if M. J. was ever married to someone named Teresa?"

The woman nods, as if this makes some kind of sense. "I know he was married, but I heard it ended badly."

"In what way?" I say.

"That's all I know," she says. "I heard it from Julie. Poor girl's been trying to get him to ask her out for a decade. I assumed he was gay, but she said she thought he was married before, thought he might even have a kid."

Flynn seems to intuit that I've lost the ability to speak, because he takes the lead and asks her where we might find this M. J. Croft.

"He works at Tito's," she says. "Tito's Auto Repair." She looks at the clock behind her. "He's probably there now."

"Thank you so much," I say. "And, you know, good luck with your business. I hope things pick up."

"Oh, I'm not worried," she says.

This seems like such an irrational response that I wonder about her sanity. Then I wonder about *my* sanity. Then I decide it's time to leave.

Flynn reaches across the desk to shake her hand. I notice her nails, which are thickly painted in graded shades of pink. "What was your name?" he says.

She looks confused. "Princess," she says, as if the answer should have been obvious. And I guess it should have been.

Flynn recovers first and says, "Thank you for your help, Princess."

And then we get the hell out of there.

♪ ♪ ♪ ♪

WE PILE INTO THE VAN, BUT THEN DISCOVER THAT THE SHOP is just a couple blocks away, so we get back out and walk. It's almost 6:00 p.m., and I worry that we'll have missed him. But as we turn the corner, I see the sign for Tito's Auto Repair illuminated above an entire edge of the strip mall. There's a light on in the office, and I hear a grinding sound coming from the shop in back.

I stop walking, but Cameron nudges me forward, and I only lose one step. Flynn reaches the door first and holds it open for us, so I'm the first to step through into the unadorned office, which smells faintly of cinnamon pot-pourri. Through the door that leads to the shop, I hear the song "Virtual Insanity" by Jamiroquai. I love that song.

The woman sitting behind the desk is a round-faced bru-nette. Like Princess, her age is difficult to determine, but not because of an excess of makeup; her skin is just uni-formly pale and unlined, like a new bar of Dove soap. She looks at us curiously, waiting for one of us to speak. But it's not going to be me.

"Are you Julie?" Flynn says. I've never been so grateful for his ability to take charge even when it's completely not his place to do so.

"That's me. What can I do for you?"

"We were sent here by Princess," Flynn says.

Her eyes brighten. "Oh, there's only one Princess," she says. "I'll thank her for the referral."

"We're actually not here with a car issue," Flynn says. He squares his shoulders, adopts his best adult voice, and says, "We'd like to talk to Martin—or M. J.—Croft."

I look at Flynn, and I get a sudden flash of who he's going to be when he grows up—someone responsible, well dressed, organized. He'll be somebody's dad, and he'll be good at it.

The woman tilts her head to the side, then says, "Who should I tell him is here?"

But before Flynn can respond, the door to the shop swings open, and a short, muscular man with thick hair streaked with gray, and a more-gray-than-not beard, steps into the office. He pokes at Julie's cheek with a greasy finger, and she swats him away. I guess she got her wish after all.

"Martin?"

It takes me a second to realize that I'm the one who said his name.

He's smiling broadly at the woman at the desk, and he's still smiling when he looks up. His eyes are almost iridescently blue, crinkled at the edges. His skin is deeply tanned. He doesn't seem like the Jamiroquai type. But I always thought that Jamiroquai doesn't look a whole lot like their sound. What's a book to its cover, anyway? Or a band's look to its sound? Or a mechanic to his taste in music?

"No one's called me that since the sixth grade," he says. His voice is resonant and gravelly. "I'm M. J. to everyone but the IRS. What can I do ya for?"

There are no more words inside me.

After a way-too-long pause, Flynn reaches across the top of the desk to shake his hand. "It's nice to meet you, sir," he says.

I sense more than see Daniel raise his eyebrows at Flynn's use of the title.

Flynn places his hand on my shoulder and says, "This is Nora." I'm shaking my head. "What?" Flynn says, looking down at me.

But my mind is still blank. Or, it's not blank, exactly. It's more like the connection between my brain and my mouth has been severed. My brain, in fact, is going a million places at once. First, I'm thinking that my eyes aren't blue, and didn't we learn in biology that blue is recessive? So, if this man were my father, wouldn't I have blue eyes? Well, not if Teresa's eyes are brown. Then my eyes would probably be brown, which they are.

But he's short. I might be half an inch taller than him.

His features are blunt, where mine are rounded. His cheeks seem to be permanently blushed.

We look *nothing* alike.

Then again, Cameron is taller than both his parents. And Daniel's older brother, who I've only met once, has hair so dark it's almost black, the opposite of Daniel's dirty blondness. Flynn looks exactly like his dad, which surprises no one. But still, genes can express themselves in strange ways.

Daniel steps forward and says, "Her biological parents named her Summer, but the couple that adopted her changed her name to Nora."

M. J.'s smile falters. This is not the expression of a father who wanted to be found.

The walls of this office will crush me if I don't get outside right now. Without another word, I turn around and head toward the door. I'm already outside, but the door is suspended at the apex of its arc.

Behind me, M. J. says, "You're Tessa's kid, aren't you?"

I turn and look at him as the door swings shut behind me.

CHAPTER 14

"Tessa?" Daniel says. "Nora's adoption papers say *Teresa*."

Cameron came outside and led me back into the office. I'm standing in the center of the room again, feeling excruciatingly aware of all my appendages and of the muscles in my face, which seem to be trembling in unison. In fact, all my atoms seem to be vibrating together at a frequency only dogs could hear. Maybe if they accelerate further, the bonds connecting them will break, and my particles will disperse, rising upward like smoke from a campfire.

This makes me remember two things simultaneously: the one time my parents took Irene and me camping (Irene loved it; I did not), and my physics final, which I am definitely going to fail.

"Tessa hated being called that," M. J. says. "Thought it made her sound like a saint, which she certainly was not." He says this last thing almost to himself, then realizes it might have been inappropriate, considering the audience. "Most people didn't know Teresa was her legal name."

"*Was?*" Daniel says. "Is she—?"

"Oh, no," M. J. says. "As far as I know, she's still alive. Though, we don't keep in the closest touch. I've only seen her once in—" He appears to do the math in his head, then realizes the answer to the math question is standing in front of him. He looks at me. "In sixteen years."

"But what do you mean by *Tessa's kid*?" Flynn says. "Doesn't that make you Nora's father?"

"That's a complicated question," M. J. says.

No. It isn't.

He looks at Julie, who's gazing at him with an expression full of equal parts love and concern. I wonder if she'd still be as crazy about him if she knew he abandoned me. Or maybe she does know. Maybe she's secretly glad—no irritating stepkids to get in her way.

I don't know where that thought even comes from. It's like everything angry, sad, and mean is bubbling to my surface at once. Because as I stare at M. J. Croft, all I can think about is the fact that he didn't want me enough to keep me. He didn't know that I'd be adopted by wonderful people who would love me in the best way they know how. He didn't know where I'd end up, and he didn't care.

"Why don't you kids come to our place for dinner?" he says. He looks at me. "I assume you came looking for your biological parents, but also for answers about who you are. I'm sorry, but I can only help with one of those."

I don't know how to process this. If this is Martin, then

he should be *it*. This should be where the journey ends. These should be the arms I run to. But he's threading his fingers through Julie's and saying, "I've got to lock up, but we'll meet you around front."

When they disappear through the back door, my body goes limp. If it weren't for Cameron and Daniel wrapping their hands beneath my elbows and guiding me outside, I think I might actually collapse. But Flynn opens the door for us, and then we're out in the sunset-pink parking lot, and Cameron is saying, "I think Nora might puke." And Daniel's saying, "No, she won't. She'll think she's going to puke, but she won't." And he's right.

When M. J. and Julie reappear around the edge of the building, I take a deep breath and lead the way to their truck. Once we're pulling out onto the main road, I even manage to lean forward and say, "Thank you for talking to me. I appreciate it."

"Kid, it's the least I can do," M. J. says.

I resist the urge to tell him he's right.

♪ ♩ ♪ ♩ ♪

JULIE IS A WONDERFUL COOK. AFTER EATING EXPIRED vending-machine snacks and fast food for the past two days, I can feel her grilled salmon, rosemary potatoes, and sautéed asparagus infusing my body with much-needed strength. Through most of dinner, M. J. asks us questions about how we found him, our band, our road trip. He's heard of the Magwitch, but not Horoscope. Still, he seems impressed that we're opening for any band in San Francisco. The guys do most of the talking, for which I'm extremely grateful. But when he asks about the family that adopted me, I find my voice.

"They're both attorneys." I consider going into more detail, but decide against it. "And they're very nice people." I lean forward. "I'm not looking for my biological parents because there's anything *wrong* with the parents I have. I just—" I close my eyes and take a deep breath. "I want to know who I am."

"Yeah," he says. "I get that. And I suppose some part of me always expected that you'd hunt one of us down."

I'm not sure I appreciate the predator analogy, but it's not worth dwelling on. "I don't mean to be rude," I say, "but if you're not my biological father, then who is?"

He pushes his plate away and sits back in his chair. He's looking at his hands now, which are crossed on the table in front of him. "His name was Rico."

"*Was?*" Daniel says.

"And probably still is. Though, I've made no effort to keep in touch with *him*."

Julie puts her hand on his shoulder, and his pained expression softens, just slightly. He takes a deep breath. "I'm trying to figure out where to start this story. But I think I should start with this: when Tessa told me she was pregnant, I was delighted." Julie stands and starts clearing the table, and the guys wordlessly join her in the kitchen, leaving M. J. and me alone. "We'd only been married a year, but things were already on the rocks for us. She'd convinced me to throw all our money at this bakery she was starting—"

"Croft's Confections?"

"That was it." He doesn't seem surprised that I've figured out this much. "But once she had everything set up, she lost interest in the business, and me." His jaw clenches. Whatever damage my birth mother did to this man, it runs deep. "So, when she told me she was pregnant, I thought, *This will be the thing that saves us.* And for the first couple months, it seemed like it might. She put energy back into the bakery, got into being the Earth Mother type—long skirts, no makeup. She changed her whole"—he looks for the right word—"*identity.*"

I'm having an out-of-body experience. I'm watching myself watch this man I just met tell me about my birth mother, about how she acted when she was pregnant with *me.* The strangest thing about it is that it doesn't feel strange at all. Instead, it feels like my whole life has been leading me to this moment.

"What do you mean?" I say.

He looks at me, apparently gauging how much he should say, how well I'm handling what he's divulged so far. I do my best to look emotionally stable and totally okay.

"When Tessa and I first got together, we did some pretty crazy stuff. She used to wear this thick black eyeliner, and these outfits that were held together with safety pins. Her hair was blue when I met her. Later, it was purple, then orange, but not really orange. More like—" He closes his eyes, and I feel so envious of the memory he's retrieving. "More like a tangerine." He coughs into a hand while he says, "We did some drugs." He sits forward quickly and adds, "But that all stopped when she got pregnant. And I was into it. I wanted my marriage to work. I was excited to be a father, to start this new chapter of my life. So, I grew out my Mohawk—"

"Mohawk?"

"—and sold my drum set so I could buy a ten-year-old Subaru wagon. Tessa didn't include me in any doctor's appointments or anything, but I didn't know what to expect."

He stares at his hands. I keep waiting for him to say something else, but he doesn't. While I wait, I realize there's an actual clock ticking somewhere. It's like listening to the heartbeat of the universe.

"And then what happened?"

He seems reluctant to relive the end of his story, but he goes on. "When she was nine months pregnant, she told me that she didn't want to raise her daughter in Watsonville. She wanted to be somewhere else. Hawaii, she told me. She needed to be in Hawaii. Of course, we didn't have the money for plane tickets, but I'd been to Santa Barbara and thought it was the most beautiful place I'd ever seen. So, I packed everything we owned into that Subaru and drove us down the 101, worrying the entire time that I'd end up delivering you on the side of the road."

"Did you?"

He shakes his head. "We were in Santa Barbara for

a week, and then when she went into labor in our hotel room, I drove her to the hospital, pushed her into the lobby, and there was *Rico*." A small blue vein begins to pulse in the center of his forehead. "He worked at this granola-crunchy health food store next to Croft's Confections, had white-guy dreadlocks, smoked weed twenty-four seven. The whole thing."

I wonder how many businesses have come and gone from that strip mall in the last sixteen years.

"I'd seen him a couple times, but never thought much about him," M. J. says. "But there he was, in this hospital in Santa Barbara. When Tessa saw him, she held her arms out to him and started crying, as if he was rescuing her from some"—his face contorts as he finds the right word—"*prison*."

I wonder who else knows this story, whether he's been up to the task of sharing it with even Julie. It seems to take everything out of him to say, "Rico told me he was the real father of Tessa's child, and that they were running away together as soon as you were born. He said Tessa hadn't wanted to hurt me, *but*"—he puts a bitter emphasis on that word—"she'd tried to tell me she was leaving by saying that she needed to go to Hawaii, and I hadn't gotten the hint." He presses his hands against the surface of the table. "As if all of it had been my fault."

I give him a moment to recover before I ask, "So, if they took me with them to Hawaii, then how come you're the one who gave me up for adoption?"

He drops his forehead into his hands, breathes. "I was

so shocked when she left me. They disappeared down the hallway of that hospital, and I just stood there. Once I could move again, I went back to the hotel room, broke a lamp, and then drove home to Watsonville. I figured I'd never hear from either of them again, except when she served me divorce papers, which I expected every day."

He lifts his head and meets my eyes. "But the papers never came. And then almost a year later, I get this phone call from a woman in Oahu. She said she was my wife's neighbor and that she'd agreed to watch our daughter for an afternoon, not a week. She didn't want to get Tessa in trouble, but she had her own kids to take care of." He looks back down as he says, "Tessa had taken off."

I see Daniel and Cameron peeking around the corner from the kitchen. I shake my head, and they retreat.

"So, I flew to Hawaii," M. J. says. "None of us had cell phones back then, and Tessa didn't even have an email address. I spent a few days trying to track her down, but it was like she'd never existed. I was already working at Tito's and I was running out of money, so eventually I had to go back to California, and when I did, I brought you with me." He turns his hands palms up. "I didn't know what else to do."

"And you tried to keep me for a few months," I say. "Right?"

"I did and I didn't," he says, exhaling. "I wish I could say I still wanted to rise to the occasion, but whenever I held you, I thought about Rico standing there with my pregnant wife, telling me I'd been too dense to understand that we'd been doomed from the beginning. Not that you look much like him," he adds, as if to reassure me of something. "The truth is, you're the spitting image of your mother." The word *mother* lands heavily between us, and I think he senses the wrongness of it. He looks at me. "The problem was, I really loved Tessa. She was the kind of woman that got under your skin, that could make you fall in love with her just by glancing in your direction."

He shakes his head. "I kept you for six months while I tried to track down Tessa, or even Rico, but she'd listed me as your father on your hospital records, which gave me the authority to put you up for adoption, once I was able to prove that Tessa had abandoned us both." He looks at me, and his clear blue eyes hold mine for a second before he says, "I don't know if you'll believe this, but on the day I signed the papers to give you up, I almost didn't go through with it. You were such a sweet baby. But there would have always been this cloud over our relationship. I wanted you to be with a family that would love you without all the baggage I was still carrying."

The clock ticks. M. J. and I look at each other. There are so many things I'd like to say, but what comes out is, "Did you ever find Tessa again?"

He nods. "She came back to Watsonville once about ten years ago. She didn't tell me what had happened with Rico, and I didn't ask. But she was still living in Hawaii, managing some kind of spiritual center, I think it was. She said that she'd always known I'd brought you home with me— the babysitter must have told her. When I said you'd been placed with an adoptive family, she said she knew you were with good people." He shrugs. "I don't know how she tracked down that information, but even with that much water under the bridge, I wasn't too happy to have her back in town. We finally got our divorce, and then she went back to Hawaii, and I never saw her again."

He lets out all his air, widens his eyes. "Though, a few years ago she found me on Facebook." He looks over his shoulder, then lowers his voice as he says, "Julie's not too pleased that we're connected there, but it's been *sixteen years*, and the truth is I'm happier with Julie than I ever was with Tessa. Tessa was a drug; Julie's water. You think you need one, but you really need the other."

After a pause, I say, "My biological mother is on *Facebook*?"

He nods.

"Can I see her profile?"

He pulls his phone out of his pocket, finds the right page, and then hands it to me.

As soon as I see her picture, I know that I've found her, because our faces are the same; we have the same wide brown eyes, the same short nose. Our hairlines both come to off-center points, and our lower lips are thicker than our upper lips. Her hair is wavy where mine is straight, and her cheekbones are more pronounced than mine are, but otherwise it's like looking into the future and seeing myself, age forty.

Tessa Reynoso. Her current name is *Tessa Reynoso*, and her location is listed as Honolulu. Under relationship status, I read, *Married to Roger Reynoso*. I make a mental note of this and then hand the phone back.

"You can look through it as long as you want," he says, pushing the phone back to me.

"Thanks for the help," I say, laying the phone on the table between us. "But we should get going."

Daniel and Cameron reappear around the corner, evidence of the fact that they've been listening to this whole conversation.

"Are you sure?" M. J. says, looking surprised. "You're all welcome to stay the night. We have a guest room and a sofa bed."

Julie and Flynn enter now, too. Julie takes her place next to M. J., but Flynn hovers in the background, glancing at M. J., then at me. I can feel a question on the edge of his tongue, and I need to get out of here before he asks it.

I realize now that I don't have anything with me—not my purse, not my phone, not even ChapStick. I left all of it in Flynn's van, which is still parked outside Princess Nails. Without having a plan other than *Get out of this house*, I step around the edge of the table, cross through the dining room to the tiled foyer, and close my hand around the doorknob.

"Thank you, but we prepaid for our rooms," I say, trying to keep my voice even and unemotional. "And we have to leave early." I look at Daniel and ask, "Could you order a car?"

His phone is already out. "They're close. Be here in three minutes."

"Oh, that's not necessary," Julie says. "We're happy to drive you to your hotel."

"No." I'm surprised how firmly I say this. "You've already done too much."

"Well, keep in touch," M. J. says, though I'm certain he doesn't mean it. They're just words to say.

Words, words, words—the detritus that's skimmed off the top of our minds. I hate them.

Till death do us part.

I was excited to be a father.

I wanted better for you.

Lies.

That's where I come from. I come from lies and deceit and selfish heartbreak bullshit. These are the building blocks of my existence.

I say, "Thank you. I will," because now I know that words don't have to mean anything. And then I'm outside, and the night is cool and dry. The stars spread out above me like the raised notes inside a music box.

Daniel and Cameron follow me out to the sidewalk. Flynn's still hovering on the porch, exchanging pleasantries with Julie. I'm facing the street, willing the car to show up now, before anyone else tries to speak. The air has turned cold, and I'm just wearing a thin T-shirt and jeans, but it feels good to be uncomfortable. It gives me something to think about other than blue-eyed M. J. Croft saying that every time he looked at me, he only saw Tessa's deceit.

"I understand why you'd be upset." M. J. drapes a jacket

over my shoulders. I hate how warm it is. I hate that it smells like pine sap and ocean. "It's a lot to process."

I'm not going to add more meaningless words to this night, so I say nothing.

As the car pulls up to the curb, I hand M. J. his jacket and force out, "Tell Julie thanks for dinner."

He starts to say something along the lines of *Good luck*—another meaningless phrase suggesting emotional involvement while really signifying *You're on your own*—but I'm already sliding into the back of the car, and I miss most of it. Daniel and Cameron climb in on either side of me; Flynn sits up front. As the driver pulls onto the street, Flynn looks back and asks, "Why are we leaving?" But the answer should be obvious: because that's what people do.

CHAPTER 15

*I*t's still early when we return to the Watsonville Inn. Flynn asks if I want to study for physics with him, but I tell him I think I'll just turn in. It's been a long day, and tomorrow, after all, is the Magwitch.

While Daniel takes his turn getting ready for bed, I call my parents. The sound of my mom's voice makes me inexplicably angry. It's not anything she says, really; it's just the calm, soothing way that she says it. She must sense the irritation in my voice, because she asks me if something's wrong. I tell her I'm fine, just tired, and then quickly end the call.

When it's my turn to use the bathroom, I take an unnecessarily long and hot shower. I wish I could scrub away everything—my jealousy, my anger, all of my lies. I wish I could stand under the water until my slate was washed clean.

By the time I step back out into the room wearing my

shorts and jazz festival T-shirt, Daniel's sitting on the bed, holding his acoustic guitar in his lap. He's fingerpicking something simple and sweet. I haven't heard it before, so I ask him what it is, and without giving any indication that he knows what this will do to me, he says, "It's something new I've been working on. It's about you."

I stare at him.

"Want to hear it?"

All I can do is nod.

While he starts to play, I lean against the desk and fold my arms across my chest. He sings softly, so he won't wake up Flynn and Cameron next door, but the words come through clearly.

I wish I could pretend it was a love song, but it's not. It's tender and sweet, but innocent, almost like a lullaby. It's a song for a friend who's hurting. Still, I'd like to cross the room and kiss him, since that seems to be an option, at least for tonight. But I'm not sure I could do it without losing myself completely, so instead I open my bass case and carry it over to the bed. I sit facing him and pick out the melody he's singing. My instrument isn't amplified, so it just sounds like a tinny whisper under his guitar and voice. When I shift to playing a harmony, though, the tone doesn't matter as much. The intervals chime together perfectly. I start to mess around with the rhythm, filling in spaces in the melody and leaving room while he sings. By the time the song ends, my mind is pleasantly blank.

"So?" He shifts the position of his guitar. "What do you think?"

I mean it when I say, "I love it."

He nods, pleased.

"It's different from other things you've written."

"Well, you're different from other people I've met."

Instead of responding, I invent a slow, melodic line in E minor. Daniel quickly figures it out on his guitar, then finds a complementary part to play above it. I'm not much of a singer, but I can hear a vocal part begging to be sung between the notes, so I add that in, too—just notes, not words. I hate words.

Over the next few hours, we invent dozens of riffs and progressions, and it feels almost as good as kissing him. We play covers, too. We never talk about what we're going to play; we just play it. I realize that even if his feelings for me never change, I'm still so grateful for *this*, for a friend who speaks a language I understand.

We're in the middle of an acoustic version of "Everlasting Light" by the Black Keys—I never realized how sweet those lyrics were until now—when I hear something slam shut nearby. Two seconds later, someone knocks loudly on our door.

Daniel and I look at each other. We've been playing so softly; I can't imagine that someone could have heard us. As Daniel gets up to open the door, I clutch my bass defensively, but Flynn's the one who steps into our room, and he doesn't even seem to notice our instruments. The first thing he says is, "Is Cameron in here?"

Daniel says, "No. Isn't he in your room?" but I've already got a sick feeling in the pit of my stomach. Because

I don't know where Cameron is, but I bet I know what he's doing.

"No," Flynn says. He's still wearing his clothes from today, but his hair looks messed up in front; this only happens when he's been studying or taking a test—the result of resting his head on one of his hands as he stares at a textbook or exam. "I was looking over my history notes, and he said that he was going to get some ice or something. I can't remember." He strides to the far side of our room and looks out the window. "I had my headphones on, and I just assumed he'd already gotten back. Or, I don't know. I guess I wasn't thinking about it. But when I stopped studying, I realized that he's still gone." He steps away from the window and paces toward the door. "It's been hours."

"And you're only noticing this *now*?" Daniel says.

Flynn glares at him. "Hey, I'm not his guardian. I'm not *responsible* for him."

While they continue arguing, I return my bass to its case and go into the bathroom to change back into my jeans. When I come out, I say, "Could I get into your room, Flynn?"

He looks at me. "Why?"

"I just—" I don't want to voice my suspicions unless they're confirmed. The thing is, I'm thinking about what I smelled on Cameron's shirt outside of the prison, and I'm not sure it was laundry detergent and coconut after all. "I just want to check something."

His eyebrows go up, but he's already at the door when he says, "Yeah, sure."

Daniel follows us back into the other room. I wish I could do this part without them watching, but that's not going to be an option, so I approach Cameron's duffle bag, take a deep breath, and pull it open.

The evidence, unfortunately, is right on top—half a dozen miniature bottles, the kind people buy in airports, all of them empty. Flynn and Daniel step up next to me, and soon I've allowed myself to be pushed to the side. In two minutes, they've pulled out half a dozen more small, empty bottles and deposited them on the closest bed.

We stare at them for a moment before Daniel says, "He must have run out."

Flynn doesn't say anything at first. He doesn't even seem to be breathing. But eventually he brings his fist down on the TV stand so hard that I think he must bruise something.

Daniel anticipates Flynn's reaction and swings around to face him. "We need to focus on finding him now."

"Yeah." Flynn's face is red. All his worry seems to have been replaced by rage. "Yeah, and then I'm going to kill him. We came all this way, and the night before the only gig that actually *matters*—"

I wince.

"We can talk about that another time, but not tonight. Besides, look at this." Daniel gestures at the bottles. "He's clearly got a problem."

"I'll tell you what his problem is." Flynn picks up one of the bottles and then throws it back down on the bed. It bounces off the duvet and lands on the floor by my feet.

"He's so busy trying to punish his parents for being *rich* that he doesn't even notice that he's ruining his life."

Daniel's own anger seems to be rising as he says, "You know that's not the issue."

This is the same argument they had on the night of Cameron's surprise party—same arguments, same sides, new venue. That night, Flynn said that if Cameron pulled another stunt like that, then he'd quit Blue Miles. I don't think any of us thought he meant it, but Cameron seemed to chill out for a while after. As I look at the bottles on the bed, though, I wonder if he really did chill out, or if he just hid it better.

"Then what's the issue?" Flynn says. "They didn't buy him a birthday present? They didn't see him in the school play? Nora's parents dropped her off with some nuns when she was a year and a half, and she's doing okay."

Okay is, of course, a relative term. But it occurs to me that if I *am* doing okay, then maybe that's because I was adopted by people who make it clear that I matter, who show me in hundreds of small, easily overlooked ways that their lives wouldn't be complete without me. But it would be too weird to say this out loud, especially considering the fact that I've spent this whole week searching for the people who left me with the nuns.

"If Cameron's ruining his life, then it's our job to help him get it straightened out," Daniel says.

"Like hell it's our job."

I don't like how close Daniel and Flynn are standing to each other. If I didn't know them better, I'd think one of them was about to throw a punch, and the only thing I can think to say that might defuse the tension is, "He didn't tell his parents he was leaving this week."

They both look at me.

"What?" Flynn asks. The edge in his voice is so sharp it could wound.

"He never asked his parents for permission for any of this." Neither of them speaks, so I go on. "He thought they'd get mad at him for disappearing, but they didn't even notice. He told me on Wednesday."

The sadness of this fact settles some of the energy that's been boiling around us, but Flynn still says, "And what's this"—he gestures to the empty bottles—"going to do to help anything?"

"Numb the pain?" I suggest.

But Daniel leans toward Flynn and says, "It's a cry for *help*, and if you can't see that, then I don't know what kind of friend you are."

I shift my attention to the window, mostly to avoid hearing them rehash their arguments for the thousandth time, and then something catches my eye at the back of the parking lot.

"Guys." They don't hear me. I squint at the spot, and slowly the shape becomes clear. He's sitting on the curb directly between two streetlights, which is why he was so easy to miss before. "Guys, I think he's outside."

Daniel and Flynn are instantly beside me. I point him out, and Flynn groans, but before he can say anything, Daniel and I are at the door. Flynn's right behind us, though, as we jog through the lobby and out into the dew-heavy night air. As we approach Cameron, I'm hoping that he'll look up at us, clear-eyed, and say something like, *I just went for a walk.* Or even better, *My parents called, and I came out here to talk to them.* But instead, his eyes are glassy, and what he really says is, "What's this?" He narrows his eyes at the starry sky. "Itzz not day yet."

Flynn takes a deep breath, then turns silently around and marches back toward the hotel. Daniel and I both watch him deliberately retrace his steps through the lobby and around the corner to the stairs. I guess we should be glad he refrained from telling Cameron off right this second, but it's hard to feel anything other than annoyance.

When our eyes meet over the top of Cameron's head, we both know what we have to do. We wrap our arms around his waist, helping him to his feet. Then, one precarious step at a time, we guide him back to the hotel. We're halfway there when Cameron says, "Where did Flynn disappear to?" He's overenunciating now, as if that might fool us. "Do you think he's upset?"

"My guess," Daniel says, "is that he went to bed."

I pat Cameron's back and say, "You'll sleep in our room tonight."

WHEN WE GET UPSTAIRS, CAMERON PUKES IMMEDIATELY. Luckily, Daniel's prepared with the trash can. He catches every drop, then helps Cameron into the bathroom, where he offers him mouthwash and a spare shirt to sleep in. At some point, I ask Cameron if something happened, something that set him off, but he just stares at me like I'm speaking Greek. I don't know what would be worse, anyway—if his parents did do something new to broadcast how little they care about him, or if they didn't. I don't like the idea of Cameron binge-drinking to escape a fresh wound, but I think I like the idea of him binge-drinking on a whim even less.

Once Cameron's tucked in, I change back into my pajamas, then slip into the other bed next to Daniel. His song helped me decide that I need to start pulling away, start protecting myself from probable heartbreak, but here's the thing I didn't reckon on: Daniel didn't get the memo. As far as he's concerned, nothing's changed. We're still here to comfort each other in our loneliness, as friends. In the semidarkness of our hotel room, his hand finds my cheek, and he whispers, "Thanks for finding him, Bass Girl."

Despite my resolution, I don't move away. "You're the one who did everything," I say. "Got him ready for bed, brushed his teeth. I always feel so frozen when he's like this."

Daniel takes a deep breath and lets it out on a sigh as he says, "Poor Cameron."

"What do you think Flynn will do?"

He rolls onto his back and smoothly tucks his arm under my head. Rather than resist, I let my cheek find a natural resting spot on his chest. Tomorrow night we'll be in a hostel in San Francisco, so I'll be sharing a dorm-style room with five strange women, and the guys will be in a different room altogether. Besides, I'm leaving for D.C. right after school ends. What's the harm in giving in to this moment now, when it'll be over in just a few days? I know where we stand. I can keep my expectations low.

"I don't know," he says. "Pout, definitely. Probably make some speech about responsibility and Cameron getting his act together." His arm tightens around me. "I hate it when Flynn gets all self-righteous, but who knows? Maybe it'll be good for Cameron, wake him up."

"Yeah," I say, thinking about the bottles in his duffle bag, and how quickly and furtively he must have drained them. "He has gotten out of control, hasn't he?"

"Yeah, I think he has."

We're both quiet for a while, and then I say, "You don't think Flynn will really quit Blue Miles?"

Daniel angles his face down toward mine, and our lips are just a breath apart. "Not a chance," he says. "He knows we've got something special. He's not walking away from this."

Briefly, I think about Tessa bouncing recklessly from M. J. to Rico to whoever came next. I know better; I've been taught better. But maybe nature really is stronger than nurture, maybe Descartes was right, because when Daniel leans in for a kiss, I let myself melt into him. And all those voices in my head telling me to pull back, play it safe, protect my heart? They fade into just a distant, meaningless hum.

♪ ♫ ♪ ♫ ♪

THE NEXT MORNING, MY BRAIN WAKES UP BEFORE MY BODY. I'm no longer touching Daniel, but I can feel the warmth of him radiating from the other side of the bed. I give myself several minutes to rest inside the memory of last night— the way we kissed, the way my body naturally intertwined with his—before I force myself to face facts: he doesn't love me, I'm getting way too attached, and my heart is going to be broken, imminently. I can almost hear Irene say, *Well, duh, Nora. What did you think was going to happen?* But I'm not in the mood to argue with even an imaginary version of her, so I don't attempt a retort.

Suddenly, my need to speak to Tessa is overwhelming. Somehow, I know she's the only person who would completely understand how I feel, and I have to believe that one way or another, she'd know what I should do next.

It would be easy to find her now. I know her last name. I know what she looks like. I can connect with her on Facebook, if I want to. But I also know she lives in Honolulu. Tessa Reynoso—how many of them can there be? How big is Honolulu? For a few moments, I let myself imagine buying a ticket and flying there on my own, showing up on her doorstep and saying, *Tessa? It's me. Summer.* But my parents would never allow me to travel to Hawaii by myself, especially if they knew why I wanted to go.

I roll away from Daniel so I can check my phone, which has been charging on my nightstand, but as soon as I turn over, I see that Cameron's sitting on the edge of his bed, looking disordered and a little bit green.

"Hey," I whisper. "How are you feeling?"

"I've been better." He presses his lips together, wincing at the sound of his own voice.

I look over my shoulder at Daniel, but he's still asleep, facing away from us. "How much do you remember?"

He stares at me a bit longer than is comfortable, then says, "Enough."

I go into the bathroom and fill a water glass, which I bring out to him. "Drink."

He takes the glass from me and sips.

"There should be breakfast downstairs. We can go get you something greasy to settle your stomach."

He nods at me, but after a pause he whispers, "You're in love with him, aren't you?"

I stop breathing.

He sips his water again, then says, "I saw you two last night. You thought I'd passed out, but I woke up again and saw."

I still can't respond.

"How long's that been going on, Nora?"

It almost feels like a relief to admit, "Wednesday night."

"I was afraid that might happen. You know he hates being alone." Finally, he looks up at me, and I realize that he understands much more than I would have expected. "But you are going to hate yourself for letting it happen this way."

I move toward the bathroom, with a vague plan to regroup while taking a shower, but Cameron gets shakily to his feet, shields his eyes from the light, and follows me. I could shut the door on him, but I don't. I know that I need to hear whatever he's going to say.

His voice is strained as he says, "Do you know why Darcy threw that burrito at him on Wednesday?"

I test the water, but it's still too cold.

He goes on. "She found out that during their twenty-four-hour 'break' a couple months ago"—he puts the word *break* in air quotes—"he hooked up with a girl from the volleyball team. You know Harmony Ryan?" I nod without looking at him. "Yeah. Her." He sighs. "This is what Dan does when he's insecure, or lonely. He finds someone else to be insecure and lonely with him."

"I know he's not in love with me or anything." My voice shakes on the word *love*, because even though I've told myself I knew what this was, I secretly hoped it might be different. "But I'm not some random girl from the volleyball team, either."

"Yeah, you're right," Cameron says. "He cares about you. A lot. Which makes this so much worse." He steps between me and the bathtub, forcing me to look at him. "It would have been fine if you really felt the same way about him, but I know—and you know—that you don't."

I could deny it, but what would be the point? Instead, I ask, "Do you think he knows?"

"No." Cameron sighs. "He has a unique skill for missing things like that. But you need to prepare yourself for the fact that things are going to be really hard for you when we get back to reality."

"Well, we'll have all summer to cool down, anyway," I say. "Because my parents are sending me away." The words tumble out unexpectedly.

Cameron stares at me for several heartbeats, then says, "*What?*"

The water is warm enough for my shower now. Steam has partially obscured our reflection in the mirror.

"That was the deal I made. I get to play the Magwitch, go on this tour, everything, as long as I do a summer internship in D.C."

Quickly, the steam becomes suffocating. I want to dial down the temperature, but Cameron's stare has me frozen in place.

"And it didn't occur to you to discuss this with us?"

"You know my parents. There's nothing to discuss. It's happening." My throat starts to feel tight, but I plunge onward. "That's why it seemed important to find my biological parents. I'm so sick of feeling"—the first tear falls, rolling down my cheek to my chin, where it dangles precariously—"*inferior.* They keep pushing me into a box where I just don't fit."

I'm staring hard at my feet, so I don't notice when

Cameron steps closer. I just feel his arms wrap around me. His chin settles against the top of my head. "It's going to be okay," he says.

I nod, drying my tears on the front of his shirt. "I'm sorry if I've ruined everything."

"No," Cameron says. Then he repeats, "It's going to be okay." But I don't know who it's for this time: him or me.

♪ ♫ ♪ ♫ ♪

NONE OF US SPEAK AS WE LOAD THE VAN FOR THE FINAL LEG of our journey north. Even though it's his turn to sit shotgun, Cameron opts to sit on the bench seat in back—probably because Flynn is refusing to look at him or speak to him directly. Daniel slides in next to Cameron, giving me no choice but to sit up front, even though I'd probably rather ride in the way back with the equipment.

When we stop to gas up on the edge of Watsonville, Cameron gets out and follows Flynn around to the pump. Daniel and I stay inside the van, but the windows are cracked open, so we can hear every word.

Cameron opens with, "Just say it, Flynn. Get it off your chest." He hasn't taken off his sunglasses since we left the hotel room, but other than that, he seems fairly well recovered.

Flynn's jaw tightens, but he still doesn't speak. He shoves the pump into the van and glares at his feet.

"If we're going to get through this show tonight, then we need to be able to at least speak to each other."

That finally gets Flynn to react. He's still compressing the lever of the pump as he says, "Oh, *now* you care about our show?"

Cameron rolls his wrists out in front of him. "Get it all out, Flynn. Tell me what you really think."

"You want to know what I think?" For once, Flynn uses the little kickstand to keep the pump in place so he can turn to face Cameron. "I think you're so spoiled that you don't even understand how good you have it. You don't even comprehend what you're throwing away."

Cameron takes a step back. That's not what he expected him to say.

Daniel whispers to himself, "Goddammit, Flynn." And I know what he's thinking, because I'm thinking it, too: This isn't just about Cameron's parents anymore. He has a real problem with alcohol.

But Flynn goes on. "You're almost an adult, Cam. Nine months, and then you'll be a legal adult. No one's saying that your parents are going to win Nurturers of the Year, but at some point you'll have to stop blaming everything on them. At some point, it's not about them anymore, it's about you."

When Cameron responds, his voice is so low that I have to lean closer to the open window to hear it. "This from the guy whose dad helped him rebuild a van, the guy whose mom quit her job to be home full-time when he was born."

"Yeah," Flynn says, undeterred. "The guy who's had a job since he was fourteen because money's always tight, the guy who doesn't have a trust fund to fall back on, so he has to think about his future, the guy who knows he'll have to pay for his own college education, so he takes his grades seriously, because that's the only way he'll get a scholarship. And you know what? I'm also the guy who never complains about any of it."

The pump clicks off, and Flynn jams it back into the station. As he strides toward the convenience store to get his receipt, Cameron follows him, leaving Daniel and me alone.

In the silence that follows, it occurs to me that I should warn Daniel that Cameron saw us together, just so he's aware. I say it casually, like it's really not that big of a deal, but Daniel doesn't take it that way. His first response is, "But he passed out."

"Yeah, I thought so, too. Apparently, he woke up."

Daniel stares out the window at Cameron and Flynn, who are still arguing as they stride back across the asphalt toward the van. "You don't think he'll tell anyone, do you?"

My heart sinks, because he can only be thinking about Darcy. He doesn't want her to have another reason to be upset with him, which means he doesn't think it's as over as he says.

"No, he wouldn't."

Daniel nods, relieved.

By the time Cameron and Flynn reach the van, their argument seems to have reached an impasse. Flynn gets in the front and slams his door. Cameron closes the back door softly, then sinks low in his seat and stares out the window.

The rest of the drive into San Francisco is silent.

CHAPTER 16

*B*ackstage of the Magwitch isn't much different from backstage at the Rowdy. It's bigger, sure; there are more chairs and longer hallways. But the ceilings are just as low, the floor is just as sticky, and the whole area smells just as pervasively of stale beer. There are two greenrooms, but they're individually just as small and decrepit as any greenroom I've ever been in.

The club, though, is something entirely new. The house has a ground floor with a pit in front of the stage and bar at the back, and there are two balcony levels—the middle one is dotted with cocktail tables, but the upper floor seems to be a kind of lounge, with sofas and cushy chairs. Hanging from the ceiling above the proscenium are hundreds of strands of spherical lights of varying sizes. Right now, the houselights are on and the deconstructed chandelier is off, but I imagine that tonight, it'll look magical.

The stage itself has an ornate proscenium framed by

matching towers of can lights, each the size of my torso.

And the sound system. The sound system is ridiculous. When the sound engineer asks me to play at my full strength, I feel each note reverberate deep in my bones. As I play the last measure of my run, Becca and Skeet walk onto the stage.

"Hey, whiz kids!" Skeet says. He's just wearing jeans and a T-shirt, but he still gives the impression of being clad in black leather and metal spikes. It's just his vibe.

Becca's gravitating toward the drum set as she says, "How was the drive?"

After a pause, Flynn's the one who answers: "Long."

"Not too bad, though," Daniel says.

"Good, good," Skeet says. He spins toward the front of the stage. "You ready to tear this place up?"

Becca smiles over her shoulder at us. "We're sold out."

Jos saunters out from somewhere at the back of the house, stepping into the center of the floor. The way the three of them are moving through this space reminds me of the velociraptors in *Jurassic Park*. They're exploring the terrain, marking their territory.

"Did you tell them Stellan Prescott might show?" Jos says.

My heart leaps to my throat. "Wait, really?" Stellan Prescott works for Kitten Kat Records. He scouted Horoscope, along with a dozen platinum-selling bands before them.

"Yeah, he's a friend," Skeet says, shrugging. He wraps an arm around my shoulders.

Becca laughs. "I thought we weren't going to tell them."

Jos climbs over the front of the stage. Two steps bring him next to me. I'd forgotten how enormous he is. "It's a stress test," he says. "They'll either rise to the occasion"—he folds his arms across his chest, causing his pecs to flex under his shirt—"or crack under the pressure."

Skeet squeezes my shoulder. "I'm sure you'll do fine, Carol Kaye."

I search inside myself for any sensible response, but find nothing.

"We're gonna grab food," Becca says. "But we'll see you tonight."

Food. I haven't been able to eat yet today, and I can't imagine that my stomach will ever settle enough for me to eat again.

"Don't worry about Stellan," Skeet says, following her off the stage. "He's a real sweetheart."

"Oh, yeah?" Jos says. "Want to say that to his face?"

And then they're gone.

"Nora."

I jump.

"Could you test your mic?" It's the sound engineer. Of course it's the sound engineer. I sing my first harmony line, and then the engineer says, "Daniel, could you jump in with her?"

"Sure thing," Daniel says.

I feel Cameron looking at me, but I stare determinedly straight ahead.

Then a sultry voice speaks up from the back of the auditorium, and everything stops. It's only two words—"Hey,

Dan"—but I only know one person who sounds so effortlessly sensual. When Darcy walks into view, I spin around so fast that I knock over my mic stand. It clatters to the floor with an impossible, amplified boom.

"Whoa," Flynn says. He leaps away from his drum kit and kneels down to help me lift the microphone. It's not heavy, though; the help wasn't remotely necessary. "What was that?"

"I don't know," I say. In my peripheral vision, I'm watching Daniel jump off the stage to greet Darcy. They're talking softly, intimately, but I hear him say, "What are you doing here?" and I catch the gist of her answer: "I wasn't needed for rehearsal tonight, so I flew in to surprise you." I don't hear what he says next, but she shoves her hands into the back pockets of her jeans and replies, "You know I couldn't miss your big show. No matter how things ended between us."

Flynn puts his hand on my back. His expression is full of concern. "Are you okay?"

I nod, then stand, but as I do, I become so light-headed that the edges of my vision darken. I stumble to the side, and Flynn steadies me. "What's wrong?"

I shake my head, staring at my feet. "I'm fine," I say. "Just—I'll be glad when this is over."

Flynn hesitates, then calls to the sound engineer, "Do you still need Nora and me?"

The engineer says, "Nope. I've got your levels set."

Flynn lifts my bass off my shoulder and says, "Have you eaten anything today?"

I shake my head, but most of my focus is still on Daniel and Darcy. I can't tell what they're saying, but I see Daniel leaning against the edge of the stage, laughing. I've so rarely made him laugh. I have a wild flash of regret that I haven't tried harder to be funny.

I follow Flynn through the dark, narrow corridors, which are lined with signed black-and-white photographs of all the people who've played here. I see Victor Wooten's picture, Esperanza Spalding's, Jaco Pastorius's. All my bassist heroes. I can't believe that I'm finally here, in this storied, incredible place, and all I can think about is how unfunny I've been.

At the threshold to our greenroom, I pause. Flynn goes inside and sits on the sagging velvet couch, but I don't want to be alone with him. I pull my phone out of my pocket and say, "I'm going to check in with my parents."

Flynn nods. This is an excuse he accepts. "Let's get some food when you get back," he says. In his expression, there's a shadow of what I saw outside our hotel in Reedley. It makes my stomach churn all over again. "You and I have hardly talked on this trip."

"Yeah," I say. I'm already backing away. "That sounds good."

Before he can say anything else, I turn and jog down a hallway, around the corner, and out through a back door into an alley, where I sink down against the wall and stare at my phone. I didn't really intend to call my parents, but I find myself dialing our landline. Before anyone answers, though, I hang up.

I close my phone and settle into the silence. A large rat darts out from under the dumpster to my right, then scurries along the edge of the building, heading deeper into the shadows. To my left, the alley ends at a steeply graded city street. I watch people walk past carrying canvas grocery bags, pushing children in pastel strollers. As I watch them, I wonder what each of them would say if I told them my story from the beginning. What would *they* tell me to do next?

I really thought I could handle it—a friends-with-benefits fling with Daniel. I thought I knew how it would feel, but I didn't. I expected that it would feel somewhat unsatisfactory, but exciting, like a step in the right direction. Instead, it feels like amp feedback in physical form, spreading through my bloodstream like a slow poison.

As I lower myself to the rough, cracked pavement and pull my knees toward my chest, I think again about Irene saying that she'd never waste her time on someone who didn't love her back. She made it sound so easy, so obvious. I've never wished I was my mother's daughter more.

I open the music app on my phone and search for "Blue in Green" by Miles Davis, which seems appropriately melancholy for this moment. I don't have headphones with me, so I just turn the volume up and let the song fill the alley.

This song always reminds me of the early days of playing with the band, because I was playing through the bass line when we chose our band name. Flynn asked me what the song was. When I told him, he said, "Miles Davis? Wasn't he a trumpet player?"

"And a composer, and a bandleader," I said. I was still playing through the changes. We were taking a break from rehearsal. Cameron had gone out somewhere, and I didn't think Daniel was listening. "He started out in bebop," I said. "But I like blue Miles the best—the stuff he wrote after he kicked heroin."

"Wait," Daniel said, stepping toward us. "Say that again."

I quietly repeated, "After he kicked heroin?"

"No, before that."

Cameron walked back into the room.

"I like blue Miles the best?" I said, feeling embarrassed. Back then, I was confident enough when we were playing music, but awkward in moments like this one, when we were just hanging out.

"That's it," Daniel said. "That's our name."

"It's perfect," Cameron agreed.

I looked at them. "What is?"

"Blue Miles." Daniel strummed a chord dramatically. "We're the Blue Miles."

"Not *the*," Flynn said. "Just *Blue Miles*."

Cameron held up an invisible microphone. "Introducing . . . *Blue Miles*!" He nodded at us. "We have a winner."

I think that's when I started feeling like I belonged in the band. I wish I could go back to that moment, experience that freshness all over again. Moving forward this time, I'd protect the relationships as they grew, keep all the lines between us untangled and strong.

Then again, could I have *not* loved Daniel? I'm not sure it would have been possible, when he's always felt so right. And he *would* be right, if he loved me. Which he doesn't.

I can't help thinking about M. J., who decided almost from the moment of my birth that he wouldn't try to love me, either.

The alley door cracks open, and Daniel's face appears in the gap. He sees me and steps outside. "Hey, we didn't know where you went."

The song ends, and I close the music app on my phone. In the brief silence that follows, I think, *What is it about me that makes people so certain that I don't deserve a chance?*

I've been crouching against the wall, but now I stand. The edges of my vision go black again as blood rushes away from my head. I really do need to eat something, which is maybe why I say, "There never was another guy." The words are out before I can stop them, but there's no taking them back. Even if I could, I'm not sure I'd want to. I tell myself that if no one else is willing to give me a chance, then I'll have to take the chances myself. Daniel mostly looks confused, so I take a deep breath and go on. "You were always the one I wanted to be with. You must have known that." My next breath comes a little easier, like those words have been clogging my airway for the last two and a half years.

He shakes his head. "No. If I'd thought that, I wouldn't have—" He pushes his hand through his hair. "The whole point was, we were on the same page."

"I know." My hands begin to shake, so I shove them in my pockets. "But I thought—" What? What did I think?

The truth is, *thinking* has had very little to do with it. "I thought you should know the truth, before—" After a beat of silence, I force out, "Are you getting back together with her?"

He looks like he's in physical pain as he says, "I don't know, Nora. You know how things are with us." I know she's familiar. I know that even though they make each other miserable, she makes him feel safe. "And she flew all the way up here." His eyes finally meet mine as he says, "I'm sorry."

My throat tightens. I nod, managing, somehow, to keep all the muscles in my face steady as I say, "Me, too." Even through my own disappointment, I know that at some point in the future, maybe years from now, he'll regret this.

I expect him to go back inside, but instead he steps toward me. "Would it be awkward if I hugged you?"

Friends. At least we can still be friends. And friendship is its own sort of risk.

"A hug, actually, sounds great."

He crosses the alley and wraps me in his arms. It should feel weird to be comforted by the person who's breaking my heart, but it doesn't, not in this moment. Because when it comes right down to it, we're *this* first. We were always *this*.

And then the alley door opens again, and I hear Darcy's voice say, "I fucking knew it."

Daniel steps away from me, and we both see her standing there, flanked by Flynn and, slightly behind them both, Cameron.

She steps forward until she's nose to nose with Daniel. "I *knew* it. I've *always* known it, but you told me, 'Never. Not Nora. We're just friends.'"

Daniel places his hands on her shoulders as he says, "It's not what you think, Darce," but she pulls away and hisses, "Don't touch me."

Flynn steps forward. His expression makes me think of timpani played hard and fast, and gongs. There's a whole percussion section in there, crescendoing to nowhere good. "I'm going to play this show tonight." His voice is eerily steady. "And then I'm done." He looks at Cameron, then me. "I'm done with this shit."

I know I should try to stop him, but I don't. And then he steps back through the door and disappears inside the club.

Darcy says, "How could you, Nora?" as she follows him toward the door. Right now, she doesn't look hurt or angry as much as disgusted. She pauses and repeats, "How could you do it?"

I think, *Because I love him.* I also think, *Because I'm genetically programmed to self-destruct.* I even think, *Because you two are poison for each other.* But I say nothing.

As she moves away from us, Daniel lunges after her and says, "Darce, wait." Soon, they're both out of sight.

The ground is spinning beneath me. I need to sit down, but nothing is close by, so I just sink to the pavement. Even though everything is shattering, I'm still able to feel a small stab of disappointment in *him*. For choosing her. For leaving me here alone.

But I'm not really alone, even now. Cameron crouches down beside me and says, "Nora, I am so, so sorry."

I'm too stunned for tears, and I'm way past words.

He goes on. "Darcy asked us how Dan had been on the trip, whether he'd seemed depressed, whether he'd hooked up with anyone, and I swear I didn't say anything, but she must have seen it on my face or something. I never said a word, but she guessed it. And then Flynn said, 'No way, it couldn't have been Nora,' but he saw it on my freaking face, too."

I want to rage at him, blame him, somehow. But it's not his fault. It's mine. Everything I touch is eventually ruined; everyone who should love me leaves.

"Nora, it'll blow over. You didn't do anything wrong."

But I *am* wrong. I'm *always* wrong.

"Are you going to get something to eat?"

I shake my head.

"Okay, well—" There's a long pause, but I'm not sure what he does during it. Maybe he sits, or stands, or bursts into tears. The space around me seems to be disappearing, and Cameron along with it. "I'm going to go out for a bit. Want me to get you something?"

Even though I worry about what he means by *out*, I shake my head again.

And then he's gone.

I'm done with this shit.

Rico, Tessa, M. J., Daniel, and now Flynn. Maybe, once Cameron realizes that I'm the one who destroyed everything, he'll also fade. And once my parents and Irene realize I'm not Stanford-bound, not a *real* Wakelin, they'll disappear, too. Everyone can stand me for a while, maybe even love me a little, but eventually something breaks, and they're done with this shit. And by *shit*, they mean me.

CHAPTER 17

*P*laying at the Magwitch is everything and nothing I imagined it would be.

Everything: the enormity of our sound, the energy of the audience, the power of this music we've been working on for almost three years, the ecstasy of playing it, the pride of knowing it's worthy—*we're* worthy—of this stage.

Nothing: realizing that I got what I wanted, and it ruined what mattered.

From the first note, Daniel's voice overflows with emotion; it's clear that he's singing to the one person in the building he cares about right now. She's sitting on a sofa on the top balcony. The whole room is dimly lit by the crystal orbs that drip from the ceiling—it's like we're suspended at the edge of the galaxy, floating among the stars—and yet even from here, she's clearly visible. For one paranoid moment, I wonder whether she carries the illumination within her.

Cameron, who apparently used the free time to just get some street food and then wander around the city, told me before we walked onstage that she threatened to fly home before our set, but Daniel convinced her to stay. How, I don't know. But when we play "Love You So," Daniel very nearly sobs into the microphone. By the end of the number, I think I see her stony expression soften.

Anger seems to fuel Flynn, who's playing like a drum-destroying machine. When I step toward him during my bass solo on "Figure Eight," he looks away from me and hits his snare so hard that his drumstick splinters. He drops it quickly and retrieves a replacement from a bag by his side. I mostly keep my distance after that.

Cameron's playing fast and loose, like he's finally let go of everything that was holding him back. His solo on "Fetch" is insane. He steps out toward the front of the stage and shreds his instrument, but it's not just speed for the sake of speed. What he plays is beautiful, mesmerizing.

And I'm playing like I have nothing to lose, because I don't.

And the room knows it.

And it electrifies everything.

When we reach the bass/drum break at the end of "Long Morning," which is our second-to-last song, I swing around to face Flynn again. It's an oven up here. Sweat rains off his face as he hammers on his kit. He pretends not to notice me, so I step toward him again, and almost despite himself, he leans into my rhythm. We lock eyes, and the music surges between us. For one breathtaking moment, I think that maybe we'll be okay, but then Daniel and Cameron come back in on their instruments, and the moment is over. Flynn looks away, hitting his ride cymbal so hard it looks like he wants to murder it.

Still, our set has been tight, flawless. As we play the out-chorus of "Long Morning," I think of a song by Jeff Buckley—"Last Goodbye," originally titled "Unforgiven." I hear it underneath what we're playing now, and I remember, suddenly, that Jeff Buckley only met his biological father once. He didn't know his real name was Jeff until he saw it on his birth certificate. Tears gather in the corners of my eyes, spilling over my cheeks, hopefully blending with the sweat that's streaming down from my scalp. But I'm not just crying for me this time. I'm crying for the end of my band, the destruction of these friendships, the inevitable and ongoing disappointment of my parents. I'm also crying for Jeff Buckley, because he died so young, and I can't ask him if he ever felt like I do now. He can't ever explain it to me, except in the music he left behind.

The song ends, but Cameron and I maintain a constant, pulsing tone as Daniel leans into his microphone and shouts, "San Francisco!" Sound swells up from the club floor and down from the balcony levels. "We have one more song to play for you tonight." His voice reverberates deep in my bones. After everything that's happened today, it still sends a shiver down my spine. "But first we'd like to thank Horoscope for inviting us. It's been a dream to play for you."

Daniel steps to the side of his microphone, angling his

body toward Cameron—which is to say, away from me—as he says, "I'd also like to introduce the band."

Flynn starts tapping out a rhythm as Daniel says, "On lead guitar we've got Cameron Zamani . . ." The audience applauds as Cameron plays a blinding series of arpeggios. "On drums, we've got Flynn Ross . . ." Flynn plays a brief but complex fill. "On bass, we have Nora Wakelin . . ." The audience's volume surges as I slap a bass line. "I'm Daniel Teague, and together we're *Blue Miles* . . ."

Cameron and I look at each other to get the timing of our entrance for our last song. We land on the downbeat together, and the music gushes out of me. I step toward Daniel as Cameron joins on the countermelody. I step toward him again. He sways in my direction. The energy grows, swells, peaks, and then we cut out.

The entire room seems to gasp for breath before we come back in on the chorus. My voice is stronger than usual as I sing harmony.

Neither Daniel nor Flynn will make eye contact with me; we don't even have a word. But my entire soul seems to spill across the stage as my fingers climb the neck of my bass. I close my eyes, arch my back, and let everything go.

When we play the final note, the room erupts with applause. This is not you-were-decent-enough-for-an-opener applause; this sound hits me like a wall, practically pushing me off the stage. Daniel does his usual, "Thank you! We're Blue Miles! Good night!" But I doubt anyone hears him.

The stage lights switch off abruptly, and before I've lifted off my bass, I see Flynn's shadow dart toward the wing and disappear. Daniel glances at me as he brushes past, but then he, too, is gone. Cameron and I walk offstage together. Before I step out of view, I take one last look at the audience. The houselights have brightened somewhat. I wonder who all these people are and if, a few years from now, any of them will remember our performance tonight. I wonder if Stellan Prescott is really out there and, if he is, whether he thinks we had what it takes.

♪ ♫ ♪ ♫

DURING HOROSCOPE'S SHOW, I SIT IN THE WING, HIDDEN IN the shadows, knees drawn in to my chest. I thought playing the Magwitch would change everything, that afterward I'd feel fundamentally different. But I don't really feel different at all, and things have changed, but not because of our performance. I wonder if every big moment in my life will be this much of a letdown.

Suddenly, I'm exhausted. I feel wrung out, desiccated, like I need to spend the next decade sleeping off the past forty-eight hours.

Behind me, someone shouts, "Nora," and even over the noise from the stage, I know that it's Flynn. I look back at him and wait for him to speak. "I'm leaving. Tonight. The rest of you can fly back, but I'll take your equipment if you want." He'll drive my bass, but he won't drive me. It's so

Flynn—principled, but practical. "So, do you want me to take your bass?"

I look back at him. His posture is rigid; his arms are crossed tightly over his chest. It's too dark here for me to see his face clearly, but I get the general idea. His lips are pressed into a straight line across his face. His eyes seem to be angled to the side, so he doesn't have to look at me.

I keep my voice steady as I say, "Yeah. Thanks." He doesn't move right away, so in case I don't get another opportunity to say this, I force out, "I'm sorry, Flynn. I didn't mean to ruin everything."

A long moment later, he sits down next to me, cross-legged. The position looks unnatural on him—too casual by a mile. But some of the rigidness goes out of his spine as he says, "I know this has been a rough week for you, for a lot of reasons."

I think about the lies I told Daniel, the lies I told the band, and then say, "That's not an excuse, though."

He folds his hands in his lap. "I just wish—"

When I realize he's not going to finish his thought, I look at him and say, "You wish what?" Because if there's something I could do to make this better, I'd do it. It's heartbreaking enough to know that I've lost Daniel, or that I never had him to begin with, but the thought of losing the band is what's making my throat close and my chest feel like it's being squeezed in a vise. As soon as our show was over, it struck me how isolated I am. I don't have friends outside the band. I don't even talk to my sister, not really. Somehow, I've managed to go my entire life without letting anyone get close to me. I'm sure that some shrink could tell me a dozen ways that this is rooted in some trauma from my past, or something like that, but I don't really care. Right now, I just don't want to be alone.

Flynn looks at me, and his eyes seem strangely bright, catching the stage lights at a weird angle. "I wish that you'd come to me instead." Those words send a white-hot pain through my midsection, because I suddenly realize that, yes, this night *can* get worse. Because there's at least one thing I won't be able to do to make this better.

When he places a hand on my knee, I feel its clamminess through my jeans. "Nora, you have to know that I—" He closes his eyes, moves incrementally closer to me, tries again. "I always thought that you and I were the same. You know?" I know I need to make this stop, but I can't find the words. I can't even find the breath to make words come. So Flynn goes on. "Dan and Cameron don't take anything seriously. They never have. But you and I, we *care* about things."

I need to say it. I need to get these words out. I start to say, "Flynn—"

But the words get caught in my throat, and in that pause, he takes my hand. I feel his pulse racing through the center of his palm.

"Ever since you joined the band, I've hoped that someday we could be more than just bandmates, more than friends." He finally looks at me as he says, "I think we'd be great together."

He watches me hopefully, until I slowly remove my hand

from his and manage to choke out, "You know you're one of my best friends, but—"

I lose the thread again, but he doesn't need me to fill in the blanks for him. His expression shifts from hope to horror, and it breaks all the pieces of my heart that weren't pulverized already. He's on his feet in a blink.

He chokes out, "I'll get your bass to you on Monday," and then he's gone.

♪ ♩ ♪ ♩ ♪

BY THE TIME HOROSCOPE'S SET ENDS, ALL MY GUYS HAVE left. Well, they're not mine anymore, so I guess they're doubly gone. Cameron informed me that Daniel's staying in Darcy's hotel tonight, then flying home with her in the morning. And Flynn left as soon as his van was loaded. If he drives all night, he'll be home by sunrise.

Before taking a cab back to our hostel, Cameron used his parents' credit card to book a flight home for us; we get into John Wayne Airport tomorrow morning. I have no idea how I'll explain this to my parents. My current plan is to say nothing at all.

When Skeet, Becca, and Jos stride off the stage, I'm still sitting in the wing, wondering what sort of hell I'll face at school on Monday, or at home tomorrow night. And still there's a corner of my mind that can't stop thinking about Tessa Reynoso, my verified birth mother, alive and well in

Honolulu. I can't believe I've come so far and lost so much—and gotten so close—and still haven't met her.

"Hey, Carol Kaye," Skeet says to me. "Why the long face?"

I shake my head. "It's a long story."

"Well, we have it on good authority that you impressed Stellan Prescott," Becca says.

Skeet wraps his arm around Becca's shoulders. The way they're standing together reminds me of a thousand moments with Flynn and Cameron and Daniel; I wonder if this aching sense of loss will ever diminish.

"As in, we heard him say, 'I'm impressed.'" Skeet smiles at Becca. "And trust us, that's high praise from Stellan."

I inhale deeply, giving myself a moment to live inside the possibilities of what they just said. But on the exhale, I decide that now is as good a time as ever to start spreading the news of Blue Miles's demise, so I stand, brush off my jeans, and say, "That's flattering, but my band just broke up."

"That's a shame," Skeet says, though he doesn't sound too bothered. "But Stellan specifically mentioned you. He already took off, but he wanted us to give you his card."

Skeet reaches into a pocket in his vest and produces a black business card with the Kitten Kat logo watermarked in the center. Printed along the bottom edge of the card is Stellan Prescott's contact information. Five days ago, this would have been a dream come true. Now it feels like a cruel joke.

"But I don't have a band."

Jos shrugs. "Bands break up. They get back together.

You play with some people, and then you play with others."

"Oh, wee one," Skeet says, pressing the card into my hand. "A band is like love. You always remember your first, but that doesn't mean you should settle down with them and make babies."

My first. Blue Miles was my first of a lot of things.

"Was this a sudden break," Skeet says, "or was it a long time coming?"

"Sudden."

"Like"—Skeet leans forward—"was there a fight?"

"A big one." I shake my head. "There's no coming back from this."

"Never say never, Mini-Mingus." He elbows Becca. "Bex and I were in a band together years before we formed Horoscope."

"With *Zachary*." Becca says the name with obvious displeasure.

"A good bassist can always find a group to play with," Jos says. "And you have the chops to be a great one."

I don't know how to respond to that, but it's okay, because Jos has already stepped inside their greenroom, leaving me alone with Becca and Skeet.

"You'll be all right, kiddo," Skeet says.

Becca adds, "Just keep playing."

I nod, and then they're gone, too, and I'm alone here in the belly of this mythical place, this Mecca of Music. Instead of going into the greenroom to gather my gig bag and get out of here, I step back through the hallways to the wings of the stage. People are still milling around in the pit and on the balconies, but the stage is empty, highlighted by artistically crisscrossed streams of multicolored lights. As I wrap my hands around the plush curtain, I promise myself that I'll be back someday. I'll play on that stage again.

CHAPTER 18

*C*ameron and I share a car to the airport the next morning. It's a quiet ride, because what is there to say? While we're in the car, I get a call from my mom, but I let it ring through to voice mail. I'll be home soon enough, and I'll deal with everything then. Once Cameron and I are standing together on the curb, though, he sighs and says, "I wonder what Stellan Prescott said about us."

I can't imagine why it matters anymore, but I tell him anyway. "Skeet said he wanted us to have his card. He said he was impressed."

He looks at me. "What?"

The sidewalk is crowded with people unloading their luggage, rushing through the sliding glass doors into the wide, bright airport. There's a heavy fog hanging over everything, which mutes the scene. Under normal circumstances, I'd probably be reminded of a song, but all I have inside me now is silence.

"I saw them after their set." I pull the business card out of my bag and hand it to him. "Said he wanted us to call him."

He stares at the card for a moment, then presses the heels of his hands against his eyes. "That is so depressing."

I don't know if it'll still mean anything, but I say it again just in case. "I'm sorry."

"Me, too," he says. "It took both of us to *really* push Flynn over the edge like that."

Neither of us moves. I think we both know that once we step through the glass doors into the airport, it's truly over.

Cameron tucks the card into his pocket and says, "You know what Flynn said to me yesterday, at that gas station?"

I look at him. "I mean, I heard *some* of it."

"Yeah, but after that part. When we were in there getting the receipt?" He shifts his bag into his other hand. "He said that I was so busy trying to get revenge on my parents that I was missing all these opportunities to do something worthwhile. He said that their lives clearly were not all about me, so why should my life be all about them?"

Another car pulls up in front of us, and a whole family disembarks. They unload half a dozen pieces of luggage and maneuver awkwardly around us. Still, we don't move. I'm not sure we can.

"And I hate to admit it—" He scratches the back of his head and looks to the side, clearly uncomfortable.

We're all talking constantly. So why is it so difficult to say the things we really mean?

Finally, he finishes with, "—but I think he has a point." He pulls out his phone and opens a page he must have saved there. "You know what part of the first step is? In that twelve-step program or whatever?" He must catch my expression, because he explains, "I looked it up last night."

"What is it?"

He takes a long breath, then reads, "'We admitted that our lives had become unmanageable.'" He looks at me again and says, "That sounds like a pretty spot-on description of my last few months, Nora. Flynn was right." He tucks his phone back into his pocket. "We pushed him over the edge, but he was right."

I don't know what to say, so with my free hand, I reach out and touch his shoulder. He nods once, and then finally we face the wide glass doors and step through, into the airport.

As we approach a screen to check the status of our flight, I see a different flight, headed to Honolulu, departing twenty minutes after ours. Cameron follows my gaze and then says, "Are you thinking about going?"

I shake my head. "After everything that's happened? It'd be crazy. I mean, what do I expect to find?"

He shrugs. "Answers."

We stand in silence for several seconds before I say, "But you already paid for the tickets."

"Hey, my parents' money should be put to a good use, right?"

No matter how angry I am at the Zamanis for neglecting

my friend, I still don't know how I'd feel about it. This isn't lunch, or even a split hotel room. It's a plane ticket. A *second* plane ticket. To *Hawaii*.

"They *never* called you? This whole week?"

He shakes his head, but what he says is, "Do you really want to do this, Nora?"

I look at the word on the screen: *Honolulu*. I remember the picture of Tessa that Martin showed me, how she looked so much like me that it was disorienting.

But finals start *tomorrow*. I can't just skip finals. Can I?

That wasn't his question, though. His question was, *Do you really want to do this?*

"Yeah," I say. "I do."

He nods toward the Hawaiian Airlines desk and says, "Then, let's go."

As we wait in line, he tries to insist on buying me a return ticket to Orange County at the same time, but I don't know how long it will take me to find her, or how long I'll want to stay once I do. Maybe she'll be awful, and I'll want to come home tonight, or maybe she'll be wonderful, and I'll stay for a week. (A piccolo-sized voice in the back of my head whispers, *Maybe I'll stay forever.*) Maybe I'll find her, but not introduce myself right away. Maybe I'll introduce myself, and she'll want nothing to do with me. The one thing I know for certain is that I'm not leaving Hawaii without closure, whatever that even means.

"A return ticket is like a safety net," I say.

A family steps away from the desk with their carry-ons, and we inch forward.

"Yeah," Cameron says. "Exactly."

I don't know how to explain this in a way that makes sense. (A trumpet-sized voice suggests, *Then maybe it doesn't make sense,* but I wrestle the trumpet down.) I try, "It's like a tether to home."

"So are those circular floaty things they throw to people who fall off boats," Cameron says. "So are the ropes that rock climbers use so they don't plummet to their deaths if their hands slip."

"It's a cop-out."

"It's common sense."

A couple backpackers leave their bulky gear on the conveyor belt and saunter in the direction of security. When the elderly couple in front of us shuffles toward the desk, Cameron and I are at the front of the line.

I shake my head. "If I do this, I'm stepping forward with both feet. A return ticket is one foot planted on home turf." I can see that he understands now, but he's not ready to admit it. I gently add, "I'll know when it's time to come home."

Cameron takes a deep breath, squeezes his eyes shut. As he exhales, he looks at me and says, "When you're ready, you call me, and I'll book you the first flight to John Wayne."

I tell him I will even though I'm not sure that's true. I can't keep letting him bail me out.

The elderly couple shuffles away hand in hand, and Cameron and I are summoned by a petite blond man in a teal blazer who calls out, "Next!" And five minutes later, I owe Cameron—or at least his parents—three hundred more dollars, and I'm holding a one-way ticket to Honolulu.

Our gates are close together, and I sit with him while he waits to board.

Abruptly, he says, "I should be going with you."

"No, Cam," I say. "You need to go home, talk to your parents." I look over at him. "But it means a lot that you'd say that."

Cameron sighs. "Don't worry about the band. Maybe we all just need some time."

It's the thing I wanted to hear last night, but this morning I don't really believe it. He doesn't know about that final moment between Flynn and me. I still say, "Yeah, maybe."

When Cameron's boarding group is called, we both stand. He drops his bag on the floor and gives me a rib-crushing hug. "Don't do anything reckless, Nora. Please."

I mutter into his shoulder, "Like fly across the Pacific to look for a woman I've never met who may or may not live in Honolulu?"

Cameron steps back and holds me at arm's length. "No, like not come back."

He looks so genuinely concerned that I feel sorry for him. How terrible it must be to care about someone who scares you as much as I'm scaring him right now.

As soon as I have that thought, I'm hit by a memory of my parents: When I was six years old, I tripped down our stairs and broke my arm and two ribs. The worst part about it wasn't how much it hurt, but how worried my parents were. It made me want to downplay my pain and get better as quickly as possible, just so they'd be happy again. Now here I am, stressing out everyone who cares about me, making everyone, including myself, miserable.

This doesn't change anything. I have to see this through to the end.

"I'll be careful," I say.

"Let's hang out on Friday, after finals are over."

I nod, but don't make any promises I'm not certain I can keep. Instead, I smile as comfortingly as I can and say, "Have a safe flight."

Reluctantly, he accepts this as my final answer. Another quick hug, and then three long strides take him to the back of his line. Soon, he's at the front, holding his mobile ticket over the scanner, disappearing through the tunnel toward his plane.

Alone, I walk down the wide, airy corridor to my gate. It's packed, so I lean against one of the cement columns and hold my duffle bag against my legs. When my flight starts boarding the priority passengers, my mom calls again. I stare at that three-letter word until my screen goes black. Then I open the settings on my phone and turn my location tracker off.

I tell myself I'll call my parents from Hawaii, when it's too late for them to contact the airline and cancel my ticket. Then I type "Tessa Reynoso Hawaii" into my search bar and wait. The connection is slow, probably because all the people around me are using their phones as well. The flight attendant calls my group, and I step into the line, which is moving quickly forward.

When the search results finally load, I see three hits right at the top. Two are on a website for Full Light Healing & Spiritual Learning Center. The third is on a website called Sunrise News. The first Full Light page looks like a blog post from a couple months ago. The other is a staff page for Tessa Reynoso. The Sunrise News article seems to be about a fancy restaurant in Honolulu. I click on the Full Light staff page and wait while the screen loads.

When I get to the front of the line, I fumble for my ticket. The woman scans it, then waves me forward. I'm grateful when the line stops moving, because the page still hasn't loaded. I try refreshing it, but that just makes it start loading all over. I take a deep breath and close my eyes, forcing myself to be patient. Right before I step onto the plane, the page loads, but it just reads *ERROR 404 File Not Found*. My heart starts to race, because does this mean she moved? She quit her job? Where is she now?

I go back to the search results and tap the link for the Full Light blog post.

I'm at my seat now, shoving my bulging gig bag into the overhead bin, then sliding into the window seat. A few seconds later, a couple arrives and takes the middle seat and aisle. And still the blog post is loading.

I'm being ordered to buckle my seat belt when the page finally loads. Embedded next to the text is a picture of her—the same woman from the picture Martin showed me. Tessa Reynoso, my birth mother. In this picture, her hair is long and natural; her skin glows, though she doesn't seem to be wearing any makeup. I scan the article and read about her leaving Full Light to pursue her passion for music.

My birth mother's a musician? M. J. never said anything about that. I slow down and read the post:

> We at the Full Light Center have benefited for many years from our administrative assistant's musical abilities. But now we wish her the best of luck as she continues on her journey, sharing her gift with a wider audience.

I drop my phone and then have to undo my seat belt so I can retrieve it from beneath the seat in front of me. A flight attendant appears at the end of my row. "Ma'am, we need you to remain in your seat," he says.

I hold up my phone. "I just dropped this."

"Please turn off your electronics," he says.

I say, "Sure, of course," but as he continues up the aisle to admonish other passengers, I click on the final page. It loads a little more quickly than the other two, maybe because everyone else has already turned off their phones. The article is about a musical duo called Rey-Rey. They'll be the resident musicians for Sunday brunch at Plumeria Grille near Ewa Beach through spring and summer. The members of the band are listed as Roger and Tessa Reynoso, and there's a picture of them embedded next to the text: my birth mother in a long, flowy, flower-print dress, with a large white flower tucked behind one ear, and a man who I suppose is Roger, her new husband. He's square jawed and brown skinned, with large brown eyes and a full head of salt-and-pepper hair. He's holding an acoustic guitar, and Tessa is holding a tambourine in one hand, letting it hang down by her side.

The flight attendant walks by again, and I hide my phone quickly under my leg, but the couple sitting next to me is eyeing me suspiciously. I look up the location of Plumeria Grille and see that it's in a suburb of Honolulu. It's 10:00 a.m. here, which means it's 7:00 a.m. in Hawaii. The flight is five and a half hours long. We'll land at 12:30 p.m. How long does brunch last? I wish I could call the restaurant and ask, but the flight attendant reappears at the end of my row and says, "*Ma'am*, please shut off your electronics."

He stands there and watches me as I turn off my phone, and then the plane is moving forward, rushing to the end of the runway. There's the heaviness of lifting off, followed by the lightness of flight. Fear followed by freedom. I imagine a string orchestra sustaining a long, loud note, but then the basses and the cellos and even the violas cutting out, leaving just the violins soaring above the silence.

I'VE ONLY FLOWN THREE TIMES BEFORE, ALWAYS WITH MY whole family, and always to Minnesota to visit my grandma, my mom's mom, the only other artist in our family. When I was little, I used to love visiting her; she'd take me out into her pottery shed, put on a Joni Mitchell record, and let me finger paint on her walls. We stopped visiting her after my aunt Jeanette died, but I remember that the flight was three and a half hours long and, once we passed over the mountains that separated the west coast of California from the desert beyond, the view was mostly of flat farmlands, bisected by the occasional river.

Descending through the clouds toward Honolulu is an entirely new experience. The islands seem to coalesce out of the mist. As we get closer to the ground, I see the expected flaws of civilization—graffiti, litter, cracked pavement, peeling paint—but from a distance, it could be Neverland.

As soon as the plane touches ground, phones all around me start beeping. My phone takes a minute to warm up, but as soon as I have reception, I call the number for Plumeria Grille. When a woman's voice answers, it takes me so long to respond that I'm surprised she doesn't hang up. Finally, I get out, "Do you still have live music this morning?"

The woman answers, "Yeah, they're here until one o'clock."

We landed early, but the restaurant is twenty-five minutes away. I'm not sure I'll make it.

"Is the group Rey-Rey?"

"Yeah. They'll be here on Sundays through the summer."

Faintly in the background, I think I hear a guitar accompanying an airy soprano. Is that my biological mother's voice? Is this the first time I'm hearing my biological mother's voice? My mouth has gone completely dry, but I manage to ask, "Do you know if they have any other regular gigs?"

"I know that they're locals," the woman says. Her tone has changed, like she's now holding the phone between her ear and her shoulder, completing several tasks at once. "But I'm not sure where else they play."

My phone pings multiple times in rapid succession. I glance at my screen and see a barrage of texts come through from nearly everyone I know. As I follow the couple out of our row, I read the texts, starting with Cameron's, which will probably be the least anguish-inducing.

CAMERON: Have you landed?

CAMERON: Call me if you need anything while you're there.

CAMERON: I can't believe you actually went to Hawaii.

Me, either, Cameron. I write back, Just landed. Tessa and her new husband are playing a gig nearby. I'm going to try to catch them.

He responds immediately, Really? Right now?!

Even though I'm trapped on this plane, waiting to disembark, I don't have the patience to reply. Instead, I check my mom's texts next.

MOM: Let us know when you get on the road,
and your ETA for your return. Dad's grilling
burgers tonight.

MOM: Your location tracker appears to be off.
Please turn it back on immediately.

MOM: I'm going to text the boys in your band, in
case your phone's battery has depleted.
Please text me back from one of those
numbers as soon as possible.

MOM: Flynn has informed me that you, Daniel,
and Cameron are flying instead of driving
home with him. Your phone might be off
if you're in the air. Text us when you land.
We'll pick you up.

I can tell there's a lot she's not saying in that last text.
She'll be livid that I changed my plans and didn't tell her,
and even more pissed off when she finds out we used
the Zamanis' credit card to do it. I know that my parents aren't the biggest fans of the Zamanis, but they still
won't like the idea of me spending their money, especially without asking. I have no idea what they'll do to
me when they find out I went to Hawaii. Suddenly, I'm
almost glad that I'll be spending the summer on a different coast. I say a silent *thank you* to Flynn for not spilling everything else to my parents; if he'd told them that

I spent the week hooking up with Daniel—my stomach twists as I think about it—my mom's text would have been quite different.

I text Cameron, If my parents ask you when we're landing, don't respond. I haven't figured out how to tell them.

CAMERON: Obviously.

CAMERON: Is your biological mother a MUSICIAN?
That's nuts.

Again, though, I don't have the energy to get into it. I open Daniel's texts next.

DANIEL: Call me when your flight lands.

DANIEL: We need to talk.

At first, this sends a hopeful little swell through my chest, but the more I read those words, the less encouraging they seem. *We need to talk* could mean anything. In my experience (I'm thinking about my parents again), it's rarely meant anything good.

I'd like to switch my phone off for the duration of my time here, but I need to use an app to order a car, so I just ignore the texts from Cameron that keep sliding onto my screen (CAMERON: What's the name of the restaurant? CAMERON: You're going there NOW?) as I open my car-ordering app and punch in the address of Plumeria Grille. Once the car is ordered, I sprint through the terminal, following signs for ground transportation.

I get outside just as a blue sedan pulls up to the curb. The license plate matches the one on my app, so I wave down the driver—my app says her name is Lynda—and then slide into the backseat, which smells like cigarettes and fake pineapple. As we pull away from the curb, she asks me, "Coming to visit, or coming home?"

I respond, "I guess I'm here to find out," and the weirdness of my answer doesn't seem to faze her.

I should probably be paying attention to my app, making sure she isn't driving in the wrong direction, but my breath keeps catching in my throat. I can't stop thinking about how strange it is that I've been here before, back when I was Summer and Tessa Croft was my mother, but I have no memory of it. I was here in a different life.

It occurs to me that my car-ordering app is connected to my parents' credit card. They'll see all these charges soon, and the fact that I intend to pay them back will be entirely beside the point. But I'll deal with all of that later. I look out the window at the green margin sliding past me and wonder how much of this I'll remember, sixteen years from now. My time on this island is, once again, bound to be short; I want to carry as much of it with me as I can.

LYNDA PULLS UP TO PLUMERIA GRILLE AT 12:58 P.M. EVEN though I've spent the last six hours worrying that I wouldn't get here in time, I don't get out of the car immediately. She looks back at me. "This is the place?" she says.

"Yeah." I'm holding my bulging gig bag in my lap. I wish I could bury myself inside it right now, just hide in it until I feel ready for whatever's about to happen. "I mean, I think so."

"You think so?" She glances at me in her rearview mirror. "You don't know?"

I shake my head. "I'm kind of guessing."

She twists around in her seat. "You want me to wait for you?"

I'd love to have her wait for me. In fact, I'd love to have her drive me somewhere else right this minute, back to the airport, or maybe down to the beach. I'd love to sit on the beach here, letting the bathwater-air rehydrate my heart until it's healed, or at least functioning enough to tell me what to do next. But I shake my head. "Thanks," I say. "But I'll figure it out."

I get out of the car and walk up the shell-lined path to the restaurant's front door. The building seems old. It has large, wraparound porches on both stories and a wide green lawn bordered by palm trees. As I climb the steps to the main porch, I hear the music wafting around from a deck in the back, that same woman's voice singing her soprano melodies over a simple guitar accompaniment.

Rather than approach the host station in the foyer, I step between the potted ferns that separate the tables on the porch from the entryway. I expect someone to stop me, but no one seems to even notice me weaving between the packed tables, past busy waitresses and busboys. I must look pretty disheveled, wearing the same clothes I wore yesterday and ultimately slept in, carrying my tattered gig bag over my shoulder. But no one says a thing.

I turn the corner at the end of the building, and the music gets louder, clearer. When I turn the next corner, I see that this back deck spreads out in a half circle from the main building, and at the far end of the deck, on a raised dais, a man and a woman are sitting on wooden stools. The man's playing an acoustic guitar, and the woman's holding a microphone in one hand and a tambourine in the other.

I stop moving, and a waitress crashes into my back, dropping a tray full of empty glasses, which shatter around my feet. She apologizes, but of course it was my fault. I step to the side, leaning against the railing while a team of people hurry to clean up the mess. Tessa briefly looks our way. It seems impossible that she could see me and not realize who I am, because even if I'd never met M. J. Croft, never seen Tessa's picture, even if I'd just passed her on the street, I'd know. But she doesn't seem to see me.

The song ends with a simple guitar instrumental, and then Tessa speaks over the light applause. "Thank you so much. We're Tessa and Roger Reynoso." Her voice is smooth, melodic. "You can follow us on Twitter and Instagram at ReyReyMusic. We'll see you here next Sunday."

Twitter and Instagram. I can follow my biological mother

on Twitter and Instagram. The world seems so small that it's nearly claustrophobic.

She and Roger don't have much equipment. They'll have packed everything in a couple minutes, so I don't have any more time to stand here and wonder if I should approach. The time for deciding has passed.

I step around the few tables that separate us, until I'm standing just a couple feet away from her. I clear my throat, and she looks up at me and smiles.

"Did you want to buy a CD?" she asks.

The question catches me off guard, and I freeze. She reaches into a canvas bag and pulls out a CD.

"We sell them for ten dollars online, but eight dollars here."

I can't speak, so I just nod. She holds on to the CD while I pull out my wallet and hand her several bills.

She stares at the money, looking a little worried. "Sweetie, you gave me forty-one dollars."

I clear my throat and say, "You're Tessa Reynoso?"

"That's me," she says. She's narrowing her eyes at me, and I think that she'll have to see it. She'll have to know who I am. But she doesn't.

"My name's Nora." I take a deep breath, then manage, "But you named me Summer."

The words come out as a whisper, and for several heartbeats I think she didn't hear me. My eyes are starting to burn from not blinking, but I don't want to miss even a microsecond of her reaction. And yet somehow I still miss it, because one moment she's holding the CD and the bills, and the next she's dropped both and wrapped her thin arms around my shoulders. A breeze pushes our hair away. As I see it waving behind her, I think about how similar our hair is, how similar *we* are. I think about how everyone else I know experiences this every day, and how they fail to see how magical it is.

She steps away, but keeps her hands on my shoulders. "I knew you'd find me someday." She looks at Roger, who's holding his guitar in one hand and the microphone stand in the other. He looks exactly like his picture. "This is my daughter," she tells him. She pulls me to her. Her skin is warm from the sun, and her hair smells like flowers. Or maybe this whole island smells like flowers. "This is Summer."

The words feel so wrong, because my name isn't Summer, and she is my mother, but she also isn't. But if I dwell on any of this, I'll implode, so I focus on one breath, then the next.

Roger sets down his guitar to shake my hand, and I briefly explain to them both that I met M. J. Croft, and he said I might find her here. Tessa doesn't ask about my parents, or whether or not they know where I am, or whether or not I should be here alone. She just pulls me close to her and says, "You must be exhausted."

I am. The fullness of my exhaustion spreads through my body like a vibration on a string.

"Let's get you home," she says, and there's a small piece of me that feels wrong about hearing her say that. I think about my home in California, and my parents there, worrying about me. But then she and Roger are leading the way through the restaurant, down the steps, along the shell-lined path. She's telling me that she always knew I was with good people, but that someday I'd find my way back to her. And now I have.

A few minutes later, I'm sitting in the backseat of their car, and we're following a narrow road past dense greenery. Slivers of Pacific blue are visible between the trees. "It's the perfect resolution to the song," Tessa says. "It's like a dominant chord resolving just right."

I sit back in my seat then and decide to stop worrying. Because she and I are the same. For better or worse, we're the same.

CHAPTER 19

She and Roger live in a one-bedroom house that's nestled into some shrubbery off a road leading inland from Ewa Beach. There's no air-conditioning, but there are large ceiling fans, which spin lazily in the bedroom, in the living room, and above the wraparound porch. I stash my gig bag in a corner of the living room, which is also the kitchen, then follow Tessa back outside while Roger prepares snacks.

She settles on one end of a wicker bench and pats the seat next to her. "Sit," she says. "Let me look at you."

I do as she says, and she reaches over to trace the lines of my jaw and cheeks with her cool fingers.

"I should have known you as soon as I saw you," she says. "You look just like my mother."

I think about my grandmother living in her Minnesotan suburb. A few years ago, when she came out to visit us, she gave me her old record player and dozens of records. Among them were some of the best albums of all time—*Mingus Ah Um* by Charles Mingus, *Blue* by Joni Mitchell, *Revolver* by the Beatles, *Songs in the Key of Life* by Stevie Wonder. Each record had been carefully maintained. When she gave it all to me, she said, "I always wished I'd learned to play an instrument, but the next best thing is having you as my granddaughter." She placed *Ah Um* on the turntable as she said, "I'm so proud of you, Nora. I can't wait to see who you grow up to be."

She and my mom don't get along great, so she's not a major presence in my life. But still, I press the memory away, because if I dwell on it, I'll make myself sick.

Roger comes out with a tray of nuts, dried fruit, and cheese. "Anything else I can get for you?" he asks.

"Maybe some iced tea?" Tessa says. "And why don't you call everyone?" She places her hand on my arm and says, "We should have a party, don't you think? We should celebrate!"

"Of course," Roger says. He kisses her on the top of her head before disappearing inside the house. A few seconds later, I hear him chatting on the phone, saying the words *six o'clock* and *potluck*.

I think about what M. J. said, that Tessa's the kind of woman who could make you fall in love at a glance. I see what he means now. It's there in the way Roger follows her orders, the way he's always watching her. Even I feel it— her magnetism. Everything about her is smooth and elegant, but at the edge of her movements there's a kind of energy; it's like at any moment she could leap into the air and fly away.

"So, tell me about *you*," she says. "Who did my beautiful daughter grow up to be?"

I'm not sure at all how to answer that. Who am I? I was hoping she could tell me. I think about Blue Miles, about Daniel, about all the things that have defined my life thus far, but none of them really *explain* me. When I say, "I'm a bassist," it's not because I think that's a great answer, but because I think the question is impossible.

"A bassist?" She sounds unreasonably delighted by this. "You should play with Roger and me. Can you imagine? We'd have to change our name. Rey-Rey-Rey."

It occurs to me that she doesn't even know my legal last name.

Roger brings out two sweating glasses of iced tea. When he goes back inside, I lower my voice and say, "I was wondering about Rico." She looks uncomfortable, so I clarify my question: "M. J. told me that he was my biological father. Are you still in touch with him?"

She hesitates, then says, "Trust me, sweetie. You don't want to go looking for Rico." There's a tremor in her voice, but before I can ask another question, Roger steps onto the patio and says, "They'll all be here in a few hours."

"Perfect," Tessa says, clasping her hands beneath her chin.

"Who are *they*?"

"Our friends," she says. "You'll love them, Summer." She reaches forward again and presses her palm against my cheek. "And they'll absolutely love you."

I want to tell her that I'm tired, and I have a million

more questions to ask, and I don't really like parties anyway. And she seems to have forgotten that my name isn't really Summer. But she's looking right at me, my biological mother, my indisputable kin, and saying, "When I named you Summer, I wanted to charm you, to cast a spell, like the fairy godmothers in *Sleeping Beauty*. I wanted you to never see anything but sunny days your entire life." Before I can respond, before I can tell her that things have been a bit more complicated than that, she's standing. "I'll ask Karen to tell everyone at Full Light about tonight. I can't wait for them all to meet you."

She disappears inside the house, and Roger and I are both left a little breathless, like we've been caught in a whirlwind that's just moved past. Finally, he asks, "Can I get you anything else?"

I say, "No, I'm good," but before he also goes inside I ask, "Actually, who's Karen?"

Roger takes a deep breath, then says, "She's Tessa's sister, your aunt. She runs Full Light, where Tessa used to work."

All I can think to say is, "Oh."

Roger hesitates, like there's something else he'd like to say, but eventually he follows Tessa into the house. Once I'm alone, I wipe the condensation off my glass of iced tea and think about my phone, which is currently stuffed into my bag. I'm going to be in so much trouble when I get home.

If I go home.

As soon as I have the thought, it's like the whole island pauses. It was one thing to hear a piccolo-sized voice whisper impossible things when my feet were anchored on

Californian soil, but now that I'm here, sitting on the porch of my biological mother's house, the voice is less piccolo and more trombone, and I'm having a hard time forming a convincing rebuttal.

But I can't stay here.

Why not? says the voice, a French horn now—bright, cajoling.

First of all, I haven't been invited.

She said she wanted to rename her band Rey-Rey-Rey. What more of an invitation do you need?

But she's not my legal guardian.

And by the time the courts sort it all out, you'll be eighteen anyway.

But my band—

What band?

But my family—

The family that wants you to be something you're not? The family you've never really fit into?

As I look at the gravel driveway leading to Tessa and Roger's hut, at the ferns and palm trees swaying all around me, I think that maybe this is where I belong. Maybe I can play bass for Tessa's band and fall in step with her circle of friends. Here, there's nowhere to go, but there's also nothing to hide from, and maybe that's what I've been looking for. I'd be able to leave behind my feelings for Daniel, my disintegrating band, my guilt about both. No one would make me spend the summer in D.C. or tell me that music doesn't matter.

Maybe here I'd be able to become the person Tessa

wanted me to be: Summer, an endless string of sunny days. It would certainly be a change, and maybe that's what I went looking for—a place to be a different version of myself.

♪ ♩ ♪ ♩ ♪

NIGHT FALLS SO GRADUALLY THAT IT'S EASY TO MISS THE moment when it happens. Someone has put a guitar in my hand, and I'm jamming with a large Asian man in a straw hat who's playing ukulele and a gray-haired white woman playing a beat-up guitar. A young blond guy with a deep tan is singing. I've never heard the song before, but the tempo is slow, the progression is simple, and music is the universal language. I follow the shape of the other guitarist's hands until my own hands catch the pattern. Then I'm free to just watch the party while my fingers do the rest.

On one edge of the gravel driveway, there's a long folding table, which is now piled high with fragrant dishes. Next to it, there's an ice chest filled with bottles of water, juice, and beer. Roger is standing over there, chatting with a guy who looks like he came straight from surfing. Tessa's standing on the porch with her arm wrapped around the waist of a woman with curly gray hair and weirdly luminous skin. Tessa's gesticulating with her free hand, occasionally glancing in my direction while the other woman smiles serenely at me. I stare awkwardly at the neck of my guitar. I don't usually know what to say to the people I know well. At a party full of strangers, I'm lost.

By the time the song ends, Tessa has separated herself from the other woman and is stepping inside her house, which seems to be mostly empty. I haven't had a chance to talk to her since everyone showed up, so I hand the guitar to the singer and excuse myself, moving away from the circle of musicians.

All the clothes I brought are filthy, so Tessa loaned me one of her dresses. It's long and loose, and it feels strange. I never wear dresses. I nearly trip over the hem as I climb the short flight of stairs to the porch. As I reach the front door, the woman with the curly gray hair stops me and says, tentatively, "Summer?" She's tall like Tessa and me, though her skin is paler, and her eyes are blue, framed by deep smile lines. "We're so happy to have you home with us."

"Us?"

Several emotions pass behind her eyes before she says, "I'm Karen, Tessa's sister." She hesitates, then adds, "Your aunt."

"Oh."

I know I should say something else, but nothing occurs to me. I consider shaking her hand, or hugging her, or leaping off this porch and disappearing into the moonlit forest. But before I can act on any of these impulses, Karen looks at the party behind me and says, "Introductions and"—she searches for the right word; whenever people do that, I wonder which word came to mind first, and why they deemed it unacceptable—"*linear thinking* aren't

Tessa's forte." She gestures at the crowd of people clinking glasses and laughing by the warm glow of candles and twinkle lights, which are strung from the roof to the surrounding trees. "But bringing people together, entertaining, conjuring good feelings among people—at these things, she's unsurpassable."

"I don't think I got those genes."

Her smile broadens. "You're young. You may have more in you than you realize."

There's something weirdly Yoda-ish about this woman.

"Your parents named you Nora. Correct?"

I say, "Yeah." Though, it feels weird to talk about my parents with this biological relative I just met.

"That's a lovely name," she says. "But it'll probably take a while for us to get used to it. When Tessa worked for me, I'd sometimes see her daydreaming at her desk. If I asked her what she was thinking about, she'd say, 'Summer's performing in her first ballet recital,' or 'Summer rescued a kitten and is bringing it home.'" Her eyebrows press upward, forming an expression I could probably read, if I knew her better. "I've often privately wondered where you were and what you were doing."

I want to tell her that I was never in a ballet recital and I'm allergic to cats, but it doesn't seem like the right moment.

"You've never been far from our thoughts," she adds, sadly.

I'm feeling like this conversation has taken a really weird left turn, and I'm not certain how to reverse out of it. The only thing I can think to say—because it's the only other thing I know about her—is, "You run a healing center, right?"

Karen nods. "Yes, Full Light. It's on the other side of the island, near Kawela Bay."

The obvious next question would be, *What exactly is a healing center*? But somehow that seems rude.

"And, uh"—I would give almost anything to have Flynn with me. He's the only friend I have (or is it *had* now? I don't want to think about it) who can small talk like a forty-year-old—"Tessa used to work there. Didn't she?"

"Yes, I gave her a job after Rico left."

Rico. Of course she'd know about Rico. I lower my voice and ask, "Do you know what happened to him? I asked Tessa earlier, and she said that I shouldn't—"

Karen's Yoda expression falters. After a pause, she says, "That's Tessa's story to tell." I think she's not going to say anything else, but then she steps toward me, angling her body away from the party, and says, "I'm quite a bit older than my sister. My parents didn't believe they could have more children. So Tessa was"—she looks out over the party, then back at me—"a surprise for my parents. For my father even more than our mother."

I catch the switch from *my* to *our*. "Are you saying Tessa's your half sister?"

Karen looks away again, then says, "I suppose this is my story almost as much as it is Tessa's. So, yes." She shakes her head, remembering something. "When our mother got pregnant with Tessa, my father left us. Tessa grew up thinking we had the same father, but when our mother was dying, she told Tessa the truth."

I let silence hang between us for several moments before I prompt, "Which was . . . ?"

"Tessa's biological father was nobody, at least nobody we knew. My mother didn't know his name. He was a"—again looking for the right words, the safe words—"an indiscretion, a brief reprieve from an unhappy marriage. I never blamed our mother, because I remembered what our father had been like. He was"—pause; think; edit—"a temperamental man."

"But Tessa blamed her?" I say. It occurs to me that we're talking about my biological grandmother—a woman who contributed a quarter of my genes. It also occurs to me that if Tessa never found her own biological father, then she might not have answers to all the questions I'd like to ask.

Karen nods. "It was a mistake to keep the truth from her for so long, I think. It made the revelation that much more"—she sighs—"*destabilizing.*"

I still don't understand why Karen's telling me this. I start to ask about Rico again, but she squeezes my empty hands and then steps past me. "Talk to Tessa. She's the one to tell you what you want to know."

She walks down the steps to join the party, leaving me alone on the porch, standing at the threshold of the house. I hesitate, feeling weird about interrogating a woman I've barely met. But then, that's why I'm here. So I step inside the house, determined to learn what I can.

She's not in the living room, nor is she in the kitchen, so

I move to the edge of her bedroom. It takes me a moment to see her, sitting on the side of her bed in the dark, facing the shuttered window.

"Tessa?" She doesn't move, so I step into the room and speak a little louder. "This party is really nice, but I was mostly hoping to talk to *you*."

She looks to the side, and her profile is highlighted by the dim light from the yard. "But I'm so glad you're getting a chance to meet everyone." Her voice sounds tight, like maybe she's been crying.

I hesitate, then ask, "Are you okay?"

"I'm perfect," she says, but the tremor in her voice has a different emotion behind it. That's one of the many problems with words—so often, the meaning is in the music underneath.

I walk around the edge of the bed and sit by her side. Her damp cheeks glisten in the dim light that's filtering through the perimeter of the blinds.

"Do you wish I hadn't found you?" It's not the thing I thought I was going to ask her, but now that I've said it, I realize I've been wondering about it ever since she hugged me at Plumeria Grille. Because even though she's been nothing but kind, she's seemed a little frantic, fringed with desperation.

"No, of course not," she says. "I hoped you *would* find me someday. I just hoped—" She takes a deep, shaky breath. "I hoped that I'd be different when you did."

"I don't wish you were different."

A small sob escapes her, and I find myself wrapping my

arm around her shoulders. She leans into me. "You should," she says. "Because I'm not—I never was—" I give her the time she needs, and finally she gets out, "I was never capable of being the mother you deserve."

"That's okay," I say. "I don't need you to be my mother." I only realize the truth of the words as I say them. Then I think about my real mom pacing around our house, waiting for me to call. But I'll have time to wallow in my guilt later. "I just need you to be yourself, so I can know who *I* am." I gently press her away from me. "That's why I'm here."

She nods, looks at the ceiling. I spot a box of tissues on the floor beneath the window, so I grab one for her. She thanks me as she takes it, dabbing beneath her eyes before she says, very slowly, "Rico wasn't your father." Suddenly, Karen's story about Tessa's biological father makes sense. While I wait for Tessa to continue, I notice our bare feet resting side by side on the floor. They match. "I knew it all along, but he only found out after you were born. My divorce from M. J. wasn't even final."

"How did he find out?"

"I'm not sure, actually. I wish I could say that I told him, but somehow he just knew. He took off a few weeks after you were born. I didn't blame him." With her free hand, she pinches the bridge of her nose. "After that, I became so depressed. I'd been on this manic, emotional binge for years, and then the floor fell out of everything. I couldn't take care of myself, and I certainly couldn't take care of you. I had a neighbor who helped me, but one day I wandered out of the apartment and didn't come back. She found M. J.'s number, and he came and got you—"

"Yeah," I say. "He told me about that part."

"My memory of that time is hazy. I'm not even certain that the things I do remember actually happened. All I had left was Karen. She spent weeks looking for me. When she found me, she paid for my hospital stay, then brought me back to her house on the other side of the island, eventually gave me a job. By the time I understood what had happened, that you were with M. J., it had been so long that I couldn't"—she brings her hands up to cover her face—"I just couldn't face you, or him. I knew you were both better off without me."

She looks like an ancient warrior queen with her long hair and her graceful arms and her beautiful profile. It's almost impossible to believe that what's inside could be so fragile.

Again, I can't help but think of my mom. Some people make assumptions about her because of her blonde hair, her bright eyes, her petite figure; it's when she opens her mouth that they realize, *Holy crap. I guess we'd better listen to her.* She doesn't talk about it, but I know she's had to prove her intelligence and her grit every moment of her life. I think I'd like to be like that, too—someone who's more, not less, than people expect me to be.

Eventually, as gently as possible, I ask, "So, who *is* my father?"

She crumples her tissue and lets out a long, shaky sigh before she says, "I met him at a concert."

Of course. Of course she did.

"Was he a musician?"

I'm already thinking that if she remembers the name of the band, or even where and when they played, I might be able to track him down. It shouldn't be hard to triangulate him based on the date and venue of the concert and the instrument he played. But then Tessa says, "No, he was just there with some friends. I don't know if I ever knew his name. I hardly remember what he looked like." She starts shredding the edges of the tissue. "I know what you must think of me, but I was unhappy in my marriage, and I was already having an affair with Rico, and right and wrong just didn't seem to have any meaning anymore."

I know what she means. All along, I knew I was deceiving Daniel, but I wanted him *so badly*, and that seemed like all the reason I needed.

But it occurs to me that now I'll never know the other half of my gene pool. I guess I could do a genetic test at some point to get a general idea, but it wouldn't be the same as meeting him, as understanding who he is, who his parents were, how he would have raised me, and who I might have been, if I had been his. It's yet another thing I have in common with Tessa.

But as I watch her search for a clean spot on her tissue, I realize that none of this really matters, not in the way I thought it did. I am who I am—Megan and Jerry's daughter, Tessa's spitting image, a musician, a sister, a friend, all of it and none of it at the same time. It's all a part of me, but it doesn't *explain* me.

After an indeterminable pause, I say, "It seems like you figured things out, though, with Roger."

"Yes." She lets out all her air quickly. "I guess I did."

"What was different?" I ask. If I sound a little too eager, I hope she's still too worked up to notice. "How did you get it right this time?"

She looks at the ceiling, bites the edge of her full bottom lip. I realize, suddenly, that I'm biting my bottom lip in the same way. I've never even noticed that I do that.

"Communication has always been hard for me," she says. "I never seem to know what to say." She places both her hands on the center of her sternum. "I *feel* so many things all the time, but they're jumbled up. I can't pick out which feelings are real, which are affectations based on how I think I'm *supposed* to feel, and which are fleeting blips in my chemistry."

She doesn't say anything else for a while, but I can't imagine that her secret to successful relationships ends there, so I wait. I listen to the sounds of the party that are wafting through the house. Somewhere out there, someone's playing "Blackbird."

Finally, she goes on, "By the time I met Roger, I was so frustrated by how nothing inside me seemed to make any sense. I felt like a—" She widens her eyes and spreads her hands out in front of her. "Like a curse, just glancing in and out of everyone's lives, destroying everything I touched. I felt like I needed to warn him, so I did my best to explain"—her hands drop into her lap, a gesture of surrender—"all of it. I told him the truth, about everything—my embarrassing past, my erratic inner life. And to my everlasting surprise, he didn't leave.

"Probably someone else would have left, or at least most other people. But he stayed, and he listened. When I told him I was feeling trapped, he gave me space; when I told him I felt alone, he pulled me in. And because I was being honest, he could be honest, too.

"I realized, after a while, that I'd spent my whole life trying to be perfect for everyone I was with, but because of that, they never really knew who I was. I thought I was preserving my relationships, but really I was dooming them." She looks at me. "You can get what you want, for a while, by playing a part, but you'll only get what you *need* by being yourself."

"Yeah," I say. I'm thinking about Daniel, about the years I've spent playing the part of platonic bandmate so he wouldn't guess how I really felt, and about the last few days of pretending I was in love with someone else so he'd think we needed comfort in the same way. "That makes sense."

In that moment, I know I'm going home. Staying in Hawaii would be a mask over scar tissue; it would hide the problem, but not fix it. I need to go back and actually heal my life. I need to stop lying to everyone, including myself. Otherwise, I'll always be alone.

"And your parents?" she says, tentatively. "They're good people?" She looks hopeful now, and I realize that this is just another story she's told herself, to make everything else bearable.

When I say, "The best," she squeezes my hand, and we just sit for a minute, not trying to unravel anything, but instead gazing together at the invisible tangle of thread between us, agreeing silently to let it be.

Later, we rejoin the party, and I wander back toward the circle of musicians, which has doubled in size. Roger's playing his guitar while the woman who was playing earlier sings a ballad. All around the circle, people are tapping on desiccated gourds and strumming ukuleles. Some of the instruments are a little out of tune, but it doesn't really matter. Played in a torchlit circle in the middle of Tessa and Roger's driveway, it sounds exactly right.

♪ ♩ ♪ ♩ ♪

KAREN OFFERS TO LET ME STAY AT HER HOUSE ON THE OTHER side of the island, but by the time everyone is saying goodbye, it's so late that I think I could sleep on the gravel. So, Tessa and Roger spread a couple sheets across their narrow couch, then go into their bedroom and close the door.

I would have thought I'd fall right to sleep, but once I'm alone with my thoughts, I can't stop thinking about how desperate my parents must be to reach me. I'm not looking forward to being grounded from now until my adulthood, but if I'm going to try being honest with everyone, I might as well start now.

I roll off the couch, dig through my bag, and find my

phone easily. When I try to turn on the screen, I discover that the battery is drained, so I get down on my hands and knees, searching along the walls for the nearest outlet. There's one behind the TV, but I can't reach it, so I unplug their toaster and stand nearby while my phone recharges.

Once it's powered up, I stare at it, wondering who to call first, and what to say. I'm a little surprised to discover that the first person I want to talk to is Irene. I've never known her to be confused about anything. Usually this irritates me, but right now I could use some of that certainty.

I draft several different messages to her before I finally send: How're things going there? How much trouble am I in?

She writes back immediately: Thank goodness you're okay! Mom and Dad were going to go to the police in the morning.

> IRENE: Cameron will only tell them that you took a detour on the way home, but that you're PROBABLY safe. Mom and Dad are losing their minds.

> IRENE: Where are you?

I hesitate, not sure how to answer that. Finally, I land on: Hawaii.

> IRENE: HAWAII?!

IRENE: What are you doing in Hawaii???

I hesitate again. But then remind myself: honesty. So, I write, I found my biological mother.

Half a second later, my phone rings. Irene's voice sounds impossibly close as she says, "You *what?*"

"Yeah," I say, whispering. I'm not sure how thin these walls are. "She lives in Honolulu." My phone's battery is now at twenty percent, so I unplug it and carry it outside to the porch. I sit on the steps, watching a low crescent moon hook the tops of the trees at the edge of the driveway. Somewhere nearby, something squawks. In the distance, I see the bright, organized lights of the city.

"So, you're in Honolulu." I think I hear Irene close a door. She's probably in her room now, stepping toward her desk. "With your biological mother."

"Yeah."

I'm expecting her to say something like, *How could you do this? Mom and Dad are going to murder you.* But instead she says, "What's she like?"

I think about my interactions with Tessa thus far, the ups and downs of her moods, her effervescent intangibility, and sum it up with, "Like me, but crazier."

That makes her laugh.

"But nice," I add.

On the other end of the line, Irene is silent. I wish I could see her, try to decode her expression. Finally, she says, "I didn't even know you were looking for her."

"I wasn't, really, until you told me about the Summer thing."

"Is *that* how you found her?"

"Yeah." I can't tell how she's taking everything I've told her thus far, but I briefly explain the whole process.

When I finish, she says, "Wow. That's some legit sleuthing." But she doesn't sound impressed. She sounds . . . sad. After a moment, she says, "So, when are you coming home?"

"Soon," I say, thinking about Cameron, about how much I'll owe the Zamanis if I ask him to buy me one last plane ticket. I promise myself that this is the last time he bails me out. For real.

Irene seems to read my mind, because she says, "Do you need me to book you a flight?"

That possibility hadn't even occurred to me. "Can you do that?"

"I have some savings."

"Irene, I—" I feel tears pricking at the corners of my eyes. "I can't let you spend your savings on me."

"Please." She says this in the way that means, *Come on*, sounding as decisive as ever. She's at her best when she's arranging things for other people. "This is what sisters are for."

I hear a tapping sound on her end, and a moment later I get an email notification with my flight details. She asks, "Did it come through?"

"Yeah." The flight leaves earlier in the day than I would have liked, but it's probably for the best; I'll be home in time to study at least a little for Tuesday's finals. "I promise I will pay you back."

"We can set up a payment plan."

After a pause, I say, "Thank you, Irene."

"You're welcome." I'm over here on the verge of tears, and she sounds as competent and detached as ever. For once, I'm glad to have a sister who's nothing like me. "I'll tell Mom and Dad that you're safe and you're coming home in the morning. I'll let you handle the rest. Okay?"

"I owe you forever."

There's a pause before she says, "I'm glad you texted me."

"Me, too."

We say our good nights, and I wish her luck on her first day of finals, and then we hang up. But I stay outside for a while longer. I should probably rehearse what I'll say to my parents when I see them tomorrow, or what I'll say to Daniel if I ever get the chance, but instead I just listen to the island and try to dredge up some memory of having been here before.

Nothing comes to me. As far as I can remember, there's only one place I've ever called home.

CHAPTER 20

$\mathcal{T}$essa and Roger drive me to the Honolulu airport to-gether. Neither of them seemed surprised when I said I had a flight home today. I guess, what else was I going to do? Sleep on their couch forever? The first half of the drive is quiet, but then Roger turns on a local radio station, and the three of us listen to the slow guitar instrumental. When a vocalist comes in on the sweet, simple melody, Tessa softly sings along, and after a few bars, Roger jumps in on harmony. I haven't heard him sing yet, but his voice blends nicely with hers. While they sing, I sit back in my seat and watch the island go by. We're on a highway, and not a particularly pretty one. But beyond the concrete, the ocean extends forever.

I wonder if Tessa feels like she belongs here, like she's found a place where she fits. When I think about my manicured suburb, I realize that it doesn't really suit me, not deep in my core. It's trying so hard to be perfect, and the strain shows. But Hawaii doesn't suit me, either; I think if I stayed here I'd fall asleep beneath a palm tree somewhere and, like a character in a fairy tale, wake up a hundred years later none the wiser.

I begin to spin together dreamy images of an unselfconscious place edged with energy, where musicians gather in damp basements and play music until 4:00 a.m., where artists mingle and make wondrous, messy things. I wonder if somewhere, such a place exists.

Tessa and Roger both get out of the car at the airport. Roger hugs me first. His eyes shine as he squeezes my shoulders and says, "Don't be a stranger." For the first time, I wonder what all this has meant to him, and whether he wishes that he and Tessa had met when they were younger, when they might have had kids of their own.

Tessa pulls me in next. "You sure you don't want that dress?" she says. "I could mail it to you."

But as we separate, I shake my head. This morning, I put on my least dirty T-shirt and jeans, leaving my flowy dress from last night folded on the side of the couch. "This is more my style," I say, gesturing to my outfit. We stare at each other for several awkward seconds before I pull out my phone—fully charged now—and say, "I don't think I got your number."

She looks relieved as she gives it to me. I text her, This is Nora. But then I realize that this might seem strange to her, so I add, (aka Summer).

I slide my phone into the back pocket of my jeans and say, "If you're ever in California, I'd love to see you again."

"And you're welcome here, anytime," she says. "Maybe on one of your school breaks." There's no sign of pain as she says, "If it's okay with your parents."

I can't find the words to respond, but Tessa seems to understand. She pulls me in for another hug and says, "Thank you for finding me, Nora."

It's the first time she's said my real name, and that feels like all the good-bye we need. I go through security by myself, and once I'm on the plane I turn off my phone without having to be asked.

♪ ♫ ♪ ♫

I SEE MY PARENTS BEFORE THEY SEE ME. THEY'RE STANDING just beyond security at LAX, looking tired. The word *haggard* comes to mind, though I don't think I've ever used it in a sentence before. I'm not even certain why I know what it means, except that it perfectly describes how my parents look right now.

I've been trying to plan what I would say to them when they picked me up, but now that I'm here, all coherence has evaporated. I wish Irene were with them, but she's taking a final. I won't see her until she's out of school.

The words *THIS IS GOING TO BE BAD* flash through my mind in marquee neon, and I feel a brief stab of regret that I didn't linger in Hawaii a few more days. It occurs to me that I could double back to regroup in a bathroom, but the dark circles under my mom's eyes prompt me to step past the NO REENTRY sign and call out to them.

When my mom sees me, she lunges forward in a very un-Megan-Wakelin-esque display of emotion. Her arms encircle me, and my dad comes around behind to create a Nora sandwich. I quickly become uncomfortably warm, but I don't have the heart to say anything. Because even though I'm bound to be punished for turning off my location tracker, and going to Hawaii by myself, not to mention missing the first day of finals, I also know that they love me, and I can't stand the thought of causing them any more pain.

As we separate from our hug, my dad looks away quickly, but not before I see him wipe some moisture out of his eyes. My mom leaves an arm wrapped around my shoulders, which is awkward because I'm taller than she is, but I lean into her, enjoying the calm before the storm. I'm not sure when they plan to launch into the question-and-discipline part of today's agenda, but I know it's coming soon.

When we get home, I head upstairs to take a shower, and by the time I'm dressed, Irene is home. She's walking into her bedroom just as I'm stepping out onto the landing. I move toward her, prepared for a welcome-back hug, but she gently sidesteps me—it could be an accident—and says, "I'm going to put down my stuff. It's—" She glances at me sideways. "It's good to have you back." Then she goes into her room and shuts the door.

Before I have a chance to wonder what that was all

about, my dad appears at the base of the stairs and says, "Come down to our office when you're ready, Nora. Your mother and I would like to speak to you."

Even though I've been expecting this ever since we got in the car, I still feel a shudder of anticipation, both because of what they're about to say to me and because of what I need to say to them. None of it is going to be fun. But it's necessary, and I deserve it, and they need to hear it, so I say, "Sure. I'll be right down," as neutrally as I can.

After my hair is towel-dried and pulled back into a damp bun, I walk down the stairs, through the kitchen, and around the corner to the threshold of their office. As I approach, my dad pulls open the door and waves me forward.

"Have a seat," he says, gesturing to the same chair I sat in during our last conversation. My parents are positioned as they were that night, too—my mom sitting at her desk, my dad leaning against the table by her side. As I wait for one of them to start, I think about Tessa's long, complicated history, and realize how lucky I've been to have a stable home to grow up in and parents who love each other as much as mine do.

My parents have a brief, silent conversation consisting mostly of eyebrow maneuvers, and then my mom says, "Nora—"

Irene pokes her head around the door. "Can I come in?"

My dad says, "Give us a few minutes," but my mom touches his forearm and shakes her head. He reconsiders. "Actually, go ahead and join us."

I'm expecting her to ask them something specific and

quick—*Should I make dinner? Are you still able to chaperone Grad Night?*—but instead, she steps all the way inside the office and closes the door behind her. There isn't another chair, so she just leans against a wall, careful not to upset my parents' array of framed degrees and family photographs.

"Okay," my dad says. He claps his hands once, awkwardly, then looks down at my mom for help.

She seems smaller than I remember; older, too. On the computer screen behind her, I see the bolded number of her inbox tick over from 87 unread emails to 92. For a brief moment, I can almost feel the weight of everything she's carrying, and it nearly crushes me. But she speaks as serenely as ever as she says, "Nora, your father and I think we know where you went, and why you went there." I start to say something, but she holds up her hand and continues, "Irene declined to tell us where you were flying in from, but Cameron said something when we spoke to him that suggested you may have been looking for your birth parents . . ." Good grief. Cameron is *so bad* at keeping secrets. "And since only one flight was arriving today at precisely 1:25 p.m., we deduced that you went looking for them in Hawaii." She pauses, presses her lips together, breathes. "Is that correct?"

So much for my planned comments. I look down at my feet as I say, "Yes."

My mom's voice sounds somehow thinner as she says, "It was very wrong of you to go off on your own, to travel to another *state* without permission, to turn off the location tracker on your phone, but—" She inhales for several seconds, holds it, then lets it all out. "But your father and I also want to tell you—to make it clear that—"

Now *she's* the one who's struggling to find the right words, so my dad jumps in to help her. "We want you to know that you could have come to us with whatever questions you had about your—" He hesitates. "Your biological relations. We might not have had the answers, but we could have helped you search for them."

There's a pause, and when I look up, I realize that the general consensus is, it's my turn to talk. Once again, my brain is empty; all the eloquent speeches I mapped out in my head have evaporated, and all I can think to say is, "But I know it's a sensitive subject. I mean, we *never* talk about it."

Before either of my parents can answer, Irene jumps in with, "Because it doesn't matter." When I look at her, I realize that her eyes look a little red, maybe even swollen. I don't think I've ever seen her cry before; I didn't think she was the crying type. "It never mattered to me, anyway. You've always been my sister, not my *adopted* sister. My sister."

"I know that," I say. In my reckoning of all the people I've hurt this week, it never occurred to me to include her. Clearly, I could turn Being Wrong About Stuff into an Olympic sport. "But that doesn't mean I don't have questions about why—" How the hell do I say this without sounding like angst manifested in human form? "Why I am the way I am. I mean"—I look at each of them, sitting there with their identical postures, with their tidy hairstyles and their pressed, matching outfits—"I know we're a family. Obviously. But in a lot of ways, I'm *nothing* like you. I guess I just wanted to find out why."

My sister doesn't look appeased by this at all, but my mom is nodding along, as if I've made some kind of sense. Finally, she says, "I felt like that when I was your age."

Based on the way my dad's hand automatically goes to my mom's shoulder, I can tell that this isn't news to him, but it's sure news to me.

"What? Why?"

She spreads her hands out in front of her, then says, "I was the first person in my family to go to college." I'd never really thought of it like that, but I know her dad was in the sales department for a dairy company and her mom does crafty stuff with gemstones and clay, so I guess it makes sense. I'm not seeing her point yet, though, so I keep my mouth shut, and after a moment she goes on, "My dad only got a corporate job because he couldn't make a living as a painter and he had a family to support. But more than anything, he wanted your aunt Jeanette and me to be artists, to fulfill the dream he never achieved."

I can't help looking surprised, both by this revelation about my grandfather and by the mention of my aunt. I've only heard my mom talk about her a couple times, and always within the context of a rare story about her own childhood.

I chance a glance at Irene and see that she's as stunned by all of this as I am.

"You know your grandmother," our mom goes on. "She *lives* in her pottery studio. She used to paint, too, before her hands became so arthritic. And Jeanie was just the same. Even as a tiny child, she had an eye for things that I never did. And so even though I excelled in academics and got scholarships to the best schools, I always felt"— she takes a deep breath—"inferior, somehow. My parents didn't just not go to college; they *disapproved* of college. But they could see that I didn't have whatever spark lit up the rest of them, so they reluctantly subsidized my higher education."

I've never heard my mom sound this bitter before. I'm kind of enjoying it—not because I'm glad she feels bad about her childhood, but because it's something we finally have in common.

"Of course, your aunt Jeanette was a talented artist," my mom says. "And even though my parents did their best not to show it, I always knew that she was the favorite. How could she not be?"

My mom seems to get lost in her own thoughts, so my dad jumps in and says, "I hope we've never given *you* the impression that we have a favorite child, because—"

"No," I say quickly. "Not really." And it's true. They haven't. I've never doubted that they *love* me as much as they love Irene. Before I have a chance to edit myself, I say, "But there's love, and then there's acceptance, and it'd be nice to have both."

"Oh, sweetie," my mom says, wilting a little. "Of *course* we accept you."

"Then why are you making me do an internship in D.C. when I already know I want to be a musician?"

That makes them pause. In my peripheral vision, I see Irene's mouth turn upward into a half smile; it's nice to know that even if I've hurt her, she's still on my side.

Our parents look at each other, and the silent conversation this time starts with a heavy sigh and ends with a nod.

"You're right," my dad says, eventually. "Our intention was never to shape you into something you're not, but perhaps in our effort to encourage you to explore all your possibilities, we overlooked who you already are."

My mom narrows her eyes at me. "You know we're going to punish you, right? We're going to have to ground you for running off to Hawaii and breaking nearly all of our rules."

"I know." I expected nothing less.

My dad squares his shoulders, probably glad to be back on solid footing. "Effective immediately, you are grounded from all social engagements for two weeks. This summer, you will also complete forty hours of community service for a charitable organization of your choosing."

I'm already thinking that my old middle school does a music summer camp for sixth graders. I wonder if they could use a student instructor. There are worse punishments, for sure.

"However," my mom cuts in. "In light of this conversation—"

"And your compelling argument," my dad adds.

"—you no longer have to do an internship this summer, if you don't want."

Somewhere in the house, a clock ticks, and suddenly I'm thinking about M. J.—his Mohawk, his Subaru wagon, his contented suburban life with Julie. He thought he was one thing, but he turned out to be something else. I think about my mom, too, and how she's so much more, so much fiercer, than she seems.

I surprise even myself when I say, "But if I still wanted to go to D.C. . . ." Both of my parents tilt their heads to the side at the same angle, and it seems so choreographed it almost makes me laugh. But my mind is racing too fast to fully enjoy the absurdity of their synchronicity. I suddenly remember that Dexter Holland of the Offspring also does molecular biology research, and the drummer for Blur is an attorney. Mira Aroyo of Ladytron—didn't she study genetics at Oxford? And I'm pretty sure Art Garfunkel was a math teacher. I know that I want to be a musician—I *am* a musician—but maybe I don't have to be one thing or the other; maybe it's possible to be many things at once, to be more, not less. "Could I?"

My parents look at each other, then back at me. My mom says, "Of course."

"As long as your location tracker remains on *at all times*."

"Understood."

Now I'm thinking about Santa Barbara, San Francisco, Hawaii, even Reedley and Watsonville—all the places I've seen in the last few days. Each had something different to offer, a different music thrumming beneath its surface. Suddenly, the world seems enormous, enticing, and accessible.

"Then, I'd like to work for the environmental lobbyists in D.C., if that's still all right with you." I take a deep breath, then say, "Besides, Blue Miles broke up. I don't have a band to record with, even if I wanted to."

My mom's brows pucker sympathetically. "We're sorry to hear that."

My dad, though, pushes himself away from the desk as he says, "I'll make the call now. We can arrange everything else this evening." He takes out his phone, and my mom's eyes drift toward her computer. It appears that our talk is over, which is perfectly fine with me.

"Aren't we going to talk about what Nora found in Hawaii?" Irene says. The three of us look at her. "If it's important to Nora—if it's part of *who she is*—then it should be important to all of us." She seems to shrink a little, becoming unsure of herself. "I mean, I know it's Nora's business, but if it's a part of who you are"—she looks at me—"then it's a part of who I am, too."

My mom sits back in her chair. "You're right, Irene." Then she closes her eyes, like she's preparing herself for something painful. And right then, I get it. I finally understand, really understand, why my parents haven't liked talking about my adoption, why they never wanted me to know that my biological parents named me Summer. All this time, I've been afraid that someday they'd reject me, because I'm not the perfect daughter that their genetics might have produced. But meanwhile, they've been worrying

WHEN I WAS SUMMER 281

that someday I would reject them, that I'd want to shed the identity and the name that they gave me and go back to the people who gave me up.

I want, more than anything, to step across this office and cry on their shoulders and tell them that could never happen, that they're my parents, now and forever. But histrionics don't get you very far in this family. We don't speak the language of music, or tears. We speak the language of rhetoric, of reason. If I want them to know how I feel, to know *me*, I'm going to have to use my words.

Still, when Irene says, "So, tell us what happened," my first instinct is to filter the truth, to say the things they would like to hear. But then I remember what Tessa said about honesty, about being honest with Roger so he could be honest with her, and I realize that if I want these relationships to heal cleanly, then I need to tell them the truth.

So, I gather up all the music and emotion inside me—is this what Tessa meant by *my erratic inner life?*—and translate it into a story. And as the words come, I discover that I've spoken this language all along, or maybe I learned it gradually, through exposure. Maybe Tessa gave me music and my parents gave me words, and all of it adds up to an erratic soul organized by a logical mind—some combination of nature and nurture, fate and family. Summer, Nora, me.

I tell them all about Plumeria Grille, and Roger, and the house surrounded by forest, and the candlelit party on their gravelly front yard. I tell them about Tessa's insecurities, and how she'd been imagining me as something completely different from what I am. I tell them she doesn't really know who my biological father is, but it wasn't M. J. Croft, or the man she left him for. I tell them that she doesn't know who her own biological father was, either, but that her mother—my biological grandmother—was mostly German, or so she thinks. She's not entirely sure. With a shrug and a sigh, I try to tell them that I'm honestly kind of over it. Maybe what's lost isn't always better off found.

I tell them everything about the day and night I spent with her, but in the music underneath the words, I hope they can hear what I'm *really* saying:

I'm here.

I love you.

I'm yours.

CHAPTER 21

*M*y parents must have had a serious heart-to-heart with my teachers, because no one makes much of a fuss about my absence. I'm allowed to make up Monday's finals without penalty, and the rest of the week I'm actually glad to be distracted by cramming for my remaining exams. It keeps me from dwelling on the fact that Daniel and Darcy have spent every free moment on campus making out as publicly as possible and that Flynn shows no sign of acknowledging my existence again anytime soon.

By Friday afternoon, when Cameron and I head to Royal's—a burger-and-doughnut place around the corner from my house—I feel wrung out. I'm almost certain that I managed at least a B on every final other than trigonometry, but I'm not even sure why that matters. Without Blue Miles, I don't know what I'm working for.

Cameron seems nervous as he picks at his doughnut. When I ask him what's on his mind, though, he changes the subject, asks me again what I thought of her. But even now, when I've had four days to think about it, it's a surprisingly difficult question to answer.

On Tuesday evening, after I'd survived my first round of final exams and made up the ones I missed on Monday, I texted her to let her know I'd arrived safely. The next day, she sent me a clip of her and Roger playing "Here Comes the Sun" at a retirement home. Since then, we've mostly communicated via music memes.

Eventually, I say, "She's nice."

"Oh, come on. You can do better than 'She's nice.'"

I can think the words, but I can't seem to say them. I think Tessa is like that, too. We feel things we are physically incapable of speaking.

"She's a lot like me," I say, leaving out the *but crazier* part. Because who knows, really? Who knows what decisions I would have made if I'd experienced the things she experienced? Maybe I would have done everything the same. Instead, I say, "But she wears dresses."

Cameron looks at me. "Are you glad you found her?"

"Yeah," I say, dragging a fry through a little paper cup of mustard. "Definitely."

He tears off another bite of doughnut. "Did you find the answers you were looking for?"

"I think I learned to stop asking the questions."

He wipes his fingers on a napkin. "I know what you mean."

"You do?"

"Yeah. *Why am I the way I am?*" His phone pings, but he

ignores it. "The point is that you *are* the way you are. So, what are you going to do about it?"

I'm mulling over this excellent question when the door to Royal's swings open, and Daniel steps inside, looking distressed. When he sees me, he freezes, but then Darcy is there behind him, saying, "What the hell. Are we in or are we out?" She coaxes him forward, but then she sees me, too, and she backs away. "Oh, no. No way." She looks at Daniel. "Did you know she'd be here?"

He turns his whole body to face her. "No, I swear I didn't."

Cameron's opening his mouth to speak, but then Flynn enters, head down, hands in pockets. He almost runs into Darcy's back before he sees us. When his eyes find Cameron, his face flushes. "What is this?"

Daniel points at Flynn. "How'd he get *you* to show up?"

"He said he had some of my equipment to return," Flynn says. "And while we're all together, each of you owes me eighty bucks for gas."

I have outstanding debts with a truly daunting number of people.

"So, why are *you* here?" I ask Daniel.

He glances at Darcy before saying, "I asked Cam if we could talk." For Darcy's benefit, he insists, "Just him and me. He's the one who suggested the time and place."

Cameron and I have had this postfinals Friday afternoon get-together planned ever since I got back. I'm not supposed to do anything social until I get back from D.C.—part one of the multipart series, Discipline Nora—but Cameron and I figured that if my parents look at my location tracker, it'll be easy for me to explain that I stopped by here on my way home from school for a snack, which isn't, strictly speaking, a lie.

I shake my head at him as I say, "I can't believe you tricked us."

Cameron stares at all of us for a moment before saying, "We all know that it can't end this way, right? Not after we played *the Magwitch*." He slaps Stellan's business card down on the table between us. "Stellan Prescott thought we were *good*." He looks at Daniel, then Flynn. "We can still make this work."

Darcy and Daniel look at each other, and there's so much heat between them that they could be a fire hazard. Abruptly, my appetite is gone.

Finally, she says, "I'll wait outside." As she steps toward the door, she adds, "Remember, it's your choice."

This seems to mean something to him, because he nods and stares fixedly at the floor. After Darcy is gone, he weaves between the empty tables to ours, sitting between Cameron and me. Suddenly, I'm overconscious of my hands. I fold them in my lap, rest them on the table, pick up my sweating glass of iced tea.

Cameron pulls out the last remaining chair and says, "Come on, Flynn. One more band meeting, and then, if you really want, we'll never bother you again."

Flynn stares at the chair indecisively, but eventually he sits down on my left, Cameron's right, directly across from Daniel. He pushes his chair all the way back to the window, as far away from us as possible, and stares petulantly at his lap.

After a beat of silence, Daniel looks at Cameron and says, "Now what?"

Cameron shrugs. "I have no idea. I wasn't sure we'd get this far." He presses his palms flat against the table and says, "A lot of stuff went down last weekend, but we can talk through this." He swallows, then looks at Flynn. "I know you're sick of dealing with my shit, and I don't blame you—"

"It's not just that, Cam," Flynn says. His tone surprises me. The edge of anger is gone, and all that's left is exhaustion. "You've got legitimate reasons to be angry with your parents. But the thing is"—he takes a deep breath—"I don't have time for this anymore. I'm not—" His eyes lift to me, briefly, and I know what he's thinking about: backstage at the Magwitch, his fingers briefly weaving through mine. "I'm not the person I needed to be, if this was going to work."

In the pause that follows, I want to say *I'm sorry*, but I don't know what exactly I'd be apologizing for, and, in the end, I think he's right. As I glance at Daniel, I think that maybe none of us were who we needed to be, if this was going to work.

Flynn—ever the efficient one—clears his throat and then looks at Cameron. "Do you really have something to give back to me, or was that just something to say to get me here?"

Cameron reaches into his backpack, which he brought in from the car, and pulls out a quarter-inch cable. Flynn looks at it for a second before he takes it. It occurs to me that these moments are little thresholds; once we pass through them, we can't ever go back. It seems like he's thinking the same thing as he stands and takes the cable out of Cameron's hand, because his voice is weak as he says, "You can all send me the gas money later. You know how to find me." Then, without looking at any of us, he pushes through the exit and disappears around the corner.

The three of us sit in silence for several seconds, and then Daniel lets out a long, strangled sigh before saying, "Actually, I need to go, too."

His words don't surprise me, but they still hurt. I guess somewhere deep inside me, I still believed we could make it work—him and me, the band, all of it. Cameron's the one who insists, "Nothing that happened this weekend has to be a big deal. We can all cope, right?"

"No, Darcy's making me choose," Daniel says. "Her, or the band."

Cameron looks like he wants to hit his head against something. "You said you two were done forever. She threw a burrito at you. You're really going to give up this"— he doesn't gesture at himself, or at me, but at the business card that's still sitting in the center of the table, a stark reminder of what's at stake—"for *that*?"

Daniel takes a deep breath, then stands. Beneath my own multilayer heartbreak, I think I feel sorry for him, because he'll always want the thing he can't have. But haven't I been like that, too—regretting the absence of my biological parents, when my real parents were there all along?

He bites his lower lip, pushes his hand through his hair,

then looks at me and says, "I'm sorry, but I've got to try."

It's hard for me to argue with that, because I had to try, too. Maybe we all have to try. Maybe it takes getting what we want to figure out what we need. Despite the seriousness of this moment, I can almost hear the Rolling Stones rocking the outro of that song. Music really does have the answer to everything.

After Daniel leaves, Cameron stares at the business card like it's the only thing anchoring him to his sanity. I place my hand on top of his and say, "I'm sorry, Cam."

"It's not your fault."

"It really is, though."

"No. This is on all of us."

Even though I can't help feeling like most of the blame should be mine, I can see what he means. I couldn't have changed the way I felt, not about Daniel, not about Flynn, any more than they could have changed how they felt about me. I could have acted differently last week, but those feelings were always going to be there. We were doomed to be not so much a love triangle, but a love triptych—nonintersecting lines stretching out to infinity without ever having the satisfaction of a point.

After a long pause, he says, "You know what I'd do next time?"

I know what he's talking about, because my mind has gone there, too: looking back on Blue Miles, it's easy to see where the cracks started, and what I'd do differently to catch them before they spread.

"What?"

"I'd have us write a band manifesto, like a mission statement, so we know from the beginning that we're all working toward the same goal. I'd want the music to be *about* something this time, more than just self-expression or whatever."

I'd guess that he's thinking about what Flynn said to him inside that convenience store, but I don't bring it up. He's doing the steps, making his own path.

I eat another fry and then say, "We should also have some kind of five-year plan, even if we can't stick to it. Like, the goal is to play this many gigs each month, aiming to play bigger venues along the way, to be *ready* for them, anyway."

"That's good," Cameron says, stealing a fry. "That's really good." He pulls a pen and paper out of his backpack and starts making a list.

"Another thing I'd do," I say, "is make sure we *talk* to each other."

Cameron slowly writes the word *TALK* as point number three, before putting down his pen. "I know what you mean. We spent all that time together, but we never really knew what was going on in each other's lives."

When I think about Daniel's drama with Darcy, Flynn's constant annoyance, Cameron's solitary drinking, and my desperate attempts to hide my crush, I realize that we were always performing, even when it was just for each other. We were consumed by fear, and jealousy, and loneliness, and longing, but we couldn't talk about it.

That makes me think about Summer—the name that

was meant to be a charm against everything painful, everything dark, everything tainted by reality. I wonder if Tessa realized when she gave me that name that she was trying to hide me just like she'd been hiding herself, trying to wrap me in a cloak of perfection. It took her almost sixteen years to realize that if she wanted to experience anything real, she'd have to pull off her own cloak and let the world—or at least the people she trusted—see her as she really was.

Of course, I can't judge her. It took me just as long to realize that I didn't have to be—that I *couldn't* be—perfect, by anyone's definition. I'll never be an endless string of sunny days or a Stanford-bound copy of my parents. I'll never be the one Daniel wants. But I can be myself, and that's even better.

"There's always next time." I pick up Stellan's business card and pass it to Cameron. "We'll do better next time."

EPILOGUE

$\mathcal{M}$y fingers feel like they're falling down the neck of my bass as I play the extended final run of our second-to-last song for the night. Cameron is playing a line above mine, diverging into a fuguelike counterpoint. Jenna, our drummer, plays a rollicking drumbeat beneath. Her pale arms are over her kit as she lands on a downbeat. Mason, rhythm guitar and vocals, has stepped into the shadows behind her. The stage lights catch his Afro sideways, creating a bronze halo as he bows his head over his instrument. This part of the song is all instrumental. Cameron and I wrote it over the summer by emailing each other tracks while I was in D.C.

The song ends with a call-and-response between Jenna's drums and our melodic bass-and-guitar harmony. When we strike the final note together, the audience goes a little nuts, but Jenna doesn't let the beat drop. She keeps tapping her bass drum pedal, transitioning smoothly into our final song. I have a few seconds, so I grab my water bottle off my amp and take a long swig. On the other side of the stage, Cameron's focused on his guitar pedals, checking the tuning of his instrument.

Mason and Jenna are vamping through the opening rhythm as Mason says, "Thank you so much for coming out to the Rowdy tonight. You've been a wonderful audience." More applause. "Before we start our last song, I want to introduce the members of the band. On lead guitar, Cameron Zamani." Cameron plays a funky run up the neck of his instrument. "Behind me on drums, Jenna Thomas." Jenna adds a complicated fill on top of the still-driving bass drum-beat.

That's when I see him, standing on the far side of the room with a girl who isn't Darcy. I have no idea how long they've been there. They're keeping to the shadows, which makes it difficult for me to know whether he wanted me to see him or wanted to remain invisible. He leans toward the girl he's with, brushing hair back behind her ear before he leans down to kiss her. I look away.

"On bass, Nora Wakelin!"

After I slap my bar of solo, Mason says, "And I'm Mason Benick."

Our new band name comes from something Cameron texted me over the summer, when we were trying to figure out how to find a drummer and vocalist/rhythm guitar player to replace Flynn and Daniel. He wrote, They've obviously got to be kick-ass musicians. But I also just want to find some good people.

CAMERON: I think we could work with someone
who still needs to grow as a musician,
but not someone who still needs to
grow a whole lot as a human being.

As soon as I saw the words, I knew they were perfect. I quickly wrote, That's it!

CAMERON: What's it?

ME: Our new band name!

CAMERON: As a Human Being? I don't know. Kind
of wordy.

ME: No, before that!

CAMERON: Kick-Ass Musicians? We'd be setting
expectations pretty high . . .

ME: GOOD PEOPLE!

There was a pause during which I knew he'd be sitting in his bedroom in California, saying, "We are *Good People!*" to an imaginary audience. Eventually, he wrote back, I like it!

Now, Mason leans in to the microphone and says, "We are Good People! Have a beautiful night, Huntington Beach, and get home safely." Then he steps away from the mic as he shouts to us, "Let's go!"

That's Cameron's and my cue to come in on the rest of the intro. As I play the first notes, I glance back at the spot where I saw Daniel, but he and his date have ducked out. I wonder what he told her about us. That he used to be in the band? That he and the bassist once had an ill-advised fling? More likely, he said nothing.

The music, as always, pulls me back. I step toward Jenna, locking my rhythm with hers. Cameron sways toward us. Mason doesn't play on this section, so he pulls his microphone out of its stand and steps backward, completing our pulsing circle. I feel myself let go of my awareness of the place Daniel vacated; it doesn't matter anymore. It isn't important. In my final blip of consciousness before I dissolve into the music, I understand that he was one brief note in the symphony of my life, which will be composed of melodies I can't yet imagine, melodies sweeter than anything I've heard or played before.

Acknowledgments

Thank you to my parents for playing Beatles music early and often, for subsidizing my exorbitantly expensive education, and for surrounding me with books and musical instruments. Thank you to my Grandpa Bud for teaching me about chord inversions, the importance of structure, and persistence.

Thank you to my sister, Emily, for reading many drafts of many novels long before I ever wrote this one, to my brother, James, for being a delightful collaborator and true original, and to my sister-in-law, Katie, for always being one of my most enthusiastic readers, critics, and cheerleaders. Thank you to all the friends and family who have understood the importance of this work in my life.

Thank you to every teacher who instructed and encouraged me, especially Dan Robbins, Paula Cizmar, and whoever sat on those grant committees at USC. Massive special thanks to my thesis director, mentor, and friend, Richard Bausch, and to everyone at Chapman University who participated in awarding me that fellowship. It changed everything.

Thank you to the many writer friends who have helped me along the way, especially to Kat Yeh, who told me to write this book and then showed me how to make it better, to Jim Hime, whose specific brand of generosity is unicorn-rare, to Lori Snyder, whose Splendid Mola writing retreats have been a precious haven, and to my PACT partner and soul-sister, Amber Alvarez, who has been there every step of the way to comfort, motivate, and inspire.

Thank you to Nora's agents, David Hale Smith and Liz Parker, who took a chance on both of us, expertly guided us to safe harbor, and continue to advocate for us. Double, triple, and quadruple thanks to Liz for the early edits, frequent pep talks, and constant emotional and professional support. Thank you to everyone at InkWell Management, especially to Stephen Barbara, who read an early draft and offered invaluable counsel. And thank you to the entire team at Verve Talent & Literary Agency, especially Sara Nestor, for welcoming both Nora and me into your ranks and charting our course into deeper waters.

Thank you to my editors, Leila Sales and Kendra Levin. To Leila, for seeing potential in my writing and in Nora, but having the wisdom to know we needed a better plot; you've given my family much more than a book deal. To Kendra, for generously coaching Nora across the finish line, and for welcoming her into such prestigious company.

Thank you to the whole Viking crew, especially to Ken Wright for his fearless leadership, to Marinda Valenti, Sheila Moody, and Janet Pascal for catching and correcting my many mistakes, to Kate Renner for turning my Word doc into a real book, to Kelley Brady for the beyond perfect cover art, to Aneeka Kalia for her faith and assistance, to Maggie Rosenthal for bravely taking the wheel when we needed an interim captain, and to Gerard Mancini for reading with an eye to authenticity. You are a dream team.

In telling Nora's story, I never presumed to represent a broader adoptive experience. From what I've seen, each adoption story is as unique as each adoptee. But to all readers in search of their roots or questioning the origin of their identity, thank you for being exactly the person that you already are, for caring about Nora's journey, and for reading. You are part of her family now.

Words are too poor an instrument to properly express my love and appreciation for my best friend, my husband, my partner. Brandon, this book wouldn't exist without you for reasons both obvious and unseen. I am grateful for whichever ingredients—family or fate—contributed to your being. What can I do for you?